W9-BSK-638

FEEDING
Christine

Bantam Books

NEW YORK TORONTO LONDON

SYDNEY AUCKLAND

FEEDING *Christine*

by BARBARA CHEPAITIS

FEEDING CHRISTINE

Book design by Laurie Jewell.

ISBN 0-553-80165-1

Bantam Books are published by Bantam Books, a division of Random House, Inc. Its trademark, consisting of the words "Bantam Books" and the portrayal of a rooster, is Registered in U.S. Patent and Trademark Office and in other countries. Marca Registrada. Bantam Books, 1540 Broadway, New York, New York 10036.

PRINTED IN THE UNITED STATES OF AMERICA

To Marietta and Angelina Ranalli,
Teresa and Emilia DiRosa
With thanks for their courage—

And to my mother.
No names, no dates,
Can't prove a thing.

Simple gestures, taking place on the surface of life, can be of central importance to the soul.

—THOMAS MOORE,
Care of the Soul

ABOUT COOKING

THE BEST THING ABOUT PEOPLE IS WHAT HAPPENS between them, and for Teresa DiRosa the best thing that happened between them was food, which she believed should be cooked *alla famiglia,* with stories and songs to help the work move along. That was why the women who worked with her catering business, Bread and Roses, always cooked together for the annual holiday season open house.

This event was no small affair. Through the course of the night more than two hundred people would pass through Teresa's house, where she insisted it be held. She was the cook, she said, and a cook should feed guests from her own kitchen.

For weeks ahead of time Delia Olson, Teresa's childhood friend who couldn't cook at all but who took care of the books and the PR, would be busy with invitations, press releases, and the extra burden on the accounts. Amberlin Sheffer, the baker, would be hard-pressed to make enough raisin and carob cookies, which she only hoped were healthy enough to balance the egg- and sugar-filled dadaluce Teresa insisted on. And Christine DiRosa, Teresa's niece by her sister Nan, put in a good deal of overtime getting the decorations and serving scheme in order.

It was a cold December. Ice settled into the air early and determined to stay around. Snow fell, but only enough to dust the lawns and branches with shifting glitter. The women were in the usual state of disarray commonly known as daily life. Delia was cheerfully balancing the demands of children and husband and friendship and work, but she was a cheerful sort of person. Amberlin, who was more solemn, was solemnly negotiating a serious relationship as it advanced toward commitment. Teresa was maintaining her pride in spite of being recently divorced and stoically facing an empty house now that her son was in college. And Christine was perfecting a replica of a castle in stained glass as a wedding gift for her fiancé.

As they gathered in Teresa's kitchen, all of this would be rolled out with the sheets of dough and pounded into tenderness with the veal. Amberlin and Teresa would have their usual argument over whether to put a marischino cherry for a nose on the Rudolph cake. Delia would light candles everywhere, and Christine would sing in a high, sweet voice to the Christmas carols on the radio. Teresa and Delia would pause and listen, tasting sorrow and joy when they heard Nan's voice in her daughter's song.

It was the season of miracles in Teresa's house, and while none of the women particularly expected a miracle, neither did they think they'd be needing one.

They were wrong.

Thursday

TERESA'S KITCHEN

TERESA DIROSA STOOD IN HER KITCHEN KNEADING dough at the long counter next to the sink, staring out the window. The smell of garlic and olive oil competed with fresh-brewed coffee, and the radio was on the sixth day of Christmas, which irritated her.

"Give your gifts and shut up," she said to it. For herself, she preferred "Gesù Bambino," especially for kneading bread.

She'd been at the bread making for the Bread and Roses party much of the day. She had the focaccios, and now was working on the plain Italian. She wouldn't make the Tuscan grape until Saturday, since that wouldn't keep as the others would. There would be other breads, of course, but Amberlin would bring them—amaranth and corn bread and something with a lot of seeds that she called To Your Health Bread.

Amberlin always shook her head at all the work and said, "Teresa, use the machine. It's more efficient." But Teresa preferred the feel of dough in her hands to efficiency, at least when she had time.

Light snow danced outside the big picture window in the breakfast nook. Today was only a little warmer than yesterday, and all the trees on her suburban block were sheathed in ice that coated their branches like layers of glass. If she were to walk on the grass outside her kitchen, she would feel the powdered sugar of snow give way to thin, crunching sheets of ice candy, which coated the grasses she'd let grow so long this summer that the lawn police had come after her. She was breaking an ordinance, they told her. For unrestrained growth of grass. That carried a $350 fine, and a fifteen-day jail term.

She mowed reluctantly, only after her son told her it would be the final embarrassment in his last summer before college if she had to go to jail for not mowing her lawn. She felt as if she were shaving a prisoner's head as she watched the bristly blue, yellow, and gold flowers disappear beneath the blades. Wild thyme and mint wafted spiky scents as she bruised them, catching her attention like her name whispered near her ear. After she mowed, she lay on the stubbles, which felt dry and sad, as she did.

She pressed a finger against the corner of the window, melting a patch of frost that gathered there. Summer was far away. Soon the lavender and gold sky would melt into the deep wine of darkness. The little pink Christmas lights would blink in the living room. The house was quiet and empty. She supposed she should enjoy it while she could.

Tomorrow, her huge kitchen would fill up with people and activity as bread went in and out of ovens, platters were filled with cookies and little crespollini and thin veal and braciole in green sauce, and the thirteen fish that were traditional to Christmas Eve, though that was still two weeks away.

But she wanted to remember her grandmother this year, so she would have raw oysters and clams to slide down the throat, crisp cold shrimp to dip into cocktail sauce, smoked salmon and mussels, and herring in mustard sauce. Then, for the fried fish there would be the smallest pieces of smelt she could find, rings of squid and squares of ginger trout alongside fried flounder smothered in green sauce. And, of course, there would be the seafood salad, with lobster, crab, and conch.

Amberlin and Delia and Christine would stay over tomorrow, as they always did on the night before the open house. Delia said she wasn't sure if her children would come along. Jessamyn, at nine, preferred painting her nails with her friends to spending time with her mother and adult company. At twelve, Anthony was wrapped in the long cocoon of prepuberty. He liked video games and mumbled a lot. Of course, Teresa's own son wasn't available this year. Of course.

Teresa clucked her tongue against the roof of her mouth. Her thoughts kept going to places she didn't want them to go, and she had to treat them like dogs that needed calling out of the neighbor's yard before they dug holes. She focused on the bread dough, which had ceased to be sticky and reached that point the cookbooks called elastic and smooth. She turned it over and over, pulling it into itself, pushing her hands into its soft center and turning it again. When she thought about Donnie, she was better off getting back to food as quickly as she could. Food was easier to understand and hurt her less.

She lifted the dough into a bowl, where it would rest, covered with a dishcloth, for an hour. She wished she could get in with it and rest for an hour, then have someone punch her back into shape.

A clatter at the back door brought her attention to her hands, which needed wiping before she put them on the doorknob, but she didn't need to bother. The door opened, and Delia stood inside, shaking snow out of her red curls and laughing.

"Hey," she said, her big voice rolling into the kitchen with a wave of cold. "I brought the brochures for the table, and the tablecloth Christine wanted. You know—the lace thing from my aunt Lucy. I thought I'd get it all into the living room before tomorrow, so they wouldn't get mixed up with the dishcloths." She grinned and held up two shopping bags, stomped her long feet against the mat at the door, shook out her treelike legs.

"Good idea," Teresa said. "Don't worry about your feet. It's pointless. The buffet drawer's probably safe." She wiped her hands on the pants of her coveralls and Delia walked over and slapped at them lightly.

"When're you gonna get out of that habit?" she asked.

Teresa looked down at her pants and shrugged. They bore the signs of painting and cooking and gardening, indelible remarks on the nature of her life. She could never remember to either put on an apron or wait until she got a dishcloth to wipe her hands. Always, her hands went to her pants and wiped. Always, she had something from the kitchen or the garden on her clothes. Delia, on the other hand, managed to keep life from sticking to her—or at least to her clothing. It was a trait Teresa alternately felt worthy of envy and worthy of scorn. She was certain Delia felt the same way about her.

She brushed away a strand of dark hair that had escaped from the barrette she held it back with. Her olive skin and black hair were already streaked with flour, making her large dark eyes stand out like bits of night sky peering through clouds. "At least I'm learning to put on playclothes first," she said.

"And you learned that when—last year?" Delia put her bags down and took off her coat, tossing it onto the back of the chair at the small table in the kitchen nook. She held her hands to her cheeks for a moment. Her paper-white skin had flushed an almost wine red with the cold, temporarily obliterating her freckles. When she took her hands away, the impress remained briefly, then was swallowed by color. "Cold," she said. "God, I hate it."

She pushed her shoes off carefully and left them on the mat, then brought the bags over to where Teresa stood.

It had been Delia's idea to have an open house for Bread and Roses. Good PR, she said, especially in the first few years of its existence. Now, even though the business had grown and they didn't really need the publicity, Teresa insisted they continue to have it, and at her house rather than at the Lark Street shop where Teresa usually prepared the food for big events. The shop was just downtown, only a few miles from her house, and it had the café section that could be organized into a reception area, but for Teresa being at the shop felt like work, and being in her house felt like a party.

Besides, her house was big enough, with a state-certified kitchen and not one of those Realtor's definitions of gourmet, which usually meant a side-by-side refrigerator-freezer, a Jenn-Air grill, and ducks on the wallpaper.

No. She had a double oven and stovetop, double refrigerator and full-size freezer in the cellar, and a center island with a grill built into it with another smaller oven underneath, surrounded by enough counter space for pasta to be rolled and spread even with two other people chopping and arranging vegetables. Her cupboards stayed open so the inner workings of the kitchen were visible and accessible, and all pots and pans hung from hooks just at the right length for her arms to reach.

The breakfast area, on the other side of the island, was big enough for six people. The dining and living room were one large open space just the other side of the stove wall, and the big crackling fire in the living-room fireplace always made people feel cheered, even after the snows of upstate New York turned dirty and gray.

There weren't any ducks or cows on the wallpaper either. Just an old brass-framed photograph of her great-grandmother, Emilia Campilli, sitting tall in sepia tones with her daughter, whom Teresa knew as Grandma DiRosa, on her lap. They stared at her as she cooked, ancestrally supervising Teresa's moves in the sacred realm of the kitchen.

"How's it going?" Delia asked as they passed under her shadow and into the dining- and living-room area, where a fire crackled in the hearth.

"The usual. Bread's almost done, and now I gotta worry will the fish get here fresh, and the flowers okay, and so on."

Delia arched her eyebrows knowingly. "I don't think there'll be any trouble with the flowers. Do you? I mean, Rowan's bringing the order, isn't he?"

"Don't start," Teresa said.

Delia claimed that Rowan Bancroft, who owned the garden shop where she purchased flowers for parties and plants for her garden, was interested in Teresa. Teresa claimed he was just being a good businessman with a good customer and Delia said Teresa had lost her wits if she really believed that. Teresa said she was divorced less than a year and had a right to do without her wits for a while. Delia said nuts. Sam had made it official last year, but her marriage was long dead and it was time Teresa had some fun. Teresa said Rowan wasn't her type. He wore his thick gray hair in a ponytail and had too much beard, too much in the way of eyes. Delia said she was surprised Teresa had noticed his eyes, and didn't he have wonderful hands too? Too big, Teresa said automatically, and Delia said uh-huh. So you did notice.

But the truth was, she hadn't noticed anything until Delia mentioned it, and now she felt uncomfortable, nervous, around him. Even then she felt a flush move up her face. She moved closer to the fireplace and threw a stick in, but Delia saw, and after knowing Teresa since junior high didn't have to work very hard to read the signals.

"What is it?" she asked, her whole face hungry for news. "Did he—did you—I mean, what is it?"

Teresa pointed at her, then her hand sliced back and forth through space. "Nothing," she said. *"Niènte, niènte e più niènte. Capisce?"*

Delia grinned. "I'm Irish," she said. "You know I don't *capisce*."

Teresa threw her arms up in the air. "You're about as subtle as a freight train." She went to the buffet and opened the top drawer, moved old cards and stationery out of the way. "Brochures here. Tablecloth on top. Okay?"

"Sure. Fine." Delia retrieved the brochures from the bag and stacked them neatly in the corner of the drawer, pulled out the tablecloth, and smoothed it down on top, her well-tended hands touching it lovingly. "I was thinking of giving it to Christine for her wedding present," she said a little wistfully.

"Oh, no, Delia," Teresa protested. "This has to go to your daughter, for certain."

Her aunt Lucy had brought it from Ireland, one of two handmade tablecloths of true Irish lace that her ancestors had gathered around while they discussed what to do when the famine came and they had nothing left to eat. They were the only things Delia's great-grandmother wouldn't sell, insisting that they make the passage to the new country when the time came. In its threads were the conversations that brought Delia's people here, hungry and afraid, but hanging on to their stories, woven into this cloth.

"Jessamyn'll get the one with all the people in it—you know, she calls it the story cloth because she's always telling stories about them. But I thought Christine should have this one, with the flowers. She loves it so much, and—well, she's family too, Teresa, after all this time."

Teresa's face worked around a complexity of emotions she couldn't articulate. She was always better with food than words. The language of food was so fundamental, it couldn't be misunderstood. It was difficult to miscommunicate your intent in pasta or bread.

"How about this," she suggested. "Let's make sure there is a wedding first."

"Oh, no. Trouble in loveland?"

"I think so," Teresa said.

"Y'know, you could have the good grace to pretend that makes you unhappy," Delia suggested.

"What? Did I look happy? I'm not happy when Christine's upset."

"No, but you looked excited. And I do think you're prejudiced, Teresa. You don't like James because he's a shrink, and you think all shrinks are witch doctors."

"No," Teresa said. "I don't think they're witch doctors. If I did, I might trust them."

"Nan had some good ones," Delia tried. "There was that woman—Sandy. You liked Sandy, didn't you?"

"Yeah," Teresa admitted. "I liked Sandy. She did some good."

"Well," Delia said, "so does James. He takes care of a lot of people."

"Maybe that's the problem," Teresa said. "He thinks he has to take care of Christine."

Delia took Teresa's elbow and leaned in close to her. "Let me tell you a secret," she said, "in case you didn't notice. So do you."

Teresa groaned and pulled away, bent to the fireplace and put wood in, kneeled down and watched it flame up into heat. "It's more than that," she insisted. "His family is so—so—"

"Normal?" Delia said. "Rich? Dad's big in politics, Mom's big in the social pages."

"Yeah. That's what I mean."

Delia laughed. "There's nothing wrong with money and social standing, Teresa. You make it sound like a disease."

"It's just not what we're used to. We're more—I don't know. Plain."

"Plain stubborn," Delia said agreeably.

In the argument regarding James Tyrol's admittance into the DiRosa family, Delia came down firmly on the pro side, saying that Christine deserved to have her own life, and besides, if it didn't work out, who better to divorce than a shrink. He'd provide such good alimony. She saw nothing wrong with him even if he was different from Teresa's usual family members—born of old money, his people on the continent for more generations than Teresa's family could trace back in the old country. The first time he came for Sunday dinner, he asked where she usually summered, and she wordlessly pointed past her garden to her compost heap. He gaped at her and cast sullen glances at her grandmother and great-grandmother. She cast sullen glances at him. The lines had been drawn and, as Delia said, she was stubborn. Maybe she did resent his money, his never having to work for much of anything except personal glory. Maybe she did resent the parental manner he assumed with Christine. But none of that meant she was wrong.

"Maybe I do want to take care of her," she said, "but at least I don't want to change her into something she's not."

"And you think James does?" Delia asked.

"Yeah," she said. "I do." Christine had called less than an hour earlier and asked if Teresa knew anyone else in the family who was crazy besides her mother. She wouldn't say why, but her voice was tight and angry, and Teresa assumed it was something to do with James. Afraid he's getting a lemon, Teresa thought.

"Let's have some coffee," Teresa suggested to Delia. "I'll tell you what I know so far."

ABOUT EATING LIGHT

CHRISTINE SAT IN THE PLUSH MAUVE CHAIR IN THE living room of James's condo, fiddling with a cigarette.

"Don't smoke that," James said. "Have something to eat instead."

"You sound like Teresa," Christine said, but she didn't light the cigarette.

Teresa always told Christine she didn't eat enough to keep a bird alive, and Christine reminded her that birds actually eat a great deal. Hummingbirds, for instance, require more calories than any other warm-blooded animal. Yeah, Teresa would say, right. But you still don't eat enough. You're too thin.

Christine supposed she was right. She often let a whole day pass and realized only as she was getting into bed that she'd forgotten to eat. It wasn't painful to her. On the contrary, she felt cleansed by her hunger, empty and light.

There are species of butterflies that never eat anything at all. There are great whales the size of buildings that eat only tiny plankton which they filter through their mouths as they swim. And even humming-birds get all their calories from the nectar of flowers, tree sap, and tiny insects—airy food but enough to carry them five hundred miles in non-stop flight across the Gulf of Mexico. And they find food by seeking beauty, their eyes attuned to red and orange, bright pinks and deep salmon tubes rich in sweet sustenance. Monarda, honeysuckle, fuchsia, paintbrush, trumpeter vine, morning glory, penstemon—they follow the blooming of flowers for two thousand miles in their migratory flights from Mexico to Alaska.

Christine had deep admiration for a creature capable of being sustained by something as insubstantial as nectar. Like eating light. Sifting energy from thin air. In comparison to the way humans ate, gorging on thick meats and breads, swallowing foods as heavy as stones and then wondering why they couldn't move, the hummingbird's life made a lot more sense to her.

She preferred to eat foods that didn't feel thick and heavy inside her. She liked salads and vegetables or fish cooked in bright sauces, like ginger trout, or broccoli covered with Japanese carrot salad. Even for desserts she preferred raspberry ice to hot fudge sundaes. She didn't like to taste food at the back of her throat an hour after she'd eaten it.

And when she was upset, she didn't want food at all. Often, much to the consternation of her aunt and her fiancé, she'd smoke instead. She gave James a look of apology and lit the cigarette after all, drew in smoke, felt the soothing nicotine entering her bloodstream, exhaled with relief. She had picked up the habit when she was nineteen, after she signed her mother into Adelaide State Hospital detox ward for the last time.

"You gonna be okay here, Nan?" she had asked. She never called her Mother. Always Nan.

"Sure," Nan replied, and handed her the pack of cigarettes she brought in. "Here. Take these. I won't need them."

"They let you smoke here," Christine said.

"Yeah. Maybe I don't want to," Nan said. Her hand was trembling, holding out the pack of Virginia Slims Menthol. She already had the shakes. Christine took the cigarettes and went to fill out more of the endless forms necessary for healing.

Before she went to the nurses' station, she stood on the balcony outside the common room, which had a railing that arched up over her head to keep anyone from jumping off. She stood next to a young woman in a plastic chair, huddled under a plaid blanket in the L.A. heat, and looked out over what seemed an unfamiliar landscape, though it was the Southern California where she'd spent many of her childhood years.

It was nearing Christmas, and the neon winter scenes glowed incongruously in the dry landscape. Without even realizing what she was doing, as if she'd been doing it her whole life, Christine tapped a cigarette from the pack and lit it, the cool of the menthol and the unbearable breath of L.A. entering her bloodstream at the same time. When she finished it, she went back in and signed more papers, said good-bye to her mother, and walked away from everything about that night except her cigarettes. Or so she thought.

But tonight Nan was back.

"What did Teresa say?" James asked, nodding at the phone, where Christine's hand still rested.

Christine blew out smoke. "Nothing. No family history anywhere except Nan. And I have all her papers already, so we know what they say."

Christine had just spoken with Teresa, at James's request, about her family background. Christine could almost hear the crackle of disapproval in Teresa's response, and felt once again caught between where she came from and where she was trying to go. At first she resented Teresa. By the time she hung up, she decided it would be more satisfactory to resent James.

James waved the smoke away, then pulled up a chair and sat next to her by the phone. He put a hand on her arm, smoothing her sweater. "Are you angry?" he asked.

She pulled away from his touch. "No," she said.

He laughed, then stopped himself when she whipped around to face him. She resented it that he stayed so cool during arguments, so detached. It was the psychiatric stance, and she wasn't a patient. He'd explained that conflict didn't threaten him. He saw it as an opportunity to increase healthy understanding between them. He could afford to be cool, because he didn't think he was about to be hurt. But he had promised to be respectful of her needs in the matter, and a promise should be kept.

"I'm sorry," he said contritely, "I wasn't laughing *at* you. But I do think it's important that we have all the information available to us, don't you?"

She tamped out the cigarette in the ashtray by the phone, stood up, and went into the bedroom. He followed and sat on the bed while she went to the bureau, picked up a brush, and restlessly pulled it through her hair. Because of Nan, James wanted Christine to go through some tests, genetic counseling, therapy. A personal growth opportunity, he called it. The chance to examine and resolve any residue of trauma from her childhood. Given the high correlation between psychiatric disorders and alcoholism, it only made sense, he said.

"Let's just say that your mother had a disorder—perhaps even schizophrenia, masked by her drinking." Christine began to open her mouth to protest. They'd been through this enough times that the conversation had become a script they both knew their lines to. Here was where she protested, and here was where he asked to be allowed to talk.

"Let me finish," he said. "There's no shame in it. It's an illness. Simply a genetic disorder exacerbated by environmental factors."

"First of all," Christine began, swallowing the anger she could feel rising at the back of her throat, "first of all, there's no way she was schizophrenic. She didn't hear voices. She just got low. And high. Second, what do you plan on doing about it if it's true? Trade me in for a new model?"

"Of course not. Don't be silly. Maybe she was manic-depressive, then. In her day it was often misdiagnosed, but there are some very good drugs for these sort of things today. In my position—"

"Which position is that," she said crisply, "bending over to kiss your own ass?"

He winced. "That's uncalled for, Christine."

Shame washed through her. That was Nan talking through her, or Teresa. She came from a family of women with crude minds and sharp tongues. Knives and cutting boards for dicing up the world. She didn't even know if she meant it when she said things like that. She just knew how to say them, so she did. But she knew he was sensitive about being seen as arrogant or pompous. It was such a stereotype of his profession.

But sometimes he just didn't get it about Nan. He'd never met her, so she was just an interesting case to him, and a problem in their lives that they needed to solve. Granted, he had a positive attitude about solving it, and that carried her through some painful moments, but Nan was no more than that to him. He couldn't see her as a spirit that wouldn't go away, a laugh that could lift your soul to heaven, a series of lost dreams, and finally, a certain grief Christine couldn't live with anymore.

"I apologize," she said stiffly, pushing the word out through the complexities of anger and shame.

He nodded, but he still looked hurt. "I could have a real cushy private practice pill-pushing to old ladies," he said, "but I'm in the trenches, working with the real thing. And I know what I'm talking about," he said, trying to keep his irritation within reasonable bounds in what should be a reasonable discussion. He did know what he was talking about. It was his job to know and it had gotten him the directorship of the Upstate Institute for Mental Disorders. He was the youngest man ever appointed to such a position at the institute, and proud of that too.

"I know," she said a little more gently. "I'm sorry."

He sighed. "Did Teresa upset you?" he asked.

She shrugged. "You know how she is. She won't hear anything about Nan."

James bit back on a remark. As far as he could tell, she wouldn't hear anything about anything. She had a stubborn streak a mile wide which Christine often exhibited after spending time with her, as if she absorbed it in the food Teresa fed her. She brought Christine back to her past when she needed to move forward. It was probably talking to Teresa that put Christine in this mood. Before she'd been mildly anxious and resentful, but not entirely unreasonable.

Christine pulled the brush harder through her hair, which crackled with static, sticking out and clinging to the brush. It was light and fine as a baby's. Like her, James said, fragile and full of light. He couldn't believe she belonged to the same family as Teresa and Nan when he saw their pictures. They were so dark and she was so fair. Only her eyes showed that side of her family. The rest of her belonged to whoever her father had been.

"No matter what we find out about the rest of my mother's family," Christine pointed out, "it won't tell us anything about the paternal influence, as you put it."

He leaned back on the bed and crossed his hands behind his head.

"We do what we can, sweetheart," he said gently. "Especially if we want to have a family. Don't you think that's only fair?"

She made a choking sound and coughed to cover it.

"Something stuck in your throat?" James asked.

She said nothing for a moment, then felt her hand close hard around the handle of the brush. "Fair?" she asked. "Fair?"

What did he know about fair? He was born into every possible ease, and he talked about fair as if it actually existed as a possibility. Was it fair that his family was wealthy and had sheltered him all his life, while she spent her childhood worrying about how they'd eat that day and where they'd be living tomorrow? Was it fair that her mother was a drunk, dead seven years to the day?

But she wouldn't get angry. Wouldn't yell. Yelling violated the rules of disagreement they agreed on in the beginning of their relationship. No name-calling. No yelling. No blaming words.

"Yes," he said judiciously. "Fair."

She flung the brush across the room, where it bounced against the wall and onto the bed, popping him in the chest.

His eyes got wide and he sat up and clutched his chest as if it were bleeding.

She felt horrible. Felt horror at what she'd just done and couldn't take back.

She got up, knocking her chair over, left the room stumbling. James rose from the bed and called after her.

"Christine?" he called, "Christine—what the hell is it?"

But she didn't listen. She fumbled in the closet for her bag and her coat, found them and arranged herself, then opened his apartment door and left.

As she walked down the hall, she waited to hear the door open, but it didn't. He would leave her alone for a while. That was good. She needed to be alone, she told herself. She was way over the top.

She left his condo, walked down the tree-lined path that led out onto the main street, and continued to walk out into the cold winter night. She needed to be alone and in the cold, where she could freeze out what was left of blood and family and passion and heat.

She walked fast but kept stopping to look behind her, as if someone followed. As if she might turn and see James or Teresa or even

Nan running to catch up with her. Nan, most likely, dogging her heels, her trailing ghost a strange hot breeze at the back of her neck.

Nan was inescapable. Inevitable. Flying into the middle of their relationship with her dark hair streaming, her mouth open in drunken song, flapping her unwieldy wings, the ghost of a mother-in-law to haunt a terrified James.

She walked out of the condos, through the upwardly mobile neighborhood that was just outside it, headed toward the noisier main streets of downtown. The sharpness of the air galvanized her into motion and the ice cut into her like cool flute music replacing her blood with clear water. She walked the city streets and watched the headlights of passing cars turn the trees along the side of the road into silver filigree. The streetlamps made circular webs of green and purple in the trees. Wind came up like breath, and the trees threw down their magic, ice clattering at her feet like bones.

She stopped on the corner of Harry Howard and Central and pulled a cigarette out of the pack in her pocket while she debated what to do next. She could take a cab to her apartment, take a bus to Teresa's, or she could go see Amberlin, who didn't live far, or she could keep walking to her glass-art studio, only a few blocks away. The cold wrapped itself tightly around her bones and her emotions, and she headed for her studio. That was the best place to go. It would calm her to be alone and observe light passing through glass, and cheer her to see how close she was to finishing her biggest project to date. When she thought about glass, all other thoughts quieted, the internal noise stopped.

Traffic slowed as she crossed against the light, struggling with matches and wind, and a man in a taxi cursed her soundly. She didn't respond. Her thoughts chased themselves around in circles, beating at the top of her skull and not finding a way out. James was right. Family drama didn't just go away when a family member died. Her mother was still alive in her somewhere.

James told her that women manifested schizophrenia in their late twenties. Christine would be twenty-seven this year. James also told her that it could skip a generation and appear in her children. Didn't he know it would terrify her to hear that?

And she'd been horrible to him. Horrible. Thrown a brush. She must be mad. She must be.

She pulled on the cigarette hard enough to scour her lungs clean. She heard Teresa in her kitchen, speaking with concern. "Quit, *bella.* It's not good for you." Amberlin joined her, saying, "I don't know why someone as smart as you would walk right into the trap Big Tobacco sets up for women—promoting addictions to the powerless and poor." Delia appeared, smiling sheepishly. "Can you exhale near a window, hon? Secondary smoke."

Then, of course, James had his say, lying on the bed, his trim body looking particularly fit in black bikini underwear. He spoke with concern. "For your own good, I'd like to make it a condition of our marriage that you quit smoking before the wedding."

"I prefer to wait until the stress of the wedding is over," Christine said out loud as she exhaled smoke into the lightly falling snow. A grubby man wearing several coats and fingerless gloves nodded as she passed him.

"I don't blame you, sweetheart," he croaked. "I'd like to do the same."

She ducked her head down and walked faster.

Just like her mother, she thought. Talking to herself. Throwing things at her lover. Alcoholic, schizophrenic, manic-depressive, crazy. What did it matter what you called it? *Miserable* was the best word she knew.

She reached her studio, and with shivering hands unlocked the door. Once inside, she immediately felt quieter. It was better to be here than her apartment, so unlived-in as more and more of her items made their way to James's condo. Better to be here than with Amberlin, who would notice her and ask gentle questions that ripped her guts out. And better to be here than endure Teresa's sharp gaze, which would immediately apprehend that she'd had a fight with James. Not that she minded Teresa knowing, but she did mind the small glints of triumph she'd see behind the sympathy. And she didn't want to eat any food.

She wanted to become light. Light enough so that the earth would fall back beneath her feet, and she could mount the sky to the moon that rode so calm and high above the whipping winds all earthbound creatures had to endure. Light enough to fly away from the sight of her mother's heavy dark eyes.

She took her coat off and shook out the wet and cold, rubbed her hands together. She went to the table and pulled the dust sheet off slowly, so that inch by inch she revealed the watery blue of the castle walls, the high silver and turquoise of the tower, the moss green of the drawbridge that fell over the solid cobalt-blue stream of the moat.

It had taken her months to make this castle. She'd drawn it first on endless pieces of paper, seeking perfection in form, something that would please the eye by shape alone even before she picked the glasses, the proper combination of colors and textures. And last, she began the slow and delicate process of piecing it together.

She had only to add a turret around the west wall now, and then she could present it to James. It would be their castle, perfect and pleasing. A place where all walls would be windows that let the light through to the center.

She ran a finger along the tower, where she'd fretted over getting the angles right without placing too much stress on the glass. It held, and was firm. She pulled the drawbridge up and lowered it, sighing with satisfaction. Teresa could keep her food, all made and consumed and shit away in a matter of hours. Christine preferred the more permanent satisfaction of glass and light consumed only by the eyes and capable of being reconsumed again and again without having to be remade.

She wiped her hand on her pants and reached for the glass she had ready for the turret, her eye lingering lovingly over the undulating blues of the west wall. Such subtle blues—watery, but with enough silver in them to be mistaken for stone in certain lights. Like liquid stone. The lines swam into your eyes effortlessly.

Looking at it made her calm and hopeful. James would be upset with her, but he'd forgive her. He'd understand. That's what she loved about him. He was so understanding about her pain, her confusion, her fears. After all, he knew so much about it, and had so many reassuring words to offer on the subject of emotional unbalance. They would talk it out, she would do exactly as he suggested, and they would go on to have a beautiful wedding and a life she'd dreamed about since she was a little girl. Though it might not be perfect, it would be surrounded with light and clarity and peace. There would be a seamlessness to their life, inside and out. James could help her create that. He was good at it.

She stroked her castle, her finger feeling the deepest pleasure in the cool silkiness of the glass. Then a slight hitch disturbed the motion of her hand. She stopped, and lifted her finger from the glass.

It was bleeding. There was a small line like a paper cut right at the tip. She'd been cut.

She touched the castle, blood from her finger flowing into a thin crevice where the glass had pushed against itself, cracked, and raised slightly.

As she stared, her eyes grew wide and hard. Horror washed through her, mingling with disbelief.

There was a crack in the glass.

"No," she whispered. "No." It couldn't be. She'd been so careful. Planned so meticulously. Worked so hard.

But it was. A crack in the glass. A stress fracture in her perfect glass, running down the center of the wall. She touched it, then pulled her hand back, as if burned.

"No," she whispered again, this time as an imperative to herself because she knew what she was about to do. Almost believed she could stop herself. But she couldn't.

"No," she commanded herself as she watched her arm pull itself back and swing in a perfect arc toward the table.

"No," she roared, older than a screaming storm high in the dusty hills, and her arm swept the castle off the table, swept it high into the air.

Did she mean to do this, or had her arm developed a separate will, expressing her ancestral capacity for the large gesture? The castle lifted into the air to her left and just above her. It hung there suspended by her uncertainty, waiting to know her final intent. She held as still as the moment.

She thought first of hummingbirds, their fragility and strength. She thought of the improbability of their flight, and their nightly retreat into near death, the daily resurrection of their heartbeat. Then she thought of the last time she'd seen one.

She was at Bancroft's Landscaping to get an order of herbs for Teresa. The herbs and annuals were housed in plastic-roofed longhouses, and Christine searched rows of geraniums and petunias, their colors noisy and profuse around her. Above her head hung baskets of fuchsia blossoming in arrogant purples and reds. And flitting among their blossoms was a green jewel in motion. A hummingbird.

It flew back and forth, back and forth, up and down the length of the arched plastic ceiling. She watched until she grew dizzy, and then she stopped a woman who wore a green shirt and a name tag and was watering plants.

She pointed to the hummingbird. "What's it doing?" she asked.

The woman wrinkled her nose and peered at Christine blankly through thick glasses. "What?" she asked.

Christine pointed up to the glint of green that zipped across the billowing white ceiling. The woman followed Christine's finger.

"Him?" she asked. "Oh, he's probably stuck. That happens sometimes." She picked up a flat of red petunias and walked out.

The hummingbird stopped in midair and hovered above Christine. "It's not a he," Christine said to nobody. "It's a she. See the throat? There's no red."

The unlikely machinery of the bird's wings held it suspended ten feet above her face. Then it aimed itself straight up and rammed into the plastic ceiling.

Christine gasped, waited for it to drop dead at her feet. But it didn't. Instead, it kept beating at the plastic, chirping at it scoldingly, trying to ram a hole through to the sky. Through the ceiling. Through the ceiling. Through the ceiling.

Christine began to tremble. Her hand shook as she brought it to her mouth to hold back the bile rising in her throat.

"Christine?" a voice asked behind her. "Is that you? Are you okay?"

She turned to the sound and saw Rowan Bancroft, his dark eyes regarding her solemnly. She gestured at the hummingbird.

"Oh," he said. He scratched at his head. "Yeah. They do that. Strange, isn't it? Tiny bird, great big ceiling, and she keeps throwing herself at it like it'll make a difference. Makes me wonder what I'm missing."

"But she'll kill herself," Christine said.

Rowan shook his head. "No. They do this all the time. What'll happen is she'll get exhausted. Give up. Then she'll drop down. Soon as she drops, she'll see the door. Then she'll be out."

Christine watched the castle hang suspended in the air. In her belly she felt the motion of despair, the final wall between grief and acceptance. It was a wall she'd flung herself against repeatedly, since she was a little girl. Since her mother's death. It was a wall she didn't want to bruise herself on anymore.

She let out a long breath of air, dropped her arm to her side, and watched the castle fall, slivers of glass raining up toward the ceiling in a storm of beauty and impossible rage.

TERESA'S KITCHEN

"WELL," DELIA SAID AS SHE PUT HER COAT ON TO leave, "if he's gonna pass her up because he's worried about Nan's genes, I'll have to eat every nice word I ever said about him."

Teresa picked up a fork and knife from the counter and held them out. "I hope you're good and hungry."

"Uh-uh," Delia said. "Not yet. It's probably just pre-wedding jitters. I'll see you tomorrow."

She opened the door and let in cold air. With it, Teresa's cat, Tosca, came streaking into the kitchen and wrapped herself around Teresa's leg.

"I said you wouldn't like it," Teresa said, putting the utensils down and bending to stroke the small black face and listen to the complaining meows she emitted. Donnie named her Tosca when she proved herself part of the family by howling continuously throughout "Vissi d'arte," her voice resonating against the soprano aria in remarkable harmony.

Teresa put more food in Tosca's bowl and she purred gratefully as she ate. Earlier, when Delia arrived, Teresa had turned the radio off, and now the kitchen was quiet. Too quiet. Not the quiet of peace, but the quiet of absence. Teresa turned the radio back on, poured warm water into a bowl with a spoon of sugar, and added yeast. She watched it bubble into life.

From the kitchen wall, Great-grandmother Emilia watched too, with her robust baby daughter hefted on her knee, her face caught in an almost-smile. Teresa had seen that same expression on her grandmother's face. It signified pride, and a joy that was too big for words. Better to cook something and put the joy in that.

Teresa had never met Emilia. She stayed in the old country, the Abruzzi hills, after her children left for America. Teresa often wondered what that was like, to have your children go so far away and know you might not ever see them again. A whole ocean between you and them and only letters in those days for communication. At least Donnie was only a few hours away in Boston, though emotion kept them farther apart than an ocean right now. He was at the age when he had to separate, and this was complicated by the divorce, which he was still angry about. Recently he had decided to blame his mother. Maybe next year he'd be angry at his father instead.

Either way, he was gone, off into the adventure of his own life, and he wouldn't really be back until he started a family of his own, the future drawing itself to the past like water to shore.

Her grandmother, who left her country when she was a teenager and came here to this strange new world, taught her how that happened. She'd marched with the suffragettes, bobbed her hair, got a job, and got married. She learned the new world well, but she never gave up the old, even when her own daughter was busy fitting in with the world she'd been born into, taking on cultural accoutrements such as meat loaf and bologna sandwiches and even TV dinners.

But when she had a family of her own, she and Teresa's father built a house on the same half-acre plot of land where she was raised. Consequently, Teresa spent as much time in her grandmother's house as in her mother's. It was from her grandmother that Teresa learned the alchemy of cooking. In her kitchen she'd absorbed the lesson that food was sacred, a central force around which people revolved.

She remembered sitting on a high stool at the counter near the stove. Her mother was washing dishes at the sink. Grandma was making the dough for pasta, cracking an egg into the center of a well made of flour and folding the flour into the egg as she sang a strange Italian song called "Carne di cane"—the meat of the dog.

Nan, at the kitchen table, was singing too, but a different song. Dionne Warwick. "Do You Know the Way to San Jose." Something about the song made Grandma shake her head.

"Anunziata," she called to her, "come have a cookie."

Everyone else called her Nan, but not Grandma. Nan was "Merigan," she said, as if she were biting on a nail. Too American. Sometimes she'd call it "Merdegan," and Teresa's mother would scold her for using "language" in front of the girls.

Teresa could see Nan through the cutout between the stove and the big table where pasta was rolled out and where, on Sundays, Uncle Henry made loud predictions about politics and Grandpa Donato drank wine from juice glasses and Aunt Angelina rapped her wedding ring against the Formica for grace and everybody ate.

Nan looked little and lonely, sitting there by herself, even though she was years older than Teresa. She sang in a high, sweet voice, holding her hands up to the light that poured in through the windows. Her pretty fingers with their painted pink nails danced in the air, weaving something substantial out of sound and light. Teresa watched them, fascinated, until her grandmother nudged her.

"Don't pay her attention," she whispered. "Watch this."

Teresa was called back to her grandmother's hands, large and gnarled like fleshy old roots. But her fingers had the delicate knowledge of what precise motion to make, how to fold the dough and lift it and prod it into life.

The sound of slow feet squeaking across the old wood floor interrupted the quiet motion of her grandma's hands. Grandpa Donato came in with a smelly cigar sticking out of his mouth. Grandma raised her face, looked at him, and then at Nan.

Che fa? he asked.

Niènte, she answered as she slapped the dough hard against the counter.

The feel in the room shifted. Her mother stopped washing dishes and dried her hands on a towel. Nan was in trouble again. Teresa didn't understand it—something about a boy and going out—but it was familiar because Nan was often in trouble lately. Daddy had yelled at her earlier in the week. Now, Teresa supposed, it was Grandpa's turn. But he didn't yell.

He stood for a moment, pulling on the cigar, smoke running from it lazily as if it would rather not make the effort. Then he went to Nan and patted her cheek once. Twice. Three times.

She stopped singing and smiled up at him.

Dove? he asked her. *Dove tu'angelleti? Ascolte gli'angelleti, sì?*

Nan giggled and covered her mouth with her hand.

Grandpa shook his head and pulled the cigar from his mouth. He walked to Teresa, clapped his big red hands onto her shoulders like a shirt, and pushed his face close to hers.

"Your sister," he said in his thickly accented English, "she don't hear her angels."

"Pa," her mother said, "stop that. You'll scare her."

He unbent himself and replied in Italian, poking his cigar at her. *Parla Julia. Ascolta me. Mi dice bene.*

Then he went away. Grandma turned to Teresa's mother, who shook her head. "No, Ma. I won't. I don't care what he says. Nan doesn't need Julia."

Teresa wrinkled her nose. Julia was an old woman who lived down the street. She had very few teeth and her breath was like a dog's, only stronger. Sometimes she'd come for dinner, and Grandma DiRosa always served her first, with the best of everything. After dinner Julia would take one of the old enamel bowls and pour water into it, say some words, and then pour oil on top. The women would study the oil swirled on the surface of the water and wait for Julia to speak. She used a dialect Teresa couldn't decipher, though she knew many of the words her grandparents used. The other women would listen carefully, discuss for a long time, then pass money into Julia's hands.

Again Julia's name was said. Again Teresa's mother shook her head. At the table, Nan went back to singing. Teresa watched all the unspoken words in the gestures of their hands and the workings of their faces. The conversation concluded when her mother sliced a hand through the air. Then Grandma sighed and turned Teresa's stool toward her.

"Don't worry about it," she said. "Have a dadaluce."

She held up a perfectly round cookie, with smooth white icing and pink and blue sprinkles on top. Dadaluce. The little light cookies. Teresa's eyes grew wide. The cookie moved toward her open mouth. She closed her eyes and accepted it.

When she opened them again, Nan was standing next to her, her mouth open for a cookie. Behind her, their mother stood smiling, even though her eyes had tears pooling at the rims.

The cookie had done that. The dadaluce. Teresa picked one up and examined it. It stopped Nan singing and made her mother smile and cry at the same time. It was as if, when Grandma fed you a cookie, she put into your mouth all her best thoughts for you.

At that moment Teresa learned a central lesson of her life. She learned that kitchen magic was big magic. It could change bad feelings to good, lift hearts and soothe minds. She learned that before she was tall enough to reach the stove, and she never forgot.

Now, in her own kitchen, while the yeast bubbled in the bowl of water, she muttered words over it. Then she took the bag of flour and poured some in. She stirred, muttered more, added flour, and stirred again. The batter grew thick and became dough. She wiped her hands on her pants and dipped them in, manipulating the sticky mass, adding more flour, humming with the radio as the work progressed.

When the doorbell rang, her hands were encased in abundant goo. She raised them high. "Damn," she said, and went to the door, looked out the window, and saw Rowan Bancroft, mostly dark eyes and a beard between a wool hat and scarf.

She clutched at the doorknob with her wrists and got nowhere. "Could you open it?" she asked, and he lifted one side of his hat. She raised her hands and showed him. He nodded and turned the knob, let himself in.

"Hi," he said, knocking snow off his feet and pulling his hat off. His hair sprang to life like an animate thing.

"Hi," she said back, holding out a hand, then pulling it away. "I'm kind of messy."

He nodded. "Bread?"

"That's right." She scraped at her hands and returned the dough to the bowl while he tugged at his scarf and unbuttoned his coat.

"I see. For the party?"

She nodded.

"Be a damn cold night for it if it's like tonight."

She nodded some more. "Would you like a cup of coffee or something? Some whiskey maybe?"

"Maybe both," he said, "if it's no trouble."

"Oh. No. Not at all," she lied, because it was trouble. Looked like trouble to her, anyway, the way he leaned on the counter with his elbows and smiled, his eyes all attention on her. It hadn't yet occurred to her to ask him why he had come. People came over and visited for no reason, and when they did you didn't ask them why. You just gave them something to drink or eat.

But Delia was probably right after all. She usually was, seeing things Teresa managed to miss. Not much stuck to her, but not much got by her either. Teresa let things go by because she didn't want to be involved in any trouble.

"No trouble," she said, and left the dough momentarily to pour coffee into a cup, get milk and a bottle of whiskey from the stash in the dining room, and bring it to him. He stood at the counter and fixed his cup.

"Sit," she said, waving at the table. "Relax."

He wrapped his hands around the cup, warming them. They were large hands, but they held things softly. She noticed that at his garden shop. Leaves and petals and coffee cups rested gently in his hands.

"Will you sit too?" he asked.

She pulled her eyes up from his hands and blinked. Her face felt unnaturally warm. "I have to finish the bread. But I can talk while I work. Was there something special brought you here?"

His eyes lingered for a long time on her face, but he pressed his lips together and was quiet for a moment. She started pushing the dough around in the bowl hard.

"I was on my way home," he said. He had a quiet voice, and he often paused before he answered a question, as if he was really thinking about it. "I thought I'd double-check on your flowers. You want red and white only, right? Separate vases?"

"That's right," she said. "That's just right."

He sipped on his coffee and nodded. "I was thinking about it today, looking at the Peace Rose. You know, they're a kind of peachy color. I thought maybe I should suggest it, then I said no. The only other flower I'd like to see right now is squash blossoms."

"Squash blossoms?"

"That's right. Then I'd know it was summer."

She smiled. Great golden cups of sunlight spread themselves across his home garden in the summer. She'd seen them last year when she stopped at his house to pick up transplants of the wild strawberries that grew under his oak tree. She'd marveled at how many he had and asked why he wanted that much zucchini. He said he didn't. He just liked the blossoms.

So she picked a basketful and showed him how to make fried blossoms. How to use them in risotto and soup and pasta primavera just like she'd been taught.

"But in the summer, whiskey and coffee doesn't taste as good, does it?" she asked.

"You're right. It's good tonight. My father used to drink this on cold nights. Irish coffee."

"Not so Irish," she said. "My grandfather liked the same thing. And my father. Probably the Irish stole it from the Italians."

Rowan laughed, a solid sound, like stones tumbling down a hill. "We didn't steal anything from the Italians, except maybe their women."

Teresa picked the dough up and slapped it against the counter, flipped it over, slapped it again. Rowan cleared his throat as if getting ready to make a speech. She felt every muscle in her back and shoulders tensing.

"Teresa," he said, "I know your son's away at school, and—well, the divorce and all—so I wondered—" He paused, and though she felt his eyes on her, she kept her face down, concentrated on the dough, picking it up and slapping it down.

He continued. "I wondered if you need any help this year. I know how hard you work to put this party together, and without your family, I thought maybe you'd need an extra hand, or driver, or something."

"Oh," she said, pressing into the dough and holding still. She didn't expect that. Not at all. "Oh. That's very nice of you, Rowan. I might need somebody around to do the things Sam used to."

She saw a grin form itself on his face and felt her own face go hot again. "I didn't mean it that way," she said quickly. "I mean, I didn't mean anything—oh, shit, you know what I mean."

"I'll take it in the best possible way," Rowan said. His mouth stopped grinning, but his eyes didn't. He took another long sip from his cup and plunked it down hard on the table. "And I should go. My daughter's coming home from school Sunday and I don't think I cleaned my house since she left. Probably I'll get her for only a few nights before she's racing out after some friend or other. Strange, isn't it? When they grow up?"

Teresa put the dough in the bowl. She washed her hands at the sink, dried them on her pants. "Yeah," she said. "It is."

Such extravagant closeness followed by such extravagant leaving. She was in the early phases of adjusting to it, and felt Donnie's absence like a relentless darkness in her heart. Or maybe it wasn't so much his absence as the absence of his childhood, gone so suddenly after so many years of just being there in her life. She tried to explain to Delia, but Delia didn't want to think about it yet. She always said it was best to avoid reality as long as possible. Amberlin hadn't had children yet, so she understood only in her head, not her heart. And Christine was still trying to grow up and away from her own mother's legacy.

"Does it get easier?" she asked quietly, trying to sound light but failing.

Rowan paused in getting his coat on and brought his broad face around to stare at hers. He paused, asking himself something, and answered with a quick nod. It seemed like he had a lot of practice with talking to himself, but very quietly. "It gets more familiar," he said, "like it's supposed to be this way. And then it gets kind of fun to have your own life back. No worries about homework or what time they'll get in, or where you have to be. It's like being twenty again, with more sense."

Rowan smiled as he pulled his hat and scarf back on and she went over to the table, stood next to him, waiting to see him out. He put one of his large hands on her shoulders, as softly as he'd hold a leaf or a cup of coffee.

"Teresa," he said, "what I said—about being here to help out—that's not just for the party. I want you to feel free to call on me anytime. Okay?"

Teresa felt something stirring in her belly. A warning, maybe. It blocked the possibility of any words emerging from her brain to her mouth, and so she smiled tightly, nodded. For the first time in many years, she wished more than anything for a cigarette.

"Okay?" Rowan asked again.

"Sure," she squeezed out. "Sure."

He lifted his hand, turned the doorknob, and was gone.

She pressed her palms against her belly and took in some air. Then she turned back to the counter and leaned on it. *"Che fa?"* she asked. *"Che fa?"*

She poked a finger in the bread contemplatively.

Her husband—no, her ex-husband, she had to remember to call Sam her ex-husband—once said that her hands were sexy when she made bread. He came home from school early one day while she was making Tuscan grape bread, a harvest bread from the Etruscans, and started tickling the back of her neck. So sexy, he said. Like a young Etruscan goddess.

It was early May, and she had very small artichokes cooking. She and Sam had no babies yet because she'd miscarried again and was taking the rest of the year off from teaching to recuperate. Sam came home from work early, and she was punching the dough down, and one thing led to the other on top of her long butcher-block table, and she'd had to clean dough and oil off her feet when they were done.

That bread tasted better than any other time she'd made it, though Sam was reluctant to let her share it, as she usually did, with the paper delivery boy.

She told the story to Amberlin and Delia, and they paused slightly before they bit into the bread she'd just served them, but by then Sam was gone. Besides, in Teresa's kitchen, once they had their first bite of rosemary garlic chicken or venison with currant sauce, they didn't much care who had sex in it.

She shook out a new dish towel and laid it over the bread dough.

"Rowan Bancroft, you're a fool," she said firmly. For as long as she'd known him, he was a widower, and from what he said he'd been one since his children were small. Why would he want to start that mess all over again? That involvement, so full of possible pain. A magic that couldn't sustain itself in the face of reality. He *was* a fool, and she was going to put the dough in the refrigerator and get some sleep.

Her phone rang and she picked it up.

"Hello?" she asked.

"Hello?" the male voice on the other end asked back.

"Donnie?" Even her skin tone lifted, she was so happy at the thought.

"Teresa?" the caller responded.

"Oh," she said, her face falling into grimmer lines as she recognized the voice. "James."

"I'm looking for Christine. Is she there?"

To Teresa he sounded tense, distracted. "You two have a fight?"

Fight was the wrong word, he told her. They'd been discussing some things.

"Of course," she agreed, rolling her eyes. "I meant to call it an opportunity for conflict resolution and increased understanding. But she must be resolving it somewhere else, because she's not here."

"If she calls—"

"I'll tell her you were concerned about her personal growth."

"Just tell her to call me, Teresa," he said sharply, and hung up.

She listened to the dial tone for a moment, then put the phone down. Judy Garland sang "Have Yourself a Merry Little Christmas" on the radio. The song made her taste sorrow at the back of her throat. She turned it off.

She lifted the dishcloth off the bread dough and pinched off a blob before putting the bowl in the refrigerator. She plucked a piece of rosemary from her windowsill plant, turned off the kitchen light, and went to the living room, where the flames in the fireplace curled up toward the sky. She tossed the bread and rosemary into the flame. It blackened and sizzled, transformed into heat and gas and air.

Having said her prayers for her kitchen and all those she loved, she went upstairs to sleep and dream of bread.

ABOUT BREAD

When Christine was a little girl she was taught that during mass the communion host was divinely transformed into the body of Christ, which was the bread of life.

Although to her mind the thin white wafer the priest placed delicately on her tongue bore no resemblance to bread, she understood it was important magic.

She thought the whiteness of the host was what a pure, unsinning soul must look like. A soul with sin on it would be stained with black spots that would come out only in the wringer washing machine of purgatory. Christine was afraid she'd forget her instructions from Sunday school and chew the host, and this would be felt as an offense in heaven. That fear was realized when Nan's attendance at church became sporadic, and she insisted Christine go to mass and bring home communion to her.

Christine would hold the host lightly in her mouth, and when she got back to her pew take it out and break it in two so she could bring half home to her mother in a napkin.

Every time she did this she imagined Jesus' screams as reverberating between church and the seat of the Most Holy Father in heaven.

"It's not right, Nan," she told her mother.

"Yes it is, honey. I need to take communion."

"Then go to church and get it," Christine protested.

Nan shook her head. "I can't. I just can't. C'mon, Christine. It's not that big a deal."

They often fought that way, as if they were siblings rather than mother and daughter. Nan was only nineteen when Christine was born, and she never felt old enough to discipline her. Christine never felt Nan was reliable enough to let her do so.

"What about my soul?" Christine argued back. "If God hears Jesus' screaming when I break him in half, won't I go to hell?"

Her mother shook her head. "It's only a venal sin. Tell it at confession."

So Christine did. "Bless me, Father, for I have sinned," she said. "It's been a week since my last confession and I've disobeyed my mother twice."

She didn't explain that both times it had to do with taking her mother's bottles of whiskey and pouring them down the drain. She'd thought long and hard before deciding whether this was stealing or disobedience, and finally decided that it was stealing only if she was drinking it. Since she wasn't, it must be disobedience. Not that it helped any, since her mother would just go out and get more, but Christine found that sometimes it took her a few days, during which time they would eat better, sleep better, and sometimes Nan would even pick up her guitar and sing and play, which Christine enjoyed.

"I also had bad thoughts twice—uh, three times," Christine continued, "and I made Jesus scream once."

The pause that followed this recital of her sins always frightened her. She wondered if the priest was checking in with the Almighty Father, and what the verdict would be. Years later she would remember the feeling whenever she waited for a clerk at a store to run her credit card through the scanner. What if the machine denied her credit, and she was standing there with all her purchases on the counter, terribly ashamed at her financial inadequacy? And what if God denied her forgiveness? Would she have to kill herself? Become a nun? God would know more than the priest, who never asked for particulars. He never asked what she meant by bad thoughts, or exactly how she made

Jesus scream. She figured that meant he was letting God decide. It didn't occur to her that he just wasn't listening.

Nor was she ever taught in Sunday school that the original host was rough matzo, the Jewish unleavened bread of affliction. It would not have been white or round at all.

Teresa told her about it years later. She had researched the topic for a paper she wrote on ritual uses of food. She also told her that the making of communion hosts was now a Sister industry, with Contemplative nuns fashioning from flour and water in the silent places of prayer, perfect round white hosts that would become the body of Christ. The Eucharist, which they are not allowed to consecrate, comes from their hands.

But as a young girl who knew none of this, Christine continued to bring home half-hosts for her mother, worry about Jesus' screams projected across the celestial kingdom, and confess the sin to priests around the country as her mother moved them from place to place in search of something she could never name. Whatever she wanted, it had little to do with the waitressing jobs she was fired from almost as fast as she got them. Christine couldn't tell if she was looking for something or running away from something or just constantly lost. All she knew was that Nan drank too much, and every year too much became a little more. Sometimes she blamed her mother's drinking on her own sin. Maybe Jesus would listen to her prayers better if she wasn't mutilating his body on Sundays.

Once, on the walk between church and her home, she held the half-host up to the bright morning sun to see if she could detect any signs of blood or general distress in the body of Christ. She saw none, but she noticed the quality of light as it passed through the thin white wafer. It looked like a thin white piece of glass, brittle and fragile in her hands. She could see right through it to the shadow of a bird passing on the other side. The light was beautiful, and the clean shadow of the bird wrote a particular darkness on its snowy radiance.

She tucked the half-host back in the napkin and went home. They were living in a pretty nice apartment, since their income was being supplemented by the income of a man who found the advantages of Nan's dark beauty and exigent passion outweighed the disadvantages of her attachment to alcohol.

When she stepped inside the door, Christine knew something was wrong. She smelled something acrid and followed the scent to the kitchen, where she saw her mother standing on the table, which was laden with all manner of food. Roasted chicken, vegetables in sauces, biscuits, potatoes. All of it burnt into greasy charcoal, withered black crusts.

"Nan, what did you do?" Christine asked quietly.

Her mother brought her attention to the points of light cast by the cheap chandelier, which she seemed to be chasing with her hand across the ceiling, and down to her daughter. Her eyes found their focus and bored into Christine. She was wearing a long blue strapless silk dress—a vintage piece she'd picked up at a Salvation Army for two dollars—and no shoes. Her left foot pressed into the edge of the chicken.

"I forgot to stop cooking, Chrissy," she slurred. "*Accidente.* I hate that shit. Bad 'nough you gotta remember t' cook. Then you gotta 'member t' stop cooking."

She kicked the chicken across the room, giggled, and turned back up toward the ceiling. Christine stared at the broken carcass, flesh blackened, little curls of smoke still rising from underneath the skin.

Her mother's laughter, pretty as a song, rippled across the air between them. "Who wantsa chicken, huh? Let 'em eat cake! Is't cake? Maybeeee—light? Lesseat light, huh, Chrissy?"

She tilted her head back, her long black hair reaching to her behind, held her arms up, and took in gulps of air. Her hands hit the diamond-shaped pieces of glass hanging from the chandelier. Dust danced around her fingers, supported by golden rays of light.

Christine noticed the empty bottle of wine on the table, near her mother's feet. She'd missed one, apparently. She wondered if there was any other food in the house.

Then she remembered the communion host. She removed it from her pocket carefully and unwrapped it from the napkin. Bread was made from living creatures and it sustained living creatures. And it could change. Transubstantiate. Become the body of a man. Become glass, broken, chewed, and swallowed in utmost pain. Become shadowed by birds. Become light passing through us, as if we were glass.

She went to the cupboard and got a plate and a fork, put the host on the plate, and the fork next to the host. She took all of this arrangement and put it on the table.

"Here, Nan," she said grimly. "Have some lunch."

And that day, at the age of twelve, she refused to step foot inside a church ever again. Instead, she spent Sunday mornings at an art class, where she learned how to work with stained glass, and express something sacred in terms of color and light.

GATHERING INGREDIENTS

"ACTUALLY, QUINOA DATES BACK TO THE INCAN EMpire. It's indigenous to South America," Amberlin explained. "It's not a synthetic grain. It's just wheat free."

"Oh," the woman said, twirling a slightly greasy lock of hair around her finger. Amberlin imagined that the woman had long, thick underarm hair. Probably braided. From the scent of her, she didn't believe in deodorant either. Did political correctness, she wondered, have to include ugliness and body odor? "So is it better for you?" the woman asked.

"If you're allergic to wheat, it is," Amberlin said, trying to restrain her impatience. She wanted to flip the sign to CLOSED on the door of the Lark Street shop, get her stuff packed up for Teresa's tomorrow, get home, and get some sleep. The next two days would be nonstop work.

But the woman continued asking questions about millet and amaranth and couscous, which someone told her was coated with flour and was that bad for you? She followed Amberlin to the counter, talking talking talking while Amberlin busied herself with cashing out the register. "Excuse me if I do this now," she said. "I'm running terribly late."

"That's all right," the woman said, and continued talking.

All right, Amberlin thought, for you. The phone behind her rang, and she picked it up, smiled at the woman apologetically, and spoke into it. "Hey, Teresa. Just about to close up," she said pointedly. The customer blinked at her. "What? Sure. I'll bring the juniper berries. Someone what? A deer? Teresa, that's horrible. You're going to eat it? No. Never mind. I don't want to know what you do with the heart. Have you heard from Christine?"

She smiled, put her hand over the receiver, and asked the customer in a whisper if there was anything else. The customer shook her head, chewed the ends of her hair, and looked around her vaguely, then wandered toward the door and exited. Amberlin breathed a great sigh of relief when the little bell on the door tinkled as it opened and shut. On the line, Teresa was saying that she wasn't Christine's mother.

"Testy, aren't we?" Amberlin said. "Pre-party OCD? That's obsessive compulsive disorder, in case you wondered."

"That sounds about right," Teresa admitted easily. Sometimes Amberlin found it disconcerting how definite Teresa was about herself, and how accepting of her own faults. She envied the capacity even while she wasn't sure it was such a good thing. "Is Sherry all set?" Teresa asked.

"Yes," she said, her voice a shade less certain. "She'll be there, with guitar. She said she wouldn't miss it."

"She doesn't have to sing for her supper," Teresa said. "You told her that, right?"

"I did," Amberlin said, not mentioning that in fact she had tried to get Sherry to sit the event out. She'd be real busy, she told Sherry. Somebody had to make sure everything stayed on track, and though Delia was great at socializing, she wouldn't see to it that the coffeemaker stayed full. And once the party was rolling, Teresa just seemed to let it all go to the waiters they hired for the evening. It was mostly up to her and Christine to stay alert.

Sherry just said that was okay since she'd be working too, making music for the people. Besides, it would be a sort of milestone for the two of them to attend the event together. A public statement.

Amberlin didn't say that's what she was afraid of.

"Sherry wants to play," she said to Teresa. "She says she's already tasted enough of your art, and you should taste hers since you never get to any of her gigs."

"Okay, then," Teresa said, "I'll let her. Is something wrong?"

For someone who spoke so little about her own problems or feelings, Teresa was adept at hearing small changes in tone in other people. But for once, Amberlin didn't want to talk about it. "No," she said, "everything's fine. Just Christmas blues. And I'm not even Christian. Must be hell on you Catholic types."

Teresa admitted that it was, asked again for Amberlin to not forget the juniper berries and could she pick up the soda on the way over. It was at Beverage World, already paid for, in her name.

"If you ask nice," Amberlin said only half playfully. Now and then Teresa needed reminding not to be so officious. Both she and Delia would sometimes forget not to treat her like an employee, or, even worse, a younger sister. Often her comments about politics or the environment or relationships inspired them to pass knowing looks to each other and nod sagely. If she asked what they meant by it, they'd say nothing. Just nothing. Amberlin felt guilty relief when they did the same thing to Christine. At least she wasn't uncomfortable alone. At least she had an ally. And while Amberlin tried to engage Delia and Teresa in discussion about the motives for their behavior, Christine would just tell them to knock it off. It was time they figured out that adulthood started at twenty-one, not at forty.

"Please," Teresa said contritely. "And I do appreciate it."

"Okay. See you tomorrow."

Amberlin hung up, locked the door to the shop, and turned the sign to read CLOSED. She took in and expelled a good lungful of air, and ruffled her light brown hair as if to shake out the day. She caught a glimpse of herself in the window and saw that her hair was getting quite long. Past her shoulder blades and on its way down her back. The gold streak she'd added to it last year was growing out. She didn't know if she'd go back and have it done again. Sherry liked things natural, she said. But she didn't know why that should make any difference to her. After all, it was her hair.

Ironically, her ex-husband would have liked it streaked. He said she didn't do enough with her hair to make all that length worthwhile. He wanted her to cut it. But Sherry thought she was beautiful even when her hair was greasy and she was bloated and premenstrual. She didn't know if that was because women just understood these things better, or if it was because Sherry was so good at seeing beauty. She had an eye that caught it as it appeared, and a heart that took it in.

Maybe that came from being a musician and living a life that was about creating beauty to feed others. Sherry said she thought of herself as food for her audience, who consumed the music she wrote and played. Amberlin found the image frightening, but Sherry said it was okay as long as they kept plumping up her checking account. She was a woman to whom happiness came easily and often.

Amberlin loved that about her, though she didn't know how she managed it. She worked on the suicide hotline, and got Amberlin to volunteer too, though they had very different reactions to the people they counseled. Sherry would come home and cook a pot of pasta and watch something stupid on TV, glad to know she'd done something good in the world. Amberlin would come home and exercise furiously and worry that she hadn't done enough.

Amberlin moved around the store, closing bins, straightening jars of organic peanut butter on the shelves, covering the produce. She had things to pack in boxes. The big cappuccino maker. The hand blender that somehow had gotten left there. Boxes of cloth napkins. Things. Delia would pick her up in the morning and help her carry all the things, but Amberlin wished that next year they could just have the party at the shop. To get Teresa to agree would take a fight, she knew. She'd had to fight with her about renting the Lark Street space to begin with.

Teresa, she decided, was resistant to change. Her first answer to any suggestion of it was no. That is, unless she was initiating the change. Then she'd go ahead and act without even telling anyone what she was up to. Like her ability to see and accept her own faults, Amberlin wasn't sure if that was good or bad. She supposed there was a certain freedom in being able to act on what you wanted without pause, but it seemed unfair to her that Teresa should be so good at it, and so resistant when someone else tried it.

When Amberlin told Teresa the cooking arrangements at her house were no longer adequate to the amount of work they were doing, Teresa balked at the idea of working anywhere else. She liked being able to cook in her pajamas, she said. She liked her food to come from her own home. Amberlin said she needed to define her own baking space and she couldn't do that in Teresa's kitchen. Teresa fretted and fumed for a week, until Amberlin threatened to quit, and then Teresa did an immediate about-face. Within a week they secured a lease on the Lark Street property, which was already equipped from a previous restaurant.

Now, besides preparing for most events in the kitchen here, Amberlin had opened a storefront that sold her baked goods and organic baking supplies. This was her baby to manage, and she felt good about what it added to the business.

She had met Teresa four years ago when she was teaching an adult ed class in nutritional baking that Teresa took. She brought strawberry muffins to class, Teresa tasted one, and offered to hire her on the spot.

"I can't bake like this," she told Amberlin. "I have to buy from places. I want my own baker. Can you just do this sort of thing anytime you want?"

Amberlin had laughed, nervously wondering who this woman was and what she was after. "Of course. It's not magic. It's just baking."

Teresa pointed a work-roughened finger at her. "That's magic. I'll hire you if you're interested."

Later, Teresa said she did get it right. She knew enough to hire Amberlin, who could always get it right. Who always insisted on getting it right.

Amberlin loved the precision of baking. The more complex the recipe, the more eager she was to try her hand at it. She could remember vividly her first croissant—the intricate layering of butter and dough, the folding and refolding in just the right geometric progression to create pockets of air surrounded by fluffy pastry. She felt as proud as an Olympic skater who had just landed a triple axel when the croissants emerged from the oven sweet and airy and moist. Perfect.

In college she had studied the imperfect science of sociology, and then married the stockbroker who said she should do more with her hair, but that didn't last long, and in the meantime she started working on an organic farm. She wasn't much of a gardener, because she wasted time on unnecessary precision in placing seeds in the ground, and was so concerned to get every weed, she often took out the plants she was trying to protect.

But she came up with great recipes for the fruits and vegetables the farm produced. The farm owners started paying her to make them so they could sell them in local stores. When she split with her husband she moved onto the farm for a while, but she missed town life and was glad to meet Teresa and work among people rather than chickens and corn.

The door rattled, and Amberlin walked to it, pulled the shade back. Sherry's long, angular face was pressed against the glass, her tongue stuck out, and her eyes rolled up. She clawed the window, her fingers squeaking on the pane.

"You're an idiot," Amberlin said, "and we're closed."

"No," Sherry said, her voice muffled by the glass between them. "I have to have an amaranth carob chip cookie or I'll die." She clutched at her throat and rolled against the door. Amberlin turned the key and pulled the door in, and Sherry fell in with it, landing right in her arms.

"Hi there," she said. "How's your day been?"

Amberlin laughed, then let her go. She caught herself just in time.

"Better than yours, I think," Amberlin said. "At least I'm still sane." She closed the door and pulled the shade. "I thought you had a gig tonight. In Massachusetts."

"I do," Sherry said. "Just on my way. I wanted to stop and give you something first."

Amberlin closed her eyes and held her hands out. Nothing went into them, but she felt warm lips pressed against hers. Something slipped into her sweater pocket. She opened her eyes and reached into her pocket. Pulled out something cool and smooth. A key.

Amberlin stared at it, puzzled. "You bought me a car?" she asked.

"No, dopey. It's a key to an apartment. One I happen to know will be available on January second, because I know who's moving out. And it's cheap and it's big and you'll love it. So—let's move into it."

Amberlin frowned at the key. "Move into it?"

"You and me, baby," Sherry said. She grabbed her arms and twirled her a half circle, but Amberlin didn't want to be twirled. She wanted to stand still.

"You want to move in with me?"

"No," Sherry said. "I want you to move in with me."

Amberlin took a step back and stared at the key in her hand. "I'm—I'm—"

"Flattered?" Sherry suggested. "Thrilled?"

Amberlin said nothing.

"Okay," Sherry said. "Maybe stunned? Petrified?"

Amberlin laughed nervously. "I didn't know we were going that way, Sherry."

"After two years, which way should we go?" she said, her voice softer now, its enthusiasm caged in quiet.

"Has it been that long?" Amberlin asked, rubbing the key in her fingers.

"It was just after the holiday show at the Café Open. You asked for my autograph. Remember?"

Amberlin nodded. She remembered. She'd never asked for an autograph before. Then they went and got beer at a dive bar, danced to jukebox music while portly men in flannel stared. Amberlin liked her, found herself laughing and at ease with her. Sherry didn't live very far away, so they met again casually, for coffee, for a movie. Then Sherry cooked dinner for her, and Amberlin grew unaccountably nervous and knocked over her cup of chocolate mousse. Sherry made light of the mishap, scooped it up with her finger, and started eating it. Amberlin laughed and joined her. Then, somehow they'd ended up licking mousse off each other's fingers. And tasting sambucca off each other's lips.

Their lovemaking was filled with surprises of pleasure. And to combine that with a warm and consistent friendship was beyond what she'd ever thought possible. But the biggest surprise of all was seeing herself as bisexual.

Granted, she'd had crushes on women in high school and college, and she was always aware of women as attractive, but she thought she was strictly hetero. She didn't dislike sex with men so long as it was with the right man, though even before she was married she noticed that it rarely was. She blamed her difficulty on the gender problems that plagued the culture in general. Men didn't know how to name or explore their feelings. Women didn't know how not to. Put the two together, and you've got a perfect formula for disaster. She supposed bisexuality was the inevitable result.

At least, theoretically she explained it that way. It all seemed different somehow when it was in the particular, about a specific person whose face brought you joy.

"Look, if you don't want to, that's okay," Sherry said. "Only you've been saying you want to move, and how nice it would be to have a bigger place."

"I guess I didn't think about it that way," Amberlin said. "Don't get me wrong. It sounds great, only it's a big decision. I want to think about it."

"Sure," Sherry said, her voice a little tight. "Listen, I gotta run or I'll be late for my gig. I'll see you at the party."

"Right," Amberlin said. She leaned down and kissed her quickly on the lips. Put the key back in her hand. "Here. You hang on to this for now, okay?"

Sherry exited, and the last Amberlin saw of her face, it was trying hard not to express disappointment.

"Merry Christmas," Amberlin groaned when she was gone. "God, I hate the holidays."

She went to the phone and dialed Christine's number. Christine would be the right person to talk to about it. She'd understand. She'd confessed her own jitters about marriage and commitment. Christine wouldn't make fun of it, or take it lightly. The phone rang twice, three times, four times, and then the answering machine picked up.

"Hey—it's winter. Leave a warm message, but wait for the beep."

"Hi, Chris," Amberlin said. "Listen, I need advice. I'll try you over at James's, and if you get either message, give me a call at home, okay?"

But when she tried James, he was terse and said no, she wasn't there either. Amberlin closed up shop and went home.

AFTER SHE BROKE THE CASTLE, CHRISTINE SAT ON THE floor and stared at the pieces of glass for a long time. She may have fallen asleep, because when she looked around and noticed where she was, the moonlight was gone, and the sounds of the traffic patterns had gone still. She swept up the glass, left the studio, and stood looking up and down the street. She wanted to go home.

Home? Where was that? California, where her mother was buried? Her apartment, half empty, with nothing but sour milk and one beer, one egg in the refrigerator? Where was she going under a dome of sky that was a thick white sheet waiting to crumble into snow?

Through the ceiling? Through the ceiling. Through the ceiling.

The deep night was beautiful with quiet snow, but beauty was a knife to slit her wrists with. Everything was beautiful except her. She had smashed what she loved best. She was no better than Nan.

As she stood on the corner, wondering what to do, a bus pulled up and opened its doors. It seemed like an omen and she got on it, rode it uptown, and got out close enough to James's condo that she wouldn't fall asleep before she got her car. Then she drove to her own apartment and let herself in, closed the door behind her.

Her phone machine beeped at her urgently, and she automatically went to it and pressed the button to retrieve the messages, though they didn't interest her. Amberlin needed advice. James called to say he hoped she felt better. Teresa asked her if she'd stop and pick up the napkins she had on hold at the Party Place.

It was cold. She'd turned the heat down, not wanting to waste energy when she was gone. Cold and empty and unlived-in. But it was her home, and there must be something there that would make her feel better. Something to make this ache go away. She went into the kitchen and opened cupboards, the refrigerator, the freezer. All dull and empty. She went to the bathroom and opened the medicine cabinet. Aspirin, Midol, vitamin E cream. Nothing that would help.

She went to her bedroom and jerked open her bureau drawers, thinking maybe some sleeping pills, but she didn't have any. Maybe whiskey, but she never kept any. And her things, beautiful things, weren't of any comfort. She needed a drug that didn't exist. She'd never been addicted to anything except cigarettes, and even they weren't dulling the pain. Heroin addicts must feel like this when they can't get their bag, she thought, opening her closet, thrusting apart the hangars holding her clothes to reveal boxes piled in the back.

There were boxes of photos, boxes of sketches for glass projects, boxes of books she was beginning to pack up, and a brown cardboard box labeled ADELAIDE STATE HOSPITAL. That was the box the hospital sent her after her mother died. Committed suicide, she corrected herself.

She'd never told anyone about the box. Not Delia or Teresa or Amberlin or even James. She thought they wouldn't understand why she kept it, unopened, for seven years, stuffed in the back of her closet. She wasn't sure she understood. But she knew that if she told James, he'd want her to sort through it, and she didn't want to. Amberlin would suggest a ritual of some kind, with everyone gathered around to support her. Delia would shudder and say throw it away. Don't hang on to the dead. And Teresa—who grieved for Nan as much as Christine did though in a different way—she would stroke the outside of the box. Her dark eyebrows would crease down and her lips would go tight. Then she'd turn away, go to the stove, and make chicken soup. If Christine asked her what she should do, she would say burn it, or bury it and plant a tree on top.

But she wouldn't have held on to it unopened for seven years. She would have either opened it or disposed of it. Christine hadn't been able to do either.

Seven years was enough time for all her cells to have changed. It was time enough for her to be done grieving over her mother's death, wasn't it? She pulled the box out, sitting on the floor with it. A strip of packing tape held it closed, and she twisted her fingers against it for punishment, working it until it was a thin thread that she finally snapped with her teeth so that the cardboard tongues of the box gaped open.

First she saw the thin nightgown, which humiliated her. It was a discount nightgown she had bought her mother during her last hospital stay. Didn't she realize how cheaply made it was? Couldn't she afford better? It seemed better than the hospital-issued uniforms, or at least an attempt at normalcy, but she felt now what poor comfort it must have been, just like the worn blankets of Christine's own childhood bed, which were scratchy and of no solace. Then and now, to lie back in exhaustion against thin sheets brought forth only a labyrinthine agitation that drove away even momentary rest.

There could be no rest and nothing to make it right. No drugs, no food, no prayers could repair the ugliness of her life, and Nan's life, which was still held in this cardboard box in her lap. Nothing is connected to anything, she thought. Her art, James, making a life, not just worthless but incomprehensible. Her life was cast with absent-minded viciousness by a mad god, all its parts meaningless and unrelated. James was right when he said she could end up like her mother. And he was right when he didn't comprehend the beauty of Nan's life, because it didn't exist. Neither was there any beauty in her own that she wouldn't someday smash and ruin.

She reached in again, needing to touch what pierced her, and set her hand on something small and flat wrapped in newspaper. She tore it open and saw a photo of herself in a brass frame, a smiling, stupid, and ridiculously arrogant young woman. Head back, hair in the wind, mouth open as if she were talking or laughing, as if there were anything to talk about or laugh about.

She knew nothing then except hope, which was cruel and relentless, telling her lies about her mother getting well, her loneliness ending, life being enough while you waited for the good to come your way. She flung the picture across the room and paid no attention to the crack of glass against the wall, but continued to dig into the box, her agitated hands unwrapping a hot water bottle, toothbrush, slippers, deck of cards, stained glass parrot—an ugly thing she'd made in a moment of anger and guilt, both of which showed in the bird's strange eye and curved beak. Then a pair of rhinestone reading glasses, two gold crowns, two clothespins made into dolls, a bundle of letters, and a bundle of underwear. Christine sifted through it all, her flimsy inheritance, until her hand touched an object wrapped in heavy tape and she knew, finally, that this was the reason she'd opened the box.

It was the gun.

It was small and silver. Wrapped up with it was a box of bullets. Her mother had smuggled it into the rehab ward inside the hollowed-out pages of a Bible. Nobody checked the Bible for weapons. And Nan had been in good spirits when she checked in, talking and joking about getting it right this time and never having to do this again. When the hospital called and told her Nan had shot herself, she thought briefly of suing them, but that would mean going back to California, staying there emotionally and physically. She couldn't bear it.

"Do you want it?" the nurse asked her the day after her mother put it in her mouth and pulled the trigger. "I mean, when pathology's through with it. We can send it to you with the rest of her things."

Want it? Christine couldn't begin to make sense of the question, much less formulate an answer. "Send me everything," she said at last. "Just send me everything she had."

It had remained in the unopened box that she hadn't even looked at until that day.

It was surprisingly heavy, surprisingly smooth, and when she lifted it and looked into the barrel, the sorrow drained away from her into that small round passage. A reversal of birth, she thought. Go back into the tunnel and maybe come out some other end and try again. Maybe not. But it didn't matter. Holding the gun, she felt light. It was heavy, she was light. Her mother was with her, calmly, like those rare moments of their lives when they really shared something like a bedtime story or an ice cream cone.

When she was six, she brought home a baby bird that fell out of its nest. She got an eyedropper to give it bread soaked in water, went out and found worms to squish in with the bread, but no matter what she did, the bird wouldn't eat. Within a day, it died, and she sat and wept over its wretched little body, featherless and flightless.

"It's okay," Nan told her. "That little bird is okay now."

"Didn't it hurt?" Christine asked.

"Dying's easy," her mother told her. "It's living that's hard work."

Sitting in the pristine streetlight that angled in through her bedroom window, the smooth, cold gun in her hand, Christine felt completely light and empty. Her mother's words sounded free and easy, whispered by an angel with great wings and a soft voice. Dying is easy. Christine inhabited a state of light, and she understood now why Nan's spirits had been good when she checked into detox.

There was relief available. A way out. But she wouldn't do it like her mother, with no explanation, no good-bye. She'd do it right. She'd write something—letters to Teresa and Amberlin and Delia and James. And she'd go and say good-bye to Teresa. Christine would go see her and think of some words to say that meant good-bye and it isn't your fault, without telling her what she intended to do. Then she would drive far away, up into the mountains, to a place where she wouldn't be found. In fact, she could write the letters so they'd never know if she'd killed herself or simply decided to leave. They wouldn't have to feel guilty and torn up. They could imagine her somewhere far away, happy, on her own.

That seemed right and felt good, and Christine felt her pain leaving her. She was already adrift from her own life. Unconnected, the cord between herself and her pain sliced cleanly away until she was free of it. Emptied of life and all its searing emotions.

She got a pen and paper and wrote two letters—one to James and one to Teresa. She put them in envelopes and addressed them. The one for James she propped against her bureau mirror. The one for Teresa she put in her purse.

The night glided toward morning like a dark skater going across a white ribbon of ice toward home. Day would arrive, regardless of her absence or presence. She put bullets in the gun, put the gun in her purse with the letter, stood up, and left her home.

ABOUT LOVE AND WINGS

CHRISTINE TURNED TO TERESA AT THE TWO MAJOR crises of her life—when Nan died and when she wanted to kill herself—for a very good reason. Teresa was the only person she knew who loved Nan without question and without pause for breath. She knew Nan's life, and loved her not in spite of her problems, but because of them, knowing that Nan's problems grew from the same source as her strength. Nan's blessing was her curse, and they both knew what it was.

Nan was born with wings.

Now, wings are wonderful because they'll take you as high as you dare go, to explore worlds few people ever see. And when you return, the people around you can breathe a little better, because as your wings move the air, they bring the memory of what you've experienced, a scent of the visions you've seen.

But wings aren't suited to modern times. They get caught in doors. Seat belts don't accommodate them. They stick out of voting booths, and disturb the people in back of you in line at the bank. And although they might look feathery and soft in all the pictures, they're actually sharp as knives.

There are ways of learning how to deal with all these problems, but those who could have taught this to Nan didn't speak the same language and had forgotten much in moving from the old country to the new. Maybe if she had gone to see Julia, that old hag, Julia would have explained the right way to hold her shoulders so the weight didn't crumple her back. How to use them. When to use them. Whom to show them to. Whom to hide them from.

Old ladies like Julia had that kind of knowledge, and the villages they came from were accustomed to people with wings. They would accept them, pick them up and dust them off if they tripped over them, help them fly again, and enjoy the benefits of having a winged one nearby. But Julia never spoke to Nan about her wings, and though Grandpa Donato and Grandma DiRosa tried their best, they were out-volumed by the television and the cars and the general noisiness of the New World.

So Nan drank to stifle the pain she endured from the blades of her shoulder to the center of her heart, which is where wings are attached. She would periodically lose her world, not sure how to carry it and fly at the same time, just as unsure how to prevent herself from flying because it was her nature to do so.

Teresa and Christine, no matter how angry they were at Nan, or how sad they were about her, recognized that she had wings, and they loved her for it.

When she was sober, she would cook and clean and be loving and smart and fun. Even when they didn't have money, she knew how to make food a treat. Christine remembered her going out into the park near an apartment they rented in Denver, Colorado, and picking all the edible flowers she could find. Young dandelions and violets, nasturtiums and borage she stole from someone's window box. She put them on a plate for Christine, an edible bouquet. Or she'd go out early and snip squash blossoms from a neighbor's garden, make batter, and fry them for breakfast.

When Christine was very little and Nan was still singing in cafés and bars, she'd tuck her into bed on the nights she didn't have a gig and lie at her feet, singing her songs or telling her stories about her childhood—the big house and the little house. She'd tell how her own mother cooked an unvarying weekly menu of chicken on Sunday; Monday, chicken casserole drowned in mushroom soup; Tuesday, hot chicken sandwiches; Wednesday, meat loaf; and Friday, fish. The only unpredictable days were Thursday and Saturday, when they ate with Grandma.

That would lead to elaborate stories about her great-grandma DiRosa, whose memory lingered, she said, in the shape of Christine's eyes and the tilt of her chin.

"You have her chin," Nan said. At the age of five Christine would touch her chin, trying to figure out if that was okay, to have a body part that belonged to someone else, and if she'd have to give it back.

"It's the way you hold it," Nan would say. "And her eyes too. Not the same color, but the same shape, and the same way of looking at things. She saw everything."

Sometimes, instead of family stories, her mother would make up stories about castles and fairies with wings so bright you couldn't look at them because you'd go blind. But you could wish on them, and maybe they'd give you a castle of your own. Christine was quite young when she started seeing, in her mind, the exact castle she would choose.

As Christine grew older, she noticed that her mother's speech would get slow and stumbly more often. Sometimes her mother couldn't make the notes in a song, or she'd stop talking in the middle of a sentence and just snore at the foot of the bed till morning.

Mom's drinking, she learned to say. Drinking again. Oh, well.

It became okay, because it had to be. If she threw up, Christine knew how to clean it. If she passed out at the bottom of the bed, her unconscious form would keep Christine's feet warm. It was fine as long as she didn't lose her job and they didn't have to move again. But she always did, and they always had to.

Christine was a teenager before she learned to be angry about it, and then her fury was razor sharp, and she was perpetually angry at her mother for all the moves and the boyfriends and the absence of things like money and food and sanity. She told her in as many ways as she could that she hated her, hated the life they led, wished she had gotten a normal mother instead of Nan.

By the time Christine was seventeen they'd lived in twenty-three states with about as many different men, and they were back in California on the heels of a boyfriend Nan was sure would stick around.

He played fiddle, and they were going to start a duo. They left Wyoming at his insistence, because he had some connections in California, but then he took off with Nan's favorite guitar and their television set.

Christine screamed at her mother. Screamed out her hate and her rage and all of everything that she ever felt from the bottom of her toes on up.

Nan sat in a ripped-up plaid upholstered chair with her thin hands on her lap and listened, her big dark eyes drinking it all in silently. Then she got out a newspaper and started reading it.

"Are you listening to me, Nan?" Christine panted at her, slapping at the newspaper. "Do you hear anything I say? You let that asshole do that to you, and we're broke and neither one of us has a job, and there's nothing to eat but some old Wheaties."

Nan raised her eyes to her daughter and her face shone with light. "Get your best dress on, sweetheart. We're going to a wedding."

Christine just blinked at her. Nan pointed to a paragraph in the paper about a high-society wedding in Malibu that evening. The guest list was at least five hundred people, and it was being held at the Blue Wave Hotel, one of the swankiest in an area known for swank.

"You've got to be kidding," Christine said. "I mean, they'll arrest us at the door."

"Why?" Nan said, her eyes glittering mischievously. "We're the East Coast cousins they haven't seen in years. I mean years and years."

And her excitement, her mischievousness, were infectious. Christine, grumbling, went and put on the only good dress she had, which was a vintage black taffeta studded with rhinestones they'd picked up at a secondhand shop in a lucrative period last summer. Nan got out a red silk that made her eyes look black as coal. They curled each other's hair and put on lipstick and tried a lot of different eye shadows and giggled. They were low on ready cash for a taxi, so they took a bus as far as it would go, walked the rest of the way, and were admitted without difficulty to the best party in town.

Nan talked to everybody. She'd waltz right up to people she'd never seen before with her hands out, saying, "Oh, my God, is that *you*? It's been so long, I hardly knew you."

Whoever she approached inevitably took her hands and looked nervous at not remembering her and eventually gave her enough information that she didn't even have to pretend.

She brought home an architect that night. He stayed around for almost half a year, and they ate well for a long time after that.

That was Nan.

Christine knew she had wings, because she so often saw them take her mother soaring, and so often saw them fail. And Christine was aware that Teresa was the only person left in the world who had seen the same thing.

Teresa remembered her feeling of pride in her big sister when her parents told all the family that Nan was leaving high school a year early to study music at Hartwick College on full scholarship. It seemed to redeem or perhaps explain any problems Nan had had in the past, and gave them all hope for what she would be in the future. Teresa had gone around telling all her friends that her big sister was almost famous.

After a year in college Nan decided what her career really needed was California. That was where all the real music happened, and that's what she wanted to make. Real music. Like Joan Baez and Joni Mitchell and Janis Joplin. She needed to go to Berkeley.

She got another scholarship, and during the year she actually attended classes, she wrote home long letters about how the sides of the hills near the bay were dotted with paintbrush and the skimming dance of hummingbirds that would buzz right up to your ear to see if you were a flower. She wrote about the eucalyptus trees and how wonderful they smelled under a sun that was ringed with prisms of light. How the moon was bigger in California and the people were wonderful. How they would go to play in People's Park. She wrote about feeling like she had wings and could fly.

She called home collect and talked to Teresa, telling her how free she felt walking in the mountains. She told her about the seals in San Francisco and the people, who were all there to make music and love. Yes, the sixties were over, but the hearts of the people hadn't changed that much. Not really. Everything was still beautiful. In its own way.

She started singing at coffeehouses. A manager from RCA had come to hear her and said she had the voice of an angel, she wrote. She was leaving her dorm and moving in with him, and she didn't care if everyone disowned her. It was love.

Then she wrote that maybe he wasn't really a manager, but he would be someday, and they were happy. Soon the people at RCA would move him up the ladder, and he'd have enough clout to get her signed. Get her a contract.

Not long after that she wrote that the manager had left town to try his luck in New York. And then she stopped writing altogether.

Her parents were frantic. Teresa remembered them staying up late, sitting at the kitchen table, and talking in low voices. Grandpa Donato had died earlier that year, and Grandma was thinking of selling the big house, and their daughter was lost. They called her apartment and got a mechanical voice telling them the phone was disconnected. They got hold of the landlord, who said she left without paying the rent. No, she didn't leave a forwarding address, because if she had, he'd be after her for what she owed him.

A few weeks later they got a collect call from Nan. Teresa was in the house so she could see her mother's lip trembling, as if she were about to cry. "Yes," she said politely. Then she spoke frantically, as if she had to get the words out fast. "Where are you, honey? I see. No, we're not mad. Only worried. Well, maybe your father is a little. What? Are you sure, honey? Is that what you want?"

They brought Nan home during the year Teresa was twelve. She returned with the stars of the West Coast still in her sad eyes. She stayed for six months and regaled Teresa with stories about men and the beaches at night and smoking pot and wild music and wild love. She promised to take Teresa to California when she was older. She got a job waitressing at a diner and played a couple of gigs at coffeehouses. Then, when she had enough money she bought a plane ticket for Denver, because that's where the music scene was shifting to.

She wrote periodically, called when she needed money, called to let them know she was pregnant, and again to tell them the baby was born. A girl she named Christine Emilia DiRosa. The father—well, he wouldn't be involved, but wasn't it wonderful that the baby would carry the family name, and could they send a little something for her?

She sent postcards after that to notify them of changes of address, and pictures of Christine as she grew. Teresa would look at them and wonder if Christine would inherit her mother's wings. She would occasionally feel the tug of those wings at her own back, but wouldn't dare push them forward and out after seeing what Nan's had done. She had learned that wings were troublesome, and if you had them, it was best not to let them show.

Her mother looked old when she read Nan's cards. Her father's lips would go tight and his face would turn red. They still sent money, but they no longer sent love, and Grandma DiRosa was dead now too, so there was really no one left to do that except Teresa, who sent cards with wildflowers from the backyard pressed into them.

Teresa decided to go to college to be a teacher, which seemed safe enough, and made other friends, found women she liked and didn't like and things to do that had nothing to do with her family at all. She didn't see her sister again until she graduated, when she decided to drive to New Mexico to the commune Nan was living in with a couple, a Vietnam veteran who was on methadone and an ex-nun. Christine was at the age between childhood and adolescence, gawky and deliberately bored with the adults around her. Her face was fragile and thin, and her coloring was remarkably light, but her eyes were old and already cynical.

At a dinner of buckwheat groats cooked badly and vegetable soup that had a slightly burnt taste, Nan got very drunk on cheap wine and Christine patiently led her to the bathroom to puke and closed the door behind her.

"She's such a good kid," the ex-nun said, inhaling deeply on a joint. "I wish I had a kid like her."

"Mmm-hmm," Teresa said, watching the ex-nun watching the Vietnam veteran. She excused herself and went to the bathroom, squeezed herself in with her sister and her niece, and knelt down next to the toilet with them.

"You okay?" she asked Nan.

"Fine," Christine answered for her. "She'll be fine once she throws up."

"Me too," Teresa said. "That was a helluva dinner."

For the first time since her arrival, Christine cracked a smile, actually turned and looked at Teresa without sizing her up. "You don't like buckwheat?" she asked.

"I don't like the carbon residue," Teresa answered.

"I'm okay," Nan shouted suddenly, picking her head up. She stared, a line of drool coming out of one side of her mouth. "Teresa?" she asked. "S'at you?"

"It's me, Nan," Teresa said softly. She thought a minute, then asked, "Nan, would you mind if Christine came to visit with me for a while? I never got to spend much time with her, and I'd like it if—"

"S'fine with me," Nan answered. "Ask'er."

Then she turned back to the toilet and retched some more.

Christine turned her large hazel eyes to Teresa. The man Nan had bedded must've been a Swede, Teresa thought, to white out the dark coloring of the DiRosas. "You want to?" Teresa asked. "I'm starting a teaching job in the fall, but you could either stay with me or come back here then."

Christine looked at Teresa some more. Then she looked at Nan and shook her head. "I better not," she said. "At least, not right now. Maybe some other time? Like, I could write to you and let you know?"

Teresa nodded. "Anytime," she said. "You have family. Don't forget that. Anytime at all."

Teresa left the next day, feeling a tug somewhere between her shoulder blades and her heart. She wasn't Julia. She didn't have the magic to help Nan. She didn't have the magic to help Christine. And she didn't know what angels to call on to watch over either of them.

Friday

GATHERING EQUIPMENT

"THEY FOUND OUT DESPAIR WAS A WOMAN," DELIA said pointedly.

"What?" Amberlin asked as she pressed hard on an imaginary brake pedal. The snow was falling softly, patiently, knowing its own capacity for accumulation and recognizing that there was no need for hurry. The roads were slick, and Delia's inattention to that made Amberlin nervous. And though traffic wasn't dense on a Friday morning at ten-thirty, the drivers were.

"Despair is a woman. You know," Delia repeated, patient as the snow. "The Sistine Chapel."

"Oh," Amberlin said. "Right."

When Delia picked her up and they packed the car, she'd been saying something about a PBS special she watched with her kids on the restoration of the Sistine Chapel. Between that time and now they'd talked about many other things, mostly business, but Delia was back to her first thought as if she'd never left it. Amberlin thought her children were the cause of her meandering dialogues. For the last twelve years she hadn't been able to follow a line of thought to conclusion without interruption.

"So they what?" Amberlin asked. "Scraped off the paint?"

"Right. The painted clothes. See, at some point the Church got worried about all the figures in the Sistine Chapel being naked, so they painted clothes on them." Delia deftly cut in front of another car in order to plow up the snowy on-ramp for the thruway that would take them out of the city and to Teresa's house.

Amberlin hissed and braked through the floorboards. "Careful, Delia."

"It's okay," Delia said, looking over her left shoulder as they merged with traffic. "I'm trying to beat the weather."

"It's going to beat us," Amberlin whispered. She waited until they were settled into the middle lane before resuming regular breath and speech. "So how did they know this figure was called Despair?"

"They knew which ones were headed for heaven and which ones were headed for hell. You can tell by their faces."

"The ones going to hell look evil?"

"Actually, just upset. Like they got on the wrong bus. So they started working on Despair, taking his clothes off, and surprise—he's a she."

"I'm not surprised," Amberlin said. "Not in the least."

They swerved to avoid a dog crossing the exit ramp. Delia looked back at him, his short brown legs working furiously. "That dog's got a death wish," she said. She rummaged in the paper bag at Amberlin's feet and fished out one of the all-natural cannolis Amberlin had brought for breakfast snacks. "Wow," she exclaimed. "This is great."

"Can I ask that you do just one thing at a time?" Amberlin asked plaintively, pressing her back into the seat. "Like drive. Just drive, Delia."

"Hey, I know what I'm doing. I'm older than you."

"Not that much."

"Almost ten years. And two kids, which adds about twenty years per kid and teaches you to do more than five things at a time," Delia said. "You know they say men are the best cooks. Why? Because they concentrate. One thing at a time. I mean, they can concentrate on only one thing at a time. Michael, for example, is obsessing about his father. He is a marvelous man, absolutely low maintenance, except in this instance."

Amberlin, who felt she was concentrating on staying alive through the ride, said nothing. She'd heard all about Michael's father and the stroke he had. That it had left him without much language, though he was still okay physically. Michael wanted him to come live with them, and the talks about it had been going on for a month.

"So that's still going on?"

"Yeah. I don't know. I like the old guy, so I'll probably give in. But it kind of gives me the creeps. I mean, what if he dies and I'm there alone." She shuddered. "Anyway, I don't think men are the best cooks. Look at Teresa. Look at you. How do you do it?"

"I follow the recipes," Amberlin said.

Elaborate baking had been a Sunday-morning ritual when Amberlin was growing up, replacing church worship as a family event. Amberlin's older brother would come home at dawn from his Sunday-morning paper route and start a yeast bread and coffee cakes. Amberlin's favorite was a chocolate and coconut coffee cake, warm from the oven. It was as comforting as a down-filled pillow. Sweet as sleep.

Her brother would only let her watch at first, as the yeast bubbled, as the chocolate melted. The transformation fascinated her. Things becoming what they were not. How did that happen, and did that mean those things were no longer themselves?

Later, she would wonder the same thing about reincarnation. Why couldn't you remember from one life to the next? And if you had different bodies, different brains and hearts and eyes, were you still yourself? At what point did transformation become complete, so that you could no longer say, for instance, I am Amberlin, or this is yeast.

She'd watch the blocks of chocolate sway back and forth in the double boiler, and begin to leak a dark silk puddle around the shrinking middle until it was entirely liquid and her brother would remove it to add to the confectioner's sugar for the chocolate glaze he made. She would taste the chocolate before it was melted. She would taste it after it was melted. It tasted the same. She supposed that meant it was still chocolate.

When she got a little older, her brother let her help, and then one day she surprised him by having the bread dough rising before he returned from his paper route. He laughed proudly, woke up their mother and father, and told them, "Amberlin's taken my job. She's the baker now."

And she was. The transformation occurred as easily as that, just because the words were said. Like chocolate melting in the pan. Like eggs and sugar and flour mixing together to become batter for a cake. She was the baker.

"Hey, you gonna make those cookies? The flat ones with the pictures?" Delia asked.

"Pizzelle," Amberlin said. "Yes, of course. Teresa always has them." Amberlin wasn't thrilled about making cookies that used eight eggs and a cup of sugar, and Teresa wouldn't let her use whole wheat flour either, but they were traditional.

"Great. I got this woman from *Good Living* magazine—you know, that glossy with all the articles about how to do things like make your own cheese—and she was really interested in Teresa doing all these recipes from her grandmother. Don't let me forget to call and remind her about the party. I'm hoping she'll show up."

"That's a good magazine," Amberlin said.

"I know. I been trying to get their attention for about two years now. I don't know why, it was the pizzelle and the dadaluce that caught their ear. Who can fathom the mind of the public?"

Amberlin smiled. "You can."

Delia shrugged, but Amberlin could see a slight flush on her cheek in reaction to the compliment. Delia always liked to play her talents off as inconsequential. She didn't talk about the work she did for Bread and Roses. She just did it, in what appeared to be the most casual and offhand way.

"Did you tell Teresa about the magazine?" Amberlin asked.

Delia shook her head. "I never tell her that kind of thing until the last minute. Teresa's at her best when she's improvising. Besides, she had her hands full of bread and her head full of fretting about Christine."

"Oh?"

Delia nodded knowingly. "The lovebirds had a spat."

"About what?"

"Probably nothing much. Wedding jitters and all."

Amberlin shook her head. It was more than that, she knew from her conversations with Christine. Christine was really having second thoughts. "Do you think James is handling it properly?"

Delia gave a small laugh. "Properly?"

"I mean, he could be—I don't know—stronger. I think Christine needs reassurance. Don't you?"

"Honey," Delia said, "we all do."

"No, I mean it, Delia. James is a counselor. He ought to be able to use his skills right now to help her. Not make her more nervous. I mean, that's his job, right? And he's good at it, so he should know."

"He should," Delia agreed. "But that doesn't mean he does. They'll probably work it out though. Teresa worries more than she needs to."

"She worries about Christine only so she doesn't have to worry about herself," Amberlin said.

"Yeah?" Delia grinned. "Is that why *you* worry about her?"

Amberlin fought with a moment of anger, recognized it as a reaction to hearing the truth, and laughed. Delia had a way of saying the most unpleasant things in such a way that you had to laugh—at the crazy world, at yourself.

"Probably," she admitted. She thought about it for a minute, then clutched at the side of her seat as Delia's car slid around a curve.

"Wow," Delia said when it was negotiated. She glanced briefly at Amberlin, whose lips were pressed tightly together. "Glad there wasn't anyone behind me. Anyway, I'm more concerned about Teresa than Christine. Between the divorce and Donnie going off to college, the holidays are bound to be tough on her."

Amberlin unpressed her lips and made her face relax. "From what you said, the marriage was dead a long time ago."

"And good riddance to it," Delia agreed. "Now she can find something good for her. But Donnie leaving—that's tough." She shivered, looking into her own future. She thought she'd handle it better than Teresa, though, especially if her marriage stayed as good as it was now. She and Michael could have some fun together then, be irresponsible. Unless they had his father with them, of course. Still, by then he might be—well, she didn't want to pursue that line of thought.

It would be fine, she thought. She'd enjoy her freedom and her grown-up kids. Besides, Teresa had always had some dark spots she'd crawl into occasionally that Delia didn't understand. Places she'd go where nobody—not even Delia, her oldest friend—could find her. Delia had gotten used to just waiting it out if that happened, or coaxing her back out with a story or a joke.

"She should talk about it more," Amberlin said. "It'd do her good."

"She does," Delia said. "She just doesn't use words."

Amberlin wanted to question that, but the car slid slightly toward the barricade, and she braced herself against the back of the seat, waiting for impact. Delia straightened it out and kept going.

"Nasty roads," she commented. "You brought the big cappuccino maker? I love that stuff."

"In the back," Amberlin said, relaxing some as they continued forward.

"How did people fluff milk before they had those?" Delia asked. "Or didn't they make cappuccino? I don't know how we ever ate anything without all the equipment we use now. Toasters, microwaves, blenders. Of course, my favorite cooking equipment's the car." She patted the steering wheel affectionately.

"What?"

"For takeout Chinese, fast-food drive-throughs, picking up pizza."

Amberlin braced an arm against the dashboard. "Aren't we getting a little too close to that Taurus in front of us?"

"Huh. How'd that happen?" Delia slowed to a crawl.

Up ahead several police cars were stopping traffic. The red light flashed a brilliant warning in the falling snow. "Uh-oh," said Delia. "What's up?"

"Accident," Amberlin said flatly. "Everybody's driving badly. They should be carpooling, like us."

As traffic slowed, Delia reached into the bag and pulled out a loaf of bread, broke off a chunk with her teeth, and tossed the rest back into the bag. "Jaysus," she said in a thick brogue. "This bread is good. It's the real thing. You use a bread maker?"

"Yes," Amberlin said. "Teresa won't, but I like them. Better stop."

Delia pushed down on the brake as a policeman waved his arms at them. His officer's cap was protected from the snow with an elasticized plastic covering like a shower cap. He looked like he was imitating an old lady in a Woolworth's rain cap. He motioned for them to roll their window down.

Amberlin automatically took note of his badge. Officer Lopez. Delia automatically noted that he was cute in spite of the rain cap. "What is it, Officer?" Delia asked.

"We've got a bad accident here, and we'll have to reroute you, but it'll take a few minutes. We just arrived at the scene. Please don't attempt to maneuver your vehicle around traffic or turn it around." After this official speech, he became human and smiled a crinkly smile at Delia. She smiled back. He patted the door frame and straightened to walk back to the accident.

"Officer," Delia shouted after him. He stopped and turned but didn't walk to them. Delia stuck her head out the window. "Is it really bad?"

"Pretty bad," he said.

She shook her head. "Bad luck, huh?"

"I don't believe in luck," he replied. "Just bad driving." He touched the rim of his plastic-covered hat and walked away.

"Somebody's probably dead," Amberlin commented as Delia recranked her window.

Delia grabbed at the bread and tore off another chunk. "Probably."

"Did you know that people used to hire someone at funerals to eat bread off the dead person's body? It was a way of eating his sins so he could get to heaven."

"Jeez," Delia said, her voice muffled by food. "I'll bet Despair could've used that."

She thought of funerals she'd attended. The Irish ones, where whiskey was the primary food, supplemented by beer. And when Teresa's grandfather died, how the old ladies of the neighborhood came armed with tins of ziti and bowls full of meatballs. It seemed that something always had to be consumed when someone died. Sins, or whiskey, or sauce.

"Yes," Amberlin continued, "and at the High Holy Days, Jews cast bread into the water as a way of letting go of their sins for the year."

"Really? Did you do that?"

"Once or twice," Amberlin said.

Officer Lopez came back into view and waved them onto the side of the road and forward. Delia put the car into drive and inched ahead. They passed the completely crumpled side of a black Firebird with a red racing stripe. The windows were too dark to see inside the car.

Delia inhaled deeply and held the breath in as a stretcher with a filled plastic body bag was lifted by two men into a waiting ambulance. When the ambulance doors were closed, she released her breath.

Amberlin didn't say a word. They drove the next couple of miles slowly and in silence. The snow was sticking to the road sign as they turned onto Teresa's street. It looked like a tombstone.

CHRISTINE LEFT HER APARTMENT MUCH EARLIER THAN Amberlin and Delia got on the road, and so she managed to get a taxi and arrive at Teresa's house by nine A.M. The day appeared fine and full of light, and she remembered vaguely that the open house was the next day, but she wasn't concerned about that. She would drop off the letter, tell Teresa she wasn't feeling well and couldn't stay, then go through with the rest of her plan.

In an ecstasy of lightness she walked up Teresa's driveway and in the back door. Teresa was already working, rolling thin, smooth sheets of pasta out of the pasta maker.

"Come in, come in," she said, waving a floury hand at Christine to pull her inside when she appeared at the back door. "Close the door. It's cold." Then she looked again. "Who died?" she asked.

Christine giggled. "Nobody yet," she said.

"Oh. You look funny. Is everything okay?"

"Fine. So you started already. Can I have a cup of coffee?"

"You don't drink coffee."

"Tea. I meant tea."

Teresa shook her head as she sprinkled flour lightly on the sheets of pasta dough, then wiped her hands on her pants. "You need some food. You don't eat enough, and then your blood sugar goes down and you look funny." She made a few swipes at the stove and cupboard, and a bowl of soup appeared at the counter where Christine sat, contemplating the light in the window.

Christine blinked, surprised to find food in front of her. It looked familiar, that soup, with the bits of black pepper and green chopped-up pieces of herbs floating in the deep, thick red base.

"I can't eat that," she said.

"Why not?"

"Well, it's soup. You don't eat soup for breakfast."

"I do," Teresa said. "It's good."

Christine shook her head at it again. "I can't," she said.

Teresa looked at it, then rearranged the bowl and spoon more attractively. "Yes you can. I made it just today."

"What is it?" Christine asked, feeling herself drawn inexorably back into a place that was about recipes and eating and staying alive.

"Red soup. Roast peppers, tomatoes, garlic, broth. Red soup." Teresa shrugged. "Grandma used to make it. It was one of your mother's favorites."

The return of feeling was swift and inarticulate, a wind with ice in it that ran through her heart. She watched her arm sweep across the counter, taking the bowl with it and sending it crashing into the wall, red exploding across the sand-washed white. Teresa took one step back and frowned, her head moving with the motion of the bowl, then swinging back to Christine. Both women watched as Christine's purse took a slow dive off the counter, falling open, the heaviest object in it making its way out first.

Teresa stared at the gun. Christine stared at the gun. Then they stared at each other.

"No," Teresa said.

"Yes," Christine replied. She jumped off the counter stool and went for her purse, but Teresa grabbed her wrist and wrestled with her. They stayed that way, silently struggling, no need to explain what this meant between them, until Christine got hold of the gun.

Teresa screamed and flung Christine away, made a blind reach behind her and got hold of a frying pan, which she swung high and wide in an arc that ended at the side of Christine's head.

Christine fell to the floor and was quiet. Teresa looked up at the wall, saw her great-grandmother and grandmother smiling down at her. "You got advice?" she asked. "I'll take it."

Her hands shaking, she leaned over and felt at Christine's neck. There was a pulse, strong and steady, and Christine started to groan. Teresa ceased thinking at that point and let whatever instincts she had take over. She picked up Christine's purse, put the gun in it, and ran with it to her bedroom upstairs. She ran back downstairs, stopped at the bottom, then went back up for pillows and blankets. She ran with these to the cellar door, tossed them down the stairs, went back to Christine and got her hands under her arms and hefted her in the same direction. She was light, no difficulty dragging her across the floor, down the cellar stairs, over to the wall near the big sink.

By the time they were there, Christine was blinking, shaking her head. Not quite aware. Not totally unconscious. Teresa continued not thinking. She grabbed an old clothesline from a hook on the wall and wrapped it around the sink pipes, then around Christine's legs.

Christine stared at her legs, then at Teresa. "What're you doing?" she asked. She was confused, not sure of her words or her place.

"Niènte," Teresa said. *"Niènte."* She grabbed an extension cord from another hook and wrapped it around one of Christine's arms, tied it to a pipe behind her. Got a length of garden twine and secured her other arm. Continued to wrap the rope around Christine's middle and tied it tight as she could to the pipe directly behind her, then tied it again to the post on the ceiling.

She finished, and then bent down to her. "Are you okay? Did I hurt you?"

Christine shook her head. She blinked. She wasn't sure what was happening. She'd had a plan and now she was tied to a sink in the cellar? "What're you doing?" she whispered.

"You'll stay here. You'll stay alive."

"It won't work."

"No?" Teresa asked. "You're here, aren't you?"

Christine tried to bring her hands to the ropes at her legs and found they didn't reach. She stretched a leg against the rope and found it was taut and tight. She bit at her lip a minute, shook her head. It didn't make much sense.

Teresa raised a hand up over Christine, over the ropes, words in Italian forming in her mind and on her lips, though she didn't say them out loud, wasn't even sure what they meant. But when she was done saying them, she felt better. She took a good look at Christine.

"Stay there," she said. "Just—stay there."

Christine blinked up at Teresa. "In the cellar? In the dark?"

Teresa tensed, the outline of her slim body in the darkness nothing more than a wire with something sparking at the top. She said nothing for a long time. When she spoke, her words were precise and brief. "You'll stay here. Alive."

She put the blankets and pillows next to her. Christine sighed deeply, turned her face to them, made herself as supine as possible, and closed her eyes. That was good, Teresa thought. She would sleep. That would help.

She turned in the semidarkness and floated up toward the stairs.

Christine's voice came toward her. "Can I at least have my cigarettes?" she asked.

"No," Teresa said. "They're bad for you."

She took the stairs slowly and stopped when she reached the top. She heard noises outside the house. Voices. Laughter.

Amberlin stamped her feet firmly on the outside mat and then pushed into the warm kitchen. "Hey, Teresa," she called out.

"Hello," Delia yodeled behind her.

Teresa stepped out of the basement. Her hair was out of its barrette and she was clumsily weaving it back into a braid, matting bits of floury paste into it as she worked. "Oh, hi," she said, closing the basement door firmly behind her. "Guess it's show time, right?"

ABOUT HEART AND BRAINS

OF THE FOUR WOMEN IN BREAD AND ROSES, TERESA was perhaps the one least at home in the twentieth century. The other women understood this about her, and for the most part accepted it. Amberlin, the most ecologically minded, saw that many of Teresa's ways of living were earth-friendly and applauded them. Delia, who remembered the day in eighth grade when she stopped at Teresa's grandma's house and saw a gray mass of brains soaking in a white bowl, had learned not to blanch when Teresa chopped up chicken hearts and gizzards for sauce. Christine delicately refused to help with the sausage making, and James was still a little concerned about coming to Teresa's house for Sunday dinner. You never knew what she'd be serving, he said. And half the time, she wouldn't tell you except in some cryptic Italian nomenclature that she wouldn't translate.

Although James wouldn't say so to Christine, he was ready to believe that Teresa cooked the way she did just to offend him. But the truth was, Teresa just didn't like waste. She was a spare woman, with no wasted flesh, and she didn't like to waste words or food or to see waste, which she felt was an affront to a universe that wasted nothing. This was especially true in kitchen matters.

At her house, everything was either used or went into the compost bin, which she thought of as a form of cooking. Vegetable parts and old pasta and bits of meat would cook down into perfect earth, feeding the land it grew from and making a place for more food to grow. As she grew older, she also found the process of decomposition and the reduction of waste to its essentials to be elegant. Beautiful. An unexpected transformation of the unwanted into the necessary.

She'd learned this from her family, in which it was the custom to eat all parts of an animal, making *fritto misto* with brain and liver, preparing sweetbreads—which were the pancreas and thymus—with lemon and capers, simmering tripe and kidneys with garlic and parsley and vegetables, and all the many ways to cook heart and brains. Brains had to be very fresh, of course, and because they were mushy in texture, they needed to be firmed by simmering before you used them, either baked, broiled, sautéed, or in a frittata.

She couldn't imagine wasting organs like the brains, or the heart. She remembered her grandfather bringing home veal heart, which would soak in marinade in the sink. Heart took a lot of marinating because it's a muscle, tough and dry. Sometimes they'd grind it up and use it in sausage. Sometimes they'd tie it up with string and cook it in the oven. Sometimes they'd slice it with vegetables and a sauce that had a lot of lemon in it.

While it marinated, Nan would stand on a chair and peer at it, pick it up, and poke her fingers into the ventricles. She'd bring the encyclopedia from their living room and prop it up next to the sink, say the names of the parts to herself as she turned the heart over and over in her hands. Then she'd shake her head and go away, and if Teresa tried to follow her, she'd tell her to go away. She was thinking.

Teresa stopped making certain foods when she married because Sam didn't like them. He was raised on a farm and had memories of watching his parents clean the teeth of a calf's head before removing the ears, eyes, and snout. The dessicated, quartered head would soak, waiting to become a jellied meat they called head cheese, which he hated. Every time he had to eat it, he saw the calf's eyes looking at him.

But Teresa didn't mind knowing that her food once walked on four legs. She could kill and gut a chicken without guilt or repugnance, and in fact had a farm she went to for free-range chickens, where she did just that. They gave her the chickens cheap since she did the work herself, and that was another way of avoiding waste.

Once she came home late from a butchering session with a bag full of chickens and her coveralls spattered with blood, only to find James and Christine just pulling into her driveway. She had thought she'd have time to clean up before they arrived to take her out to dinner, which was something James insisted on doing at least once a month.

"Sorry," she said. "It took longer than I thought. One of them got away and I had to chase it around."

Christine looked her up and down and said, "I don't want to hear it."

James went white to the lips, and for a minute it looked like he'd drop. "Look out," Teresa said to Christine, who took his arm and led him into the kitchen, put his head between his legs while Teresa quickly changed.

Teresa was apologetic, but Christine could see that her eyes said "I told you so." Meaning, James liked to put up a front of strength, but it was all bravado. This was what was real about him. An inability to face blood and dead chickens. To Christine, his reaction just showed how sensitive he was, but she knew why he reacted the way he did.

When they'd started dating, James had told her the story of how he'd chosen psychiatry as a career. James's father had gotten rich and even had a few moments of fame in *Time* magazine when he perfected certain techniques in liver transplants. James, wanting to emulate him, had entered medical school with the goal of becoming a heart surgeon, since he saw that as one of the most important realms of medicine. That was cutting-edge, literally. The place where people lived and died. The place where he knew he could make a difference.

But then he found he had trouble with the idea of cutting into people. Actually putting your hand into someone and wrapping it around his heart. It was so intimate a gesture that when he observed surgery, he found his head swimming. Study sessions with cadavers began to give him trouble too. He put his hand into cold intestines and thought of the person's last meal, last bowel movement. Saw the person sitting on the toilet reading *National Geographic* and deciding where to go for lunch that day or what color socks to wear with that new gray suit. But instead of going to work, the person ended up in the morgue, under James's hand, because his heart failed while he was taking a shit. Now James had to cut him open and read his entrails for knowledge of the past, since he had no more future to worry about.

James reconsidered his career plan, and made a decision to switch on the day he did the autopsy on a four-hundred-pound man who had killed himself with a barbiturate overdose. He cut into the man's stomach and found almost a dozen undigested jelly doughnuts, some of the undigested barbiturates, and a heart-shaped locket.

When his hand first touched the locket, he couldn't place what it might be. He pulled it slowly from the goo and wiped it off, then opened it. Inside was a picture of a woman, and though he never found out if this was a mother or daughter or a secret love, he could see that her face was a shining force of goodness.

Heart-shaped face, eyes large and dark, dark hair framing perfect skin, and a mouth that smiled just enough to say "I know you. I know what you think and feel and how you're afraid at night sometimes and how inside you is a clean, clear soul wanting to soar." It was a face that could see inside and love you anyway. In spite of your petty ambitions. In spite of your tendency to keep your eye on the main chance. In spite of your inability to really think of anyone outside yourself.

That was the face he found in a heart-shaped locket inside the stomach of an obese man who'd committed suicide. And that was when he thought that maybe there were secrets to unlock without scalpels. That was when he went into psychiatry.

Sometimes he'd wondered if maybe he should have gone into counseling instead, since psychiatrists were so often shunted by the system into being pill pushers. Or so his father said when James told him he was leaving surgery for psychiatry. His father never saw the point of psychiatry.

In spite of that, James believed in psychiatry. The biochemistry of the body was the place where change could be effected through the prescription of medicines. He'd seen enough schizophrenics able to lead good lives only through medication, so he knew he was doing an important job of healing. And he'd seen enough of his private-practice patients rouse from the stupor of depression because of his prescriptions to understand the power of medicine, which could work magic where words failed.

He didn't think he could sit day after day listening to the problems of mental and emotional illness and offer no solution except words. He wanted something solid to give them. He wanted to see results. He wanted to really help. Even with Christine—perhaps especially with Christine—all he wanted was to help. Nothing more.

James had been sensible after their fight. He thought about it and realized that the pressure of their upcoming wedding was creating tension in the relationship. He called Christine's apartment and left a message of conciliation, then went to sleep. He supposed she'd be with one of her friends—Amberlin, probably, who was closest to her in temperament and only four years older. That would be good. Amberlin, like Delia, was happy about the engagement, but unlike Delia was more knowledgeable about matters of the psyche. His only worry was that she'd gone to Teresa's and gotten even more upset.

In the morning, he called again, and again got no answer. He didn't leave a message, not wanting to bother her if she needed time. He dressed and went to work, but found himself nervous and anxious as he did so.

He sat staring at his own reflection in the gleaming surface of a desk in his well-appointed office at the institute. He had three grants to edit, a meeting with the board that afternoon, and a planning meeting with the staff for an arts program he wanted to start. Waiting for him was a report on a patient—a paranoid schizophrenic who got delusional and started seeing warriors. They weren't evil warriors, he insisted, but they thought he was unworthy to join them, and he wanted to. If the doctors could give him something to make him worthy, he'd take it. James agreed. Anything to get him back on meds, which he'd stopped taking because he missed his illness. That wasn't uncommon either. Many patients missed the warriors they spoke to, the angels, the conversations with Jesus and Mary and God. James didn't blame them. It must be nice.

He checked his tie in the mirror of his desk, then clucked his tongue at Christine's photo on his desk. It was a view of her face in profile that he'd had done professionally as a birthday present. In it her delicate features were pointed pensively at a spot somewhere far away.

She wore a white muslin blouse and her hair was loose around her shoulders. It could have been a portrait from a century ago. It was classic, as was her face.

But it didn't seem to be sitting right in its frame. It was crooked. He angled it to the right. Then to the left. Then back to the right. No matter how he angled it, she didn't look happy. He sighed.

On his way to his office he'd stopped by her studio, but she wasn't there. Peering through the window at the top of the door, he could see it was empty. And he could see that the glass castle she'd been working on was gone.

Maybe that was a good sign, he thought. Maybe she'd finished it and was going to give it to him early as a way of making up for their fight. It would be a rather sudden reversal of her previous stance, but that wouldn't surprise him.

Women were moody creatures, he thought. For all the fancy terms psychiatry gave it, they were plain moody, and there was no accounting for the shifts in their moods.

He decided he would try to reach her one more time, and if she didn't answer, he'd go over to her apartment. Lunchtime.

No. He had a lunch meeting with someone from the governor's office. Someone he knew was a deciding voice in appointing directorships for the Upstate Institute. He couldn't cancel that one.

Besides, she wouldn't be home by lunchtime. She'd be with Teresa, getting ready for that ridiculous party they had every year. A lot of work for no money, and Teresa didn't need the promo anymore. She had no plans to make her business bigger, go franchise, do any of the intelligent things that might actually make her some real money. She just wanted to cook. He realized he was feeling petty about her and cut himself short. He'd call Christine's again. If she wasn't home, he'd try Teresa's after lunch. She'd be there by then.

He picked up the phone and dialed.

When her answering machine was through with its message, he cleared his throat. "Hi," he said, forcing cheerfulness into his tone. "Just called to say—well, I hope you're feeling better. And—um—if I was at all—um—inadvertently . . . I mean, if I said something you interpreted as condescension, it wasn't. And I hope you can find the reasons why you'd interpret it that way, because it's important to work this through and—"

The click and buzz on the line told him his time was up. He put the phone down and stared at her photo again. It told him nothing.

He buzzed his secretary. "Send in my morning patient," he said. "We've got some warriors to deal with."

To himself, he thought he would deal with the witches later.

TERESA'S KITCHEN

WANT A DRINK?" TERESA ASKED, PULLING DOWN THE whiskey from the cupboard. "I'm gonna have one."

Delia put her bags down, took off her coat, and shrugged. "Kind of early, isn't it?" Then, she looked around. "Jesus H. Christmas, what happened?"

Teresa startled. "What?"

Delia pointed to the red soup splattered against the wall. "Somebody get shot?"

"Yeah," Teresa said. She put a smile on her face and tried to get her heart to slow down. She laughed, hoping it didn't sound false. "I shot a soup that wasn't working."

"Very funny. What happened?"

"I was going too fast, and had a spill. You know. Whiskey?"

Delia shook her head.

Amberlin swung the door open, brought in a box, and set it on the table. "Two more to go, and I think that's it. By the way, I called Christine, but she wasn't home. Did you hear from her?"

"Sort of," Teresa said. She stared at the whiskey. For a minute she thought she was about to tell them what happened. Then she realized she wasn't. She didn't know why she wasn't, but it seemed right not to say anything just yet. Maybe later. She'd know when.

Of course, if Christine decided to scream and kick, that'd give it away, but if she stayed quiet, Teresa would talk about it in her own time and way.

"She'll be late," Teresa said. "She needed a little time out. Amberlin, you want something?" She poured a shot of whiskey into a juice glass and threw it down her throat. Amberlin gaped at her, then her face made a question aimed at Delia, who shrugged.

"You okay, Teresa?" she asked.

Teresa swallowed hard, shivered, and plunked the glass on the counter. "Fine," she said, her voice cracking a little. She walked over to the oven, put in a tray with two loaves of bread on it, and put a pot onto the top of the stove. "Get me the eggs, okay?" she requested.

"Got any orange juice?" Delia asked.

Amberlin crossed to the refrigerator, got Delia the carton of juice, and handed it to her. Delia got herself a glass, plunked herself down at the table, and took a sip. "Now's the good part," she said. "I get to watch other people work."

"For a few minutes," Teresa said. "There'll be plenty for you in a while."

"I know. But not right now," Delia said, and put her feet up on a chair. Her hardest work was preliminary to the event, and in fact she didn't have to be at this stage of the preparations at all. But she couldn't imagine not being present, and so traditionally she was assigned the task of cleaning up after the baker and cook, helping Christine set up the decorations, and dealing with late deliveries. She would also phone invitations to special customers or press people who might forget the event in the busyness of the season without her last-minute, cheerful invitation.

"Must be nice," Amberlin said as she brought the eggs to Teresa and set them down on the counter where she was working. She watched closely as Teresa poured flour from the bag into a bowl. She shook out a small mountain, considered it, then added another hump.

The whiskey burned its way through her and Teresa felt a little better. Less shaky. Christine was safe now. Probably fast asleep. She would sleep, and think better of what she was going to do. Teresa would check on her later, when the other women were busy with something.

"You're not measuring," Amberlin noted. Teresa laughed.

"You know I prefer chaos," Teresa said.

"I can't imagine what you see in it," Amberlin replied, grinning. "You done with the flour? I need to start the pizzelle."

Teresa nodded as she smoothed out an indentation in the mound of flour and Amberlin went through the cupboards for the other ingredients she needed. She carefully measured out flour, consulting a cookbook as she went. The two women worked side by side, each one following the rhythm of her own movements, not sliding into the other's or getting in each other's way. The radio played Pavarotti singing "Panus Angelicus," and Teresa hummed along with him as she stirred. Amberlin concentrated on leveling the salt in her teaspoon, mixing it in well with the flour and baking powder she'd sifted into a bowl.

"That'd drive me crazy," Teresa noted, cracking eggs into the mound. "You always gotta stop and think about it. Aren't you afraid you'll get it wrong?"

"You can't get it wrong," Amberlin said, "if you follow the directions. That's why it's so easy. What I want to know is how you manage to get it right when you don't have any directions to follow."

"If there aren't any directions," Teresa returned, "how can you get it wrong? Delia, could you pretend to do something?"

"I am. I'm taking notes for when I write your biographies," she said, and grinned when Teresa and Amberlin turned the exact same scowl on her. "I'll clean the pots and pans in a bit."

"Maybe," Teresa suggested, "in the meantime, you could watch the sauce." She pointed at the stove. Delia pushed herself up, walked to the stove, and peered into the large saucepan where chopped tomatoes simmered in virgin olive oil, redolent with garlic and basil.

"What's this for?" Delia asked.

"The priestchoker," Teresa answered as she flung a heap of mashed potatoes into the flour for the gnocchi dough. It squished through her fingers and mixed in with the flour to make a silken, smooth mass, still warm from the potatoes.

"I thought priestchoker was cookies," Delia said. "Didn't we make something called that last year, but it was cookies?"

Teresa grated Romano cheese into the gnocchi dough. "That's right," she said. "There's a few recipes named that. All different things. I guess you can choke a priest with just about anything."

"Surprising how often you seem to want to," Delia noted.

"Yeah. There's also apostle's fingers, and the pope's nuts, and—"

"I sense a little resentment," Amberlin interrupted.

"Tell it to the Pope," Teresa returned. "How's the sauce, Delia?"

"I don't know. Is it supposed to do something?" she asked.

"It's not supposed to burn," Teresa answered over her shoulder as she rolled the dough into a snakelike rope and began cutting pieces off the end.

Amberlin plugged the pizzelle iron into an outlet and let it warm while she mixed batter. Delia watched the pot, picking up a wooden spoon to stir it. Teresa chopped and rolled the gnocchi into little shells with her thumb. The radio played Handel's *Messiah*.

"Why do they play that for Christmas?" Amberlin said. "It's Easter music."

"I always thought it was school music," Delia said. "Something you had to learn for school, and the boys poked you in the back at the high notes to make you miss them. Can I stop watching this pot now?"

Teresa put down her knife, went to the stove, and gave a stir with the long wooden spoon. When she cooked, she had few words. Her focus remained tight on the necessity of temperature and time. She lifted the spoon to her mouth, put the tip of her tongue to the red sauce, and closed her eyes. She put the spoon back into the pot, muttered over it, turned the heat down, and passed her hand over the top.

Behind her, she heard Delia chuckle. Teresa turned and raised an eyebrow at her. "What?" she asked.

"You looked like your grandmother," Delia said. "Remember how we used to watch her boil down the tomatoes in the summer, and we thought she was a witch?"

A half smile crawled up Teresa's lips. "Yeah. But I don't look that old yet, do I?"

"Not that old. Just that mean."

Teresa picked up a dish towel and flipped it at Delia, who scooted out of the way. She made her way back to the counter and the gnocchi, her hands a machine making repetitive curling motions, turning out perfectly formed morsels of pasta.

"Someone's going to the store soon," Amberlin said. "We're down to two dozen eggs."

"Already?" Delia said. "That was fast. I'll go."

"No. You stay and irritate us. We'll make Donnie go back out when he gets here," Amberlin said. "When's he coming?"

Teresa's thumb paused in mid-curl, then completed the gesture. "He's not," she said.

"What?"

"He won't be home for the open house."

"Don't tell me he's going to his father," Amberlin said, aghast. "Delia, did you know about this?"

"I knew," Delia said. "I thought Teresa told you."

"She doesn't tell me anything unless I dig it out with a spoon. Teresa, he should be here."

"Delia can do the errands," Teresa said.

"For now, but then she'll have to help Christine set up. Donnie always takes over for her then."

Teresa felt herself start to shiver, and covered it with a shrug. "It's okay, Amberlin. Really. He needs to be separate for a while, that's all. Let him sow his oats in peace," Teresa said, her back to them, "without a bunch of women putting an apron on him and pinching his cheeks."

Delia looked at Amberlin. Amberlin shook her head. Delia nodded hard. Amberlin sighed.

"Teresa," she said, using her very calm I-am-about-to-mediate-this-situation voice, "Delia and I think you need to talk about this more, but she's not willing to ask you about it because she doesn't want you getting mad. We both know how Delia is about people getting mad at her. So she wants me to ask you, and that way you can get mad at me, which won't upset me at all because I'm so psychologically evolved."

She turned to Delia. "Isn't that right, Delia?"

"Sort of," Delia said, and made a face at her.

Teresa turned completely around and pointed a wooden spoon at the two of them, her mouth almost finding a smile in it. "I appreciate your concern," she said, "but there's nothing to talk about."

That was true, but not all of the truth. The rest of it was that she didn't want to talk about it. She had the habit of silence. It happened to her sometimes that whatever was bubbling up inside her most was also the thing she was least likely to talk about, as if some weight settled on it and held it down. Often she just couldn't find words to wrap around whatever she was feeling. She could describe it with her hands, or by making noises, but not by words. They were dull and heavy, stones in her belly covered in sand.

At those times silence felt best. She was trained to that by her family's habit of communicating without words. A certain tilt of the head from one end of the table to the other. Her mother's hand slicing through air. Her grandfather slapping a hand against the arm of his chair. These words she understood. The others took more time, like something cooking in a slow oven.

But Amberlin continued to stare at her. She wanted words. Teresa sighed. "Look, I'm upset about it, but what can I do? He's gotta find his own way through this. And if we need help, Rowan said we could call him."

"Oh, my," Delia said, grinning. "When did he say this?"

"He stopped by last night, and don't start, Delia. Just don't, okay? I gotta concentrate." She wiped her hands on her pants and squinted her eyes at the clock. "Okay. Let's start the ginger trout. That's better if it sits in its juices overnight."

Teresa opened the refrigerator and pulled out a bulky white package, brought it to the counter, and split open the paper with a knife.

"Mmm. My favorite. And I love the way Christine puts 'em on the platter so they look like a school of little fish. Where *is* she anyway? You said she'd be late, not absent, and it's past noon."

Teresa's hand slipped, and silver-backed fillets poured like water onto the floor.

"Shit," she said. "Piss and corruption."

Amberlin scrambled over to her to help, and Delia stood, held a hand up for silence. "What's that?" she whispered.

The women paused in the middle of their next gesture, Amberlin's hand closing tight on a fish, Teresa's hand poised over a fillet.

Scratching. The sound of scratching on the other side of the cellar door. Teresa, kneeling on the kitchen floor over the heap of fish, went white.

The radio played the alto solo "He Shall Lead His Flock." The clock ticked. Teresa blinked at Delia. A pitiful meow floated to them.

"The cat," Teresa whispered. "It's the cat in the cellar. She smells the fish." Color came back into her face and motion resumed.

"Goodness," Delia said as they piled the trout into the sink for washing. "I don't know why that spooked me so." She jumped again as the phone rang.

"Leave it," Teresa said. "The machine'll get it."

They listened to Teresa's voice talking, the sound of someone clearing his throat, and then James.

"Teresa," he said in a tone that sounded false even to Delia, "I suppose you're not answering since you're busy getting ready for the party, so I'll just say happy holidays to you all, and could Christine give me a call when she gets her hands out of the flour for a minute? Thanks."

Teresa rolled her eyes.

"What," Amberlin asked, "was that about?"

"James and Christine," Teresa said over her shoulder. "They had a fight."

"I told you," Delia said. "Did it get worse?"

"Yeah. I think they're not talking to each other. Or at least, she's not talking to him right now. That's why she wanted a little time out."

"Time out?" Delia said, sounding a little panicked. "What's that mean? She's got a lot to do here."

"Just—she wanted to be alone a little to think," Teresa said. "It's not a big deal. I mean, what's the worst that could happen? They don't get married."

"It's the holidays," Amberlin said seriously. "Too much pressure. We don't let people just feel what they feel. I mean, you have to be so damn happy, and I for one resent it. I can't tell you how busy the hotline is this time of year. Suicide rates rise like homesick angels."

Teresa started, and let go of the spoon she was stirring with. She cursed as its handle dipped below the line of polenta bubbling thickly in the pot. She picked at the end of it to retrieve it.

"Do they?" she asked carefully.

"Absolutely," Amberlin said with authority. She regularly regaled them with statistics and stories from the suicide hotline. Usually Teresa liked to hear it, and Delia found a gruesome satisfaction in it as well. Amberlin felt a little guilt at using the stories to entertain her friends—after all, these were people's lives at stake—but she told herself it was therapeutic to get it off her chest this way. Often she'd get advice from

James on ways to handle different kinds of callers. "I'd be working there tonight if it wasn't for this. We call in all the workers. Sherry's working a double shift for me."

Teresa smiled warmly. "Nice of her," she said.

"I'll bet it's just cold feet," Delia said.

"Marrying a shrink's a bad idea. They always remind you of your problems."

"Yeah," Delia said. "You marry a doctor, you always got symptoms."

"That's not fair," Amberlin said. "And what's it say about your marriage, Teresa?"

A slight pause in the rhythm of conversation cued Delia in that Teresa wasn't happy with the question. Teresa took the polenta from the stove and poured it into a cooling tray as she answered lightly, "I was married to the principal of an all-girl school. I always felt like a virgin."

Delia giggled and Amberlin groaned.

"Work, *signorine*. Let's get some work done," Teresa said, waving her spoon over her shoulder at them. "Christine will get here in her own time. And while we're waiting, Delia can do something."

Delia sighed, and took her feet from the chair. "Like what?"

"Silverware. Cleaned and counted."

Amberlin took her place at the counter, mixing and measuring, while Delia went to the sink. The radio played Christmas music and the kitchen was warm and light with their motions and their singing as they worked. If Teresa seemed tense and distracted, that was normal for the day before the party. There was still a lot to be done and a lot to be kept straight, with a pile of onions being chopped for one dish on the right-hand side of the counter and herbs being rinsed and ground up on the left for another, not to mention the gnocchi drying in the middle and Amberlin's tins of carrot cakes that still had to be baked and decorated.

Amberlin had also set up a plate of food on the table for the women to pick on as they worked. No real lunch or supper would be made. They'd just break periodically for a cannoli or a piece of fruit or—Delia's contribution—deviled ham sandwiches on white bread with green olive-slice eyes and pimento smiles, cut in the shape of snowmen.

The afternoon wore on toward dinnertime, and even Delia had to hustle to keep order behind the constant motion of cooking. Teresa would chop peppers. Delia would sweep the leavings into the compost bucket. Amberlin cracked eggs into bowls, made batter, and used it up. Delia would rinse out the bowls for immediate use by Teresa, who was making the green sauce.

The hand blender would get taken out and used. Delia would rinse it and put it back. At three o'clock she traded orange juice for beer, then left it on the table, next to a half-eaten snowman. The women worked.

"Hey," Delia said, watching Amberlin mix honey and a little red wine in a bowl, "are you making the ceci cookies? They're my favorite."

Amberlin nodded and poured the liquid into a mash of chickpeas. Teresa came and looked over her shoulder. "They mashed fine enough?" she asked. She'd done them by hand yesterday, as was traditional.

"Plenty fine," Amberlin said, working the dough.

"Put chocolate in," Delia insisted, going over to look. "I like the ones with chocolate. They're the best. What's that you call them, Teresa?"

"Cauciune di San Giusèppe," Teresa said. "St. Joseph's cookies."

"Yeah. You used to make them right around St. Patrick's Day when we were kids."

Teresa nodded. "St. Joseph's feast day—March nineteenth." Then, for Amberlin's benefit, she added, "Joseph's the patron saint of death, so he gets a lot of customers. Certain families prepare a thirteen-course meal for whoever can come on his feast day."

"And the families that do this, they're something sacred," Delia added.

"Sacre famiglia," Teresa said. "Families that've had a miracle. It was a way of saying thank-you. My grandmother's family was one."

"What was the miracle?" Amberlin asked.

"Nobody remembers anymore," Teresa said. "Grandma always told me it was time to get a new one, so we'd have a story to tell."

"I love that story. You know how some stories are like certain foods. No matter how much you have, you can always have it again?" Delia reached her finger into the bowl and swiped some filling. Amberlin swatted at her. Teresa went back to the stove, where she was putting together a tuna and tomato sauce for the polenta.

"What's your favorite holiday food?" Delia asked Amberlin.

Amberlin sighed. "Which holiday?"

"Christmas, of course."

She pointed to herself. "Me atheist Jew. Remember?"

"She remembers," Teresa said. "She just likes to hear you talk about it."

She told them every year, like reciting a litany, that her mother was a Jew and her father a politically scrupulous atheist maniac who bore the burden of all white men's guilt. His two children were educated in all cultural holidays, and expected to respect them rather than celebrate them. Certainly he wouldn't let them take part in a holiday that was about consumerism and false promises, and wouldn't let his daughter believe in the capitalist god Santa Claus. They did believe, however, in exposing their children to all cultures. As Amberlin said later, you need only one exposure to be immune, and if she was skeptical about most cultural practices, it was probably her father's fault. She was immunized young.

"That's right," Delia said. "I like to hear you talk about it, because your family took you places, at least. I was stuck in Aurora Falls eating pot roast and potatoes and overcooked vegetables. Until Daddy died and we moved to upstate New York, where Mom had some relatives. Not much more exciting, I can tell you."

"Hey," Teresa said. "That's where you met me."

"Like I said." Delia grinned and stuck her tongue out at Teresa, who blew a raspberry back.

"And we were never in the same place from one Christmas to the next," Amberlin said, then grinned. "I remember they took us to Mexico one year. Me and my brother bought flaked coconut and sprinkled it in front of the hotel to look like snow. I thought my mother'd kill us for that one."

"But don't you love the holidays?" Delia said rapturously. "Everyone has a different attitude, and there's lights and singing and parties and food. I used to go to midnight mass and sit next to Bess Mitchell, and the singing was like magic. You remember, Teresa?"

Teresa nodded absentmindedly and said, "Necco wafers."

Delia laughed. "Right."

"Necco wafers?" Amberlin asked.

"You know. The candies in a roll. The pink ones tasted like Pepto-Bismol. Awful. But the yellow ones were yummy."

"What about Necco wafers?"

"We used to play communion with them. Y'know, body of Christ and all that, and put one on my tongue, and I couldn't talk or eat or do anything until it dissolved." She nodded toward Teresa, who was switching her concentration between the tuna and a sauté of mushrooms and onions, and didn't notice.

Amberlin shook her head. "My parents took us to all the churches and temples so we could see what people did. There was no mystery at all. I got to have Hanukkah in Israel one year, and Christmas in Germany the next. I preferred the latkes to the strudel."

"That's what I mean," Delia said. "You *went* places while I was eating Necco wafers. And Teresa at least had all that Italian stuff. But she didn't have Santa Claus."

"No Santa Claus," Teresa agreed absentmindedly. "We had Befana. She brought presents on Little Christmas in January. And she was a witch."

The phone rang, and Teresa glanced at the clock. Almost four and getting dark already. Somehow the day had passed.

"Bet that's Christine," Delia said, making a grab for it. "Hello?" Teresa and Amberlin watched her face. "Oh, hi, James," she said, nodding at them. "What? No, she's not here yet."

Delia listened, her face scrunching up into a question, then confusion. "I haven't got a clue what you're talking about, James. What letter?" She listened, and her eyes got bigger. "Call the police?" she asked.

Teresa took a step forward, then stopped. She held her hand out, and Delia handed her the phone.

"James," she said. "It's Teresa. Talk to me."

Her face remained tight and still as she listened, her head bent down, nodding now and then. After some time she shook her head. "No," she said. "That would be pointless, and I don't think it's—it doesn't sound to me like—James, listen to me. I don't want you over here."

Delia waved a hand frantically up and down. Amberlin took a step closer to the phone but really couldn't do anything else. Teresa's lips got tighter as she listened. Then her head snapped up and she said clearly, "Here. Talk to Delia about it. I don't have time for this nonsense." And she handed the phone back to Delia.

"James?" she said, and listened. "Well, she is busy, James. I don't know. Yes, she does care about her, but I don't think the police—yes, all they'd do is tell us she's an adult and can go wherever she wants. Okay. I'll tell Teresa. When Christine comes, I'll call you."

She hung up the phone and looked at Teresa.

"What?" Amberlin demanded. "What is it?"

"James says he left work early to go to Christine's apartment," Delia said, maintaining eye contact with Teresa. "She's not there, but there was a letter for him on her bureau. It said good-bye. It said she was sorry for hurting him. He thinks—he thinks it's a suicide note."

Unexpectedly, Teresa laughed.

ABOUT FREEZING AND PRESERVING FOODS

IN TERESA'S CELLAR, CHRISTINE'S EYES HAD BECOME preserved in gloom. The pale light that had turned her space murky gray throughout the day was leaving, and her world was settling into darkness. She was something Teresa had put in the cellar for safekeeping with the other preserved foods. Hot Italian peppers, bright green with spots of red spices in the liquid, curled like fetuses in their glass containers. Tomatoes canned with bay leaf and basil. More red and green. The small, jewellike jars of deep red raspberry jelly made from the brambles that grew in Teresa's yard. Two kinds of strawberry preserves—one made from her strawberry patch, the other from wild strawberries she gathered meticulously, each tiny red jewel precious and rare.

Christine knew that Teresa also had a freezer full of produce from her summer garden, and at about February she liked to open it up, take out a carton of frozen blackcaps, and breathe in the pine and sugar scent of them. Sometimes Teresa would thaw them and make syrup for Amberlin to use at the shop. Sometimes she would just take in a good lungful of summer, then put them back, pausing long enough to pat the plastic cartons of green beans that would see her through to next summer's harvest.

Teresa had received from her mother a copy of the book *The Joy of Cooking* for her wedding, and she would read it for pleasure in the bathtub or with her breakfast before she went to work teaching sixth-graders the joy of reading—which she felt was just another form of consumption. She told Christine that if she was stuck alone in the woods with a gun and a copy of that cookbook, she could survive. It told how to skin rabbits, cook muskrat, make head cheese—anything she might need. And in the absence of her grandmother, it taught her how to can and preserve foods.

Teresa believed, as it said in *The Joy of Cooking,* that modern packaging had removed our close awareness of growth and decay and the fragile balance between them. No matter what method of preservation you use, there are intricate reactions at work. Even freezing food, which seems so simple, could be disastrous. Not all foods froze well. Or, more accurately, they were so transformed by the process of freezing that they didn't thaw well. And it took a lot of energy to keep food at a steady state of zero degrees. Energy and room, because packing a freezer too tight would raise the temperature.

Then, of course, there was always the danger that one day the power would blow. Once, in an ice storm, Teresa's power had gone out for a week, and she'd lost almost everything. Ultimately, that was good. As the freezer defrosted itself, food appeared as if from other eras of her life. A duck dated 1989, from an anniversary dinner she never cooked because her husband forgot it was their anniversary and went to a basketball game instead. A few cartons of unidentifiable crumbly green things. A Swanson TV dinner she bought once and never ate. After that, she made it a point to clean out her freezer once a year. And she canned more food than she used to.

She always told Christine it was important not to be disconnected from your primary sources of food, though Christine couldn't see what difference it made whether you bought your berries at Shop 'N Save or picked them yourself. Teresa said it did make a difference, but when asked to explain how she grew inarticulate, put a basket in Christine's hand, and said, "Go pick something. You'll see."

But she didn't. Food didn't mean that much to her. Or maybe it meant too much. Nan's cooking sprees were spectacular and wonderful, but they were always followed by weeks of semistarvation, when they'd subsist on potato chips and hot dogs and Kool-Aid. There was always too much, and not enough always followed. Christine had come to understand that food was an irregular magic. It appeared and disappeared in an arbitrary way, without regard for your actions or feelings in the matter.

Christine could hear the women moving around upstairs and tried to distinguish who was doing what by the sound of their footsteps. Delia's heavy tread. Amberlin's soft walk. Teresa's quick steps. The sound of their voices, muted, words unintelligible, floated through the floorboards to her. Occasionally, she heard laughter. She wondered if they'd forgotten her, like a jar of pickles they wouldn't have to think of again until spring. She might sit here and rot, the way food did at the back of her mother's refrigerator. She put her head down on the blankets to rest it, felt the cool of the cellar floor near her face. She had a headache. She was so tired, she felt as if she were dreaming while she was still awake.

Delia's laughter, loud and raucous, rolled down through the floorboards. Amberlin's higher-pitched voice followed, and Teresa joined in with her throaty, clipped sounds. They were like three birds, Christine thought, each a different species, and it was a wonder they didn't peck each other's eyes out. She asked Teresa once how they managed to avoid getting in more fights than they did, given how different the three of them were, and she said it was like seasonings. They didn't have to be the same to mix well. What you wanted was for each one to retain its individual flavor but act in complement with the ones around it.

And sometimes, she said, the most surprising combinations worked just fine. Green beans with mint, garlic, pepper, and good, fresh extra-virgin olive oil was wonderful. Cinnamon and white sage in her venison marinade was an unexpected success.

When she grew tired of listening and looking, Christine wondered what James was doing, and if he'd gotten her note yet. She deliberately hadn't used the word *suicide* in it because she knew the word would affect him as strongly as the act. Suicide was a clinical event, not something a psychiatrist's fiancée would do.

And while she felt she needed to leave, she didn't want to hurt him. She wanted only to stop worrying about her mother and food and whether there was enough. Stop worrying about whether or not she could find it and keep it if there was. It would be easier to be food. Give herself back to the earth and be at peace.

Of course, James would still be upset. He loved her. Valued her. He would miss her. In spite of what Teresa said, he was a sensitive man. In fact, Christine thought he'd been very much affected by his own family—his charming mother, who had the stamina of a Kleenex, and his overbearing father, so full of his work and the importance of it. James's father expected a lot from his only son, and James lived under the pressure of his father's reputation, his demands, his love. The food and the hands in James's house were too heavy for him, and he needed to escape into a place where he could be as light as thought. He once told Christine that was what attracted him to her. Her lightness. The way her hair floated around her face like angels' hair. The way her eyes caught and held the light. The way she worked with glass.

And sitting in the dark, she remembered that she liked the gentleness of his hands on her face, and the way he handled her so carefully during lovemaking, showed her he thought she was precious and fragile and rare. At his best, he combined a cool superiority with tenderness. It was captivating and unlike any other relationship she'd had so far.

They had met when Bread and Roses catered a professional lunch he attended and James made it a point to come back to the kitchen and ask who made the beautiful vases that decorated the tables. Vases so delicate and precisely shaped were obviously works of art, and he'd like to get one as a gift for his mother. Christine was there waitressing, and she gave him her card. He called a week later and chose a square-cut vase made of silver and black pieces of glass, then took her out to dinner.

It was not love at first sight, but it was ease at first sight, followed by a rational decision on both their parts that they'd found a good and lasting partner in the other. You could say James was seeking light. You could say Christine was seeking something cool and steady as air. You could say both were good people, and the problems they had were something that happened between them.

Teresa would say that happened sometimes. Once, in fact, she'd said it about James when Christine was trying to pin her down as to what she had against him. Nothing, she said. Nothing against him. She was just worried about the combination.

"Some seasonings," she'd said portentously, "are not meant to be mixed."

They would never properly blend, and never properly complement each other. The resulting taste would be confused and perpetually frantic, as some marriages are. Christine thought Teresa had no right to comment given what had happened to her own marriage, but Teresa said that was different. Some flavors needed time to meld and become rich, while others started out blending okay, but over time they soured. Chemical reactions occurred. Environmental factors intervened. Things changed. It didn't taste the way it had at the start.

That was a matter of improper preservation or the vagaries of time, the former being controllable and the latter way out of control. But it was best to start with the right blend and hope for the best rather than with an awkward blend and hope for a change, since it's much easier to throw out a bad marinade than to get loose from a bad relationship. The smell clings to you. Or you cling to it, and keep adding ingredients to try to cover up the mess, and it only gets worse and worse, until someone is brave enough to dump the whole thing and start over.

Sitting in the dark of the cellar, with her wolf eyes scanning the rows of jars on Teresa's shelves, Christine could see that James would make a fine husband for the right woman. A woman who would rest her arm lightly on his, and be perfect as well as slightly fragile in all the right places. A woman who carried herself well, and asked no more of the world than that it provide her with a cozy nest, the admiring eye of a man, and dinner out at least twice a week.

None of that was much consolation. Christine had wanted to be that woman, full of light and air. For a while she felt as if she'd achieved it, held a steady state, all her flavors balanced and preserved. But she couldn't hold on to it no matter how badly she wanted to.

Instead, she was the sort of woman who screams at her fiancé and smashes glass. She wanted to be without that passion and that heat and thick darkness. She was in her late twenties, at an age of risk for insanity, and scared. Her mother's ghost hovered over her like a bad angel, whispering "I told you so," and she couldn't stop loving her, couldn't stop hating her. Couldn't stop loving and hating herself.

Upstairs, the women were cooking and laughing. It occurred to Christine that Teresa had put her here, separate and alone, as if she were food that needed preserving. Teresa was a literal sort of person, and it could well have been a literal act to put her here, where she put all her preserved foods, frozen, canned, properly spiced, and contained. As if being alone in the dark would allow her to seep into herself like the essential flavor of rosemary or mint, seeping up from the center into the dried leaves. As if she could preserve herself here, keep herself from spoiling.

At Nan's funeral, tears fell out of Teresa's eyes without needing any pushing by sobs or other sounds. She was quiet, and let them fall. Christine, for her part, couldn't cry at all. She kept expecting tears to come. When Teresa hugged her, when Nan's parents hugged her—they were her grandparents, weren't they? But they seemed so dry and used up and not like Nan. Then she thought maybe she'd cry at the cemetery, when Teresa sang the Joni Mitchell song "Blue" because Nan loved it. Or when the priest said the bit about love being "the greatest of these." But the tears, if they were there, stayed in her belly, a quiet salty pool of memory and unpoured grief.

It was an unspoken agreement between them that Christine would come stay with her, move back to upstate New York and find work here. Teresa never invited her, and Christine never took her up on her invitation. Not verbally anyway. As they left the cemetery, Teresa turned and said, "Where're your things?"

"At the hotel," Christine told her.

"Sam'll help you bring 'em over," Teresa said. "Tomorrow."

So she'd stayed with them until she found her own place, and got a waitressing job with Teresa's help. She started her stained glass work, did her work for Bread and Roses, got herself a life.

But the tears remained inside her. She was a jar full of brine, she thought, and now Teresa had put her in the cellar with the other jars. And here in the cellar, she felt the only part of her that was being preserved was her pain.

TERESA'S KITCHEN

SHE'S NOT GONNA KILL HERSELF," TERESA SAID WHEN Amberlin and Delia ogled her as if she were crazy.

"But the note—" Delia stammered.

"What did it say?" Amberlin asked. "Exactly."

"He said—um—she said she was sorry but she had to leave him. It wasn't his fault. She just had to go."

Teresa threw her hands up in the air. "There. I told you. He'd rather think she's gonna kill herself than dump him."

"Oh," Delia said. "Oh. You think?"

"What else? You know how men are."

Delia relented. She knew.

Amberlin's shoulders, which had been climbing up around her ears as the conversation progressed, receded to their normal position. "Well, then," she said. "Okay. She's dumping him." She chewed on her lip for a minute. "She's dumping him?"

Teresa shrugged. "Looks that way."

Amberlin twisted her mouth around and blew out breath. "Why?"

"I think she's not ready to get married," Teresa said. "At least, not to him. They're different."

"Then why didn't you just tell us that when we asked about her?" Amberlin said.

"I thought it was her place to do that. And besides, what if I said something, then she changed her mind? It'd make me look bad. Like I wished it on her."

"You've got a point," Amberlin mused.

"I got a few. So," Teresa concluded, "now can we get back to work?"

"Okay," Delia said. "Okay. What needs washing?"

She went to the sink and took platters and utensils from it, loaded up the dishwasher and started it running. Amberlin stacked pizzelle on a platter and unplugged the cookie press. "Ginger trout?" she asked.

"Start on the cakes," Teresa said. "I'll do the trout."

"She's really gonna dump him?" Delia asked. "Damn. I wanted to go to a wedding."

"Maybe when you talk to her, you can ask her," Teresa said. "Until then, can we drop it? Here. Chop some scallions." She picked up a knife by the point and held the handle toward Delia.

"Jeez. Careful, huh? *Cuidado.*"

"What?" Teresa asked.

"I think that means 'be careful.' In Spanish. I don't know the Italian. What is it?"

"I don't know. I never learned that word."

"Not a surprise," Delia said. She began to work, slowly and tentatively, at the scallions. "Your knives are too sharp," she said. "They scare me."

"A sharp knife is a snappy servant," Teresa replied. "That's from *The Joy of Cooking*. Chop faster and it'll go easier."

"Cuidado," Delia muttered as the smell of scallion climbed up to her nose and combined with the smell of the ginger Teresa was peeling. "Mmmm. I love the ginger trout. Hurry up so I can sneak a piece."

"You love food," Amberlin said as she beat eggs in a bowl. "Period. All food. It's a wonder you aren't huge."

"I am," Delia said, scooping a handful of chopped scallions into a bowl. "At least, I get told that a lot. Keep my voice down, don't walk so hard, talk so loud, ask so much."

Amberlin looked her up and down. "You're not huge. I mean, not like overweight in an unhealthy way, which is all that really matters. You're just not a little woman."

"Like Teresa," Delia said.

"Ha," Teresa said, and continued to cut trout into pieces, dip it into a bowl of flour. On the stove, the pan was heating up. Delia gave her the scallions, and she tossed them with the ginger into the pan and they bubbled in frothy pools of butter.

"*You* should be huge, with all this food around," she said.

"I cook it," Teresa said. "I don't eat it all."

"Willpower."

"Yuk," Amberlin said. "Maturity and willpower. They both suck."

"Big-time," Delia agreed. Teresa laughed.

"Oh," Amberlin said with feeling, turning away from the counter and facing the other women.

"What?" Teresa said. "What's wrong?"

"Nothing," Amberlin said. "Just at this minute there's absolutely nothing wrong." She swept her long arm across the room to include everything. "It's all perfect right . . . now."

Delia and Teresa stood still, heads tilted slightly as if listening to what she meant. Outside, darkness had enveloped the house and snow fell silently against the windowpanes. Inside, there was food, the warmth of the kitchen, and the warmth among them. It crackled with perfection.

Amberlin always pointed these moments out to them, these moments of perfection that were fleeting as a snowflake on your fingertip. Teresa thought it odd at first, then grew used to it, then grew to like it. After a while she learned how to spot the moments herself, though she wouldn't mention them as Amberlin did. She would savor them in quiet, as if that would make them stay longer. Delia, who celebrated all forms of joy, would smile and laugh and watch the moment pass. "We're having an Amberlin moment," she would say, and Amberlin would frown, not sure if this was a joke, then smile when she saw Delia meant well.

But they all knew the moment could only be appreciated, never held, so now they sighed and turned back to their tasks, Amberlin beating eggs, Teresa chopping, and Delia lighting more candles.

"So the hell with willpower," Delia said. "When can I eat?"

"Tomorrow," Teresa said. "All you want."

"Y'know," Delia said, "you're as bad as my mother, and I always thought she was the queen of willpower."

"She was," Teresa said. "Made good aspic though. I never got the hang of that."

"You're not proper enough, Teresa. She was. Even her food was proper."

"Your mother?" Amberlin said, surprised. Delia often talked about her children and her husband, but rarely about her mother or her father, who were both dead.

"Yeah. She made soufflés and shit like that. Salads. And aspic. She'd make these aspics for ladies' luncheons. They still had events like that in Aurora Falls, and all the ladies would show up with their hats and gloves on and talk about church stuff and gossip. I remember how straight their backs were, and how I practiced walking with an apple on my head so I'd have a straight back like theirs."

"How'd you end up so—so—"

"Rude and crude? Down and dirty? My father, probably. I mean, here he was, this important person in town, but he liked to hunt and fish and come home smelly. He'd make an enormous mess when he cooked too. Bacon grease everywhere, dishes all over the place. He'd make this turkey tetrazzini, then put fried eggs on top of the noodles and melt Velveeta real thick all over it. Odd foods and starches were his strong point," she noted.

"God," Amberlin said, "no wonder he died."

Delia moved to one of the votive candles in the window and lit it. "He died of leukemia, not overeating," she said.

She gazed into the candle flame, letting it dance in her eyes as she, without thought, was held by the dance. "Y'know, it's a funny thing about dead people. Sometimes they feel like they're close by. Like when you're talking about them, and you get a sort of shiver. I was watching a special on Discovery the other night—"

"Delia," Amberlin cut in, "you believe in ghosts?"

"Don't you?"

"Well, I know that sometimes there's this strange energy shift around death. Studies have shown that in hospital wards where people are dying there're often electrical problems, but that's different than ghosts."

Amberlin held up an empty eggshell and waved it around. "Last egg," she said. "And the milk's gone too."

"Okay," Teresa said. "Time for a store run."

"I believe in ghosts," Delia said firmly. "Like just now I had a feeling my father was close by. And then I'm thinking about Christine, and I could swear I feel her in the house somewhere."

"She's not dead, Delia," Amberlin said.

Teresa, frying fish in the big cast-iron pan, jerked her arm back and knocked her elbow into a glass bowl, which leapt off the counter and shattered on the floor.

"H. Christ, I did it again," she groaned. "Could someone take over here a minute?"

Amberlin took Teresa's spatula as Teresa knelt to sweep the glass into a dustpan. Delia stood up and watched, but could find nothing useful to do.

From Teresa's perspective she could see Delia's legs. She looked up at her. Over to Amberlin, who was turning fish and staring at her as if she had a question she wanted to ask.

She stood, stared down at the dustpan of glass, then lifted her chin high. "What?" she asked.

"What, what?" Delia said. "You're like spit on a griddle. Paranoid too. I think we oughta call James and have him prescribe something for you."

"You were looking at me," she said to Delia, then to Amberlin.

"Well, we're a little worried. It's your first Christmas alone, with Donnie away, and now Christine not showing," Amberlin said sympathetically. "Anybody might be feeling bad about that. I think you should have insisted, at least with your son. I mean, he should be here."

Teresa dumped the glass into the garbage under the sink.

"Look, don't get on me about it." Teresa raised her voice through her words and there was enough dry ice in her eyes to silence her friends. "I can't make him be here any more than I can Christine, or make my husband stay, or—"

She threw her arms up in the air, brought them down and bit on the end of her thumb, then walked out of the kitchen.

"Now what?" Amberlin said tensely. "What's wrong now?"

"She's not having a good year," Delia said, shaking her head. "I think we need to cheer her up somehow."

"We can't if she won't talk about it." She removed fish from the pan and put it on a paper-lined platter to drain. When they were done cooking all the fish, the pan drippings would be mixed with lemon and more ginger and scallions to make a sauce which the fish would soak in overnight. Tonight, a piece of trout in sauce would be good. Tomorrow, it would be excellent.

"She doesn't have to talk about it. Let's just distract her. We can—"

She clamped her mouth shut when Teresa reentered in her coat. "I gotta go to the store. Milk. Eggs. Lemons. I can't finish the trout without the lemons. What happened to all of them anyway?" She cast an accusing glance at Delia and Amberlin, as if they'd eaten them.

"No, I didn't make lemonade," Delia said. "I'll go. You stay and cook."

"No. You've got your phone calls to make, and you should start getting plates and stuff ready, and the man with the salmon might come tonight. Besides, I want to go. I don't think I've seen anything outside this kitchen for a week," Teresa said. She pulled her car keys out of her pocket and jangled them.

Amberlin frowned at Delia, who shrugged. Somebody should go with her, Amberlin's eyes were saying. She won't talk to you, Delia's shrug was replying.

"I'll go, too," Amberlin said pointedly, turning off the stove and going for her coat.

"Keep an eye on the sauce, okay?" Teresa told Delia. "In a little while, add some basil."

"Add something? How much?" Delia said, a little panicked.

Teresa held her fingers scrunched together in an Italian gesture and kissed the ends of them. "That much, three times. And don't open the cellar door. You know how Tosca is when there's fish around."

Amberlin returned, bundled and ready, and they exited in a huff of cold wind that blew into the kitchen after their departure.

"Good luck with that nonverbal thing," Delia mumbled after them. She was used to Teresa's silences and moods, and never took them personally, but tonight was something special. She understood, and she wished there was something she could do to make it easier for her. Maybe put in a call to Rowan and invite him over. At least it would distract her.

She gingerly lifted the spatula from the frying pan, slid it under a piece of trout on the platter, got it onto a plate, and brought it to the table. She'd just have a bite to eat, then make the phone calls on her list. Michael first, of course. She had to call and find out if he was bringing either of the kids to stay overnight with her.

The sudden quiet of the house disturbed her, so she turned the radio up louder and got herself another beer. She probably shouldn't, she thought, patting the curves of her hips, which gave her satisfaction at some moments and great concern at others. People said she was voluptuous and healthy, but she'd had an aunt who ended up shaped like a pear, with stubby little arms and hands that she used to flail at the keys of a piano to produce something that was supposed to be ragtime music. Delia could still see her hammering away, hips overflowing the sides of the piano bench as she sweated out a song.

Of course, Delia would never be stubby. Her long bones wouldn't allow that. But if she didn't watch it, she could get sloppy, since she was basically an animal that preferred pleasure to pain, and exercise to her was pain.

She got herself a fork and carved out a piece of the trout, brought it to her mouth and let it rest on her tongue. Wonderful, even without the sauce. She let it linger for a moment more before she chewed and swallowed, and took her time with the rest of it too.

Only after that, and when half the beer was down, did she pick up the phone and dial her home. It was busy.

"Gotta get call-waiting," she muttered. Anthony was almost a teenager, but it was probably Jessamyn using the phone. She loved to talk as much as her mother did. Even when she was a toddler, she was a talker and Delia had to remind her sometimes to stop talking long enough to put food in her mouth. She would sing her songs and talk to everything, from the time she was weaned from the breast and turned her face toward the world. She would talk to the leaves, the cupboard door, the light switches, refrigerator magnets, the water in the bath, the hotness of the soup, the air in the bubbles, to dirt, to chocolate, crackers, noodles that slurped in her mouth like string, yogurt that smeared the tray of her high chair, lids that she put on pans, laundry in baskets. She was in continual conversation, and Delia would suddenly think how hard it would be when Jessamyn left home for college. So quiet.

That was probably what had Teresa going, she thought. She and

Donnie were always close, and so the separation was even harder, since there was anger in it. Unwarranted anger, but there it was. Kids took things funny. He'd get over it, but if he didn't do so soon, she'd have a talk with him. After all, she was his godmother and had a responsibility in these matters too.

Maybe Amberlin was right. The holidays brought out too much feeling, and not all of it was about good cheer. This was the anniversary of Nan's death, and that might explain some of Christine's agitation too. Michael's father had had his stroke just before Thanksgiving last year, Delia was almost convinced, just to mess up the holidays. And her own father . . . well, at least he had survived through Christmas. But she didn't want to think about that. Not while she was alone in a quiet house. Quiet houses, houses with no sound except ticking clocks, reminded her of waiting to hear the footsteps of someone who would never again come down the stairs. That wasn't something she wanted to think about. Too much, and she never understood the point of wallowing in feelings that hurt like hell, for the sake of personal growth.

She raised her beer bottle and toasted her absent children. "Seize the day," she told them. She heard the cat scratching at the damn door, and its plaintive meow.

She tried dialing again, and this time it rang. While she waited for someone to pick up, she stared out the window into the yard, where snow made the remnants of Teresa's garden look ghostly and sad.

On the fifth ring, Michael answered.

"Hey, honey. You're home. Alone?"

"Almost, hallelujah," he said. "Jessie's staying at Nancy's, and Anthony's downstairs with a movie."

"Which one?"

"Terminator II."

"Again? And he's such a quiet kid. You think that's normal, Michael? It's like four times he's seen it now, isn't it?"

"I'd worry more if he craved Richard Simmons reruns. Look, we're all fine here, so just keep working. The kids'll hang with me tomorrow and then we'll go pick up my father before we head over."

"Your father?" she asked.

"Yes," he said, his voice assuming patience. "I'm bringing him. I told you that."

She closed her eyes and pressed a thumb against her forehead. Her stomach turned over. Michael bringing his father to the party made her unnaturally nervous. "I don't know. You think he'll be okay?"

"I think he'll be fine. It's you I'm worried about."

"Me?"

"Will you be okay?"

The nail of her thumb pressed a half-moon into her forehead. "It's not me," she said. "It's . . . Teresa. She's having kind of a rough time this year, and I don't want to put any more pressure on her."

Michael's laugh rolled over the lines. "Teresa? It won't even ruffle her hair. You know she's fine with old people, bums, invalids, crazy people. Anything but normalcy and she's in her element."

Delia felt her heart thumping hard. Michael didn't understand this. He didn't get it. His father was old and sick and he'd be here with all the people and the kids and anything could happen. What if he had another stroke? What if he died and Michael felt horrible and she didn't know how to console him? So many things could go wrong, and she wouldn't know how to handle any of them. The fear of it was in her belly, hollow and old like a story she already knew the ending to, or one of those nightmares where you know ahead of time the monster is behind the door but nobody will believe you.

"I don't understand what you're so afraid of, Delia. And don't tell me it's Teresa, because I know better," Michael said. "It's you."

"I just—I don't want anything to go wrong, that's all," she said.

"Honey, it's more than that. It's because of your father, isn't it?"

At her back, the cat clawed the basement door. The sauce bubbled on the stove. If there was more, she didn't want to talk about it now.

"I'm just a little worried, that's all," she said. "No big deal. Look, I gotta go. There's sauce I'm supposed to do something to."

He paused for a moment, and she could almost see him nodding his head the way he would when he knew she was trying to put a bright face on for him or the kids. He wouldn't push her, but he'd make sure she knew that he wasn't being fooled.

"Teresa left you with the sauce? She must be losing it," he said companionably.

"Yeah," Delia said, "smart-ass. I love you too."

She hung up and started rummaging in the cupboards for

something clearly marked basil. The problem with Teresa's kitchen was that she knew what all the herbs looked like and smelled like, so she didn't have to label them. But that wasn't much help to Delia.

"Shit," she said. "Maybe there's some in the cellar." And if there wasn't, she could grab a jar of the hot peppers, which would go great with the trout.

She opened the door, and quick as lightning the cat streaked out and was gone, lurking somewhere, waiting for her chance at the fish.

"Double shit," Delia said. "The cat." She decided to deal with that second and the sauce first. She flicked the stair light, which wasn't working. She peered down the stairwell.

"Molasses," she said. "As in dark as."

She retreated and began rummaging through drawers until she came up with a small yellow flashlight that worked if she slapped it against the side of her leg. Then she took a deep breath and began her descent.

When her father taught her how to swim, he threw her off the dock at the pond where they went fishing. Just picked her up and threw her into the water. She felt her body sink like a stone down through the murky darkness. She kept her eyes open and saw small fish swimming, but she just sank into the quiet, into the dark. Part of her thought, *I am going to drown.* But it was so quiet, it seemed all right. She probably would have drowned, except that her leg was caressed by an underwater weed, cool and silky and alive.

She looked down but couldn't see what it was, and suddenly it wasn't so quiet anymore. Suddenly she remembered the existence of sharks and piranhas and alligators. They'd eat you bit by bit. And while drowning seemed okay, being eaten did not. It was not okay. She did not want to watch parts of her disappear down the gullet of an alligator. That was not okay and she began to kick and kick, and as she kicked, she rose to the surface, to the frightened face and ready arms of her father, who was in the water and ready to dive down after her. Afterward, he took her out for an ice cream sundae with hot fudge on top, and they never told her mother what happened.

The cellar was cool and damp, murky as the bottom of the pond.

At the bottom of the stairs, the flashlight made a circle of light that showed her feet and the gray cement floor. Teresa kept dozens of jars of tomatoes and pickles, preserved mushrooms and beans and cauliflowers here in the cool dark. Jars of purple and red jams, golden and emerald-green jellies were a store of riches for the kitchen. Bottles of wine and vinegar with herbs stood in neat rows on shelves next to the freezer, where she stored even more of her garden through the cold months. Delia moved the light across the shelves but saw no mason jars filled with herbs.

She took a step forward, and the light came to rest on a nest of blankets and pillows. It seemed to undulate, like an animal turning in its sleep. She moved the light and saw that it was encased in a tangle of ropes around the big sink and its plumbing.

"What's she up to down here?" Delia muttered. She took another step forward. The light encircled the pale face and honey hair of a young woman who lay curled within the blankets.

"Christine?" Delia whispered.

Christine opened her eyes, then smiled grimly. "Merry Christmas, Delia," she said.

Delia couldn't think of an appropriate response. What are you doing here? might have been right, except that somehow she was sure Christine wouldn't answer. And besides, there was something in Christine's eyes that forbade words. In her eyes were people who wouldn't listen to appropriate questions or make appropriate responses, like the crocodiles lurking at the bottom of a murky lake. In her eyes were wells of disorder and emptiness, hungry for her. Sharks and crocodiles swam at the back of her eyes, and Delia felt her father's hand, cold and lifeless, unable to lift her from this place of darkness and death. *Daddy's dead* was all she could think, nonsensically, nightmarishly.

Delia felt the flashlight leave her hand, and felt rather than saw the ensuing dark. Inside it, she heard a low laugh, and above her, the phone rang. Delia turned toward the sound, moving through the dark as through water, arms thrashing. A ringing phone. Signs of life. She tripped on the first stair and lay, looking up. There was light at the top of the stairs. She crawled toward it, shaking, going up.

When she got to the top, she closed the door behind her and looked around.

Everything was the same as when she'd left. That didn't seem right somehow, but it was so. Nothing had burned. No sirens were screaming. Nobody was waiting to accuse her of any horrible deed. There were still loaves of bread on the counter. Platters of cookies covered with red cellophane. The coffee was still in the pot and the radio was still playing. "Angels We Have Heard on High."

And the phone was still ringing. She reached for it, but the answering machine picked up first and she decided to listen. If it was Michael, she'd talk to him, tell him, ask for help.

"This is James," his voice said, speaking crisply with an edge of anger. "Teresa, I'd like you to call me so that we can consult on the very pressing problem of Christine's disappearance. Please take this seriously, for a change."

"Mother of God," Delia whispered. Then the doorbell rang.

She thought about ignoring it but decided that would be suspicious, though of what she wasn't sure. She patted her hair. It must be messy, but then, it usually was. Part of her exuberant personality, Amberlin said. Nobody would notice anything wrong there. She opened the door.

The first thing she saw was a tree, which confused her. Trees, she knew, didn't normally ring doorbells. Not even in the season of miracles. Then, peering around the side of it, she saw the face of Rowan Bancroft, his great gray beard and mass of hair surrounding liquid brown eyes that almost asked a question. Always almost asked a question.

"Hey, Delia. Teresa in?"

She smiled. "No. She's . . ." Where was she anyway? It seemed so long ago since she'd been in the house. "At the store," Delia said.

"Oh. Well, then. If I could just bring this in. It's a plant, and it's cold, so I should get it inside."

The plant, followed by Rowan, entered the kitchen.

"Did you want to wait for Teresa? Can I get you anything?"

Rowan shifted his weight from one foot to the other. "Well, if there's coffee," he said.

Of course there is, you idiot, she wanted to shout. There's always coffee here. It's Teresa's house. Coffee and them damn hard cookies and enough food to choke a horse. And sure enough, if you look long enough, you'll probably find someone tied up in the cellar, their eyes all full of holes. Dammit.

"Sure," she said, smiling. "Sit down. I think Teresa'll be back any minute. We've got a lot to do yet."

She poured him a cup, got a washcloth to wipe the crumbs from her supper off the table, got him milk and sugar.

"Is that a poinsettia of some kind?" Delia asked, touching the plant.

"Fig tree," he corrected her. "Honey fig. Already bearing, see?"

He lifted a small golden droplet-shaped fruit in his hand for her to see.

"Fig tree. Is it for Teresa?"

That was when he blushed. "It's a Christmas present," he said. "She's a good customer."

"Sure. Merry Christmas. Where'd you get it?"

He caressed a leaf between thumb and index finger. "I grew it," he said. "I started four from seed years ago. Two made it. This is one of them. I wanted to give it to someone who'd appreciate it. Teresa—she seems to appreciate things like that."

Things like what? Delia wanted to ask. Figs? Things with roots that live in the dirt? Things that are difficult? Chaos and disaster and figs? All unrestrained behavior and growth?

"Yeah," Delia said. "She loves her garden."

Rowan smiled. "She told me she got in trouble for letting her lawn grow wild last year. Zoning board came after her."

"Mmm," Delia said absentmindedly, keeping one eye on the cellar door. "Yeah. Teresa gets a little out of hand sometimes. A little wild. Wouldn't think it to look at her, would you?"

"Not right offhand," Rowan agreed, "but once you get to know her, it's pretty easy to spot."

"I guess," Delia said.

And he nodded, as if this pleased him. As if he knew about all of these things as well.

UNRESTRAINED GROWTH

ROWAN BANCROFT STOPPED MOWING HIS LAWN three months before his wife died.

He could have given many good reasons for this, political and intellectual. He could have said that lawns were the historical symbol of oppression for his people, since the British aristocracy had kept them in Ireland to show the peasants that they had so much land, they didn't even need to work all of it. He could have said that grass was the progenitor of wheat, and deserved to grow long and wild. Or he could have said that environmentally, it was the right thing to do.

All of these reasons would have been correct, too, but none of them would have been true.

He could remember the exact moment when he stopped mowing, and in fact much of the last year of Ruth's life existed in his memory like a scene trapped inside a ball filled with water and snow that occasionally settled into clarity, occasionally was shaken into confusion. There was the initial diagnosis and the impossibility of it. Cancer. She was only thirty-one. They had two children under age ten. She couldn't have cancer. It was impossible.

She went through a year of treatments that were as ravaging as the disease, and he continued to believe that none of it was actually happening to him. He watched himself watch her grow thinner, weaker, less substantial, and all the while felt it was surely someone else this was happening to. Not Rowan Bancroft, who had a plan for his life and intended to see it through. Not Rowan Bancroft, who had a reputation for being able to make anything grow and be well.

He'd had a green thumb ever since he was a child, and any plant he touched flourished, which was why he went into the landscaping business. Ruth used to tease him that his hands made her grow and swell into pregnancy, into happiness, into life. Sometimes he stared at his hands and wondered if they'd made the cancer grow in her, dark and horrid. He was relieved when the doctors said it had to do with a drug her mother took during pregnancy to prevent miscarriage. If she hadn't taken it, Ruth would have died. Years later, though, doctors discovered the drug was dangerous. Years later. Too late.

Ruth was given chemotherapy. Some kind of antiviral therapy. They were a kind of poison meant to kill the cancer, and they made Ruth throw up and she grew thinner and thinner, which Rowan thought could be a good sign. Surely something that painful had to work. It should do something good for what it cost her.

When he took her home from the hospital after the last treatment, the doctors were beginning to shake their heads and look at him with pity, which he hated because of what it meant. She wore a red silk scarf to hide her baldness. He settled her into bed and went outside to mow the lawn. It had gotten long, because he'd been busy. Running his business, running his kids back and forth to after-school activities. Ben was in Little League. Cara was learning to ride horses. Each of them had friends and parties that still had to be attended in spite of their mother's illness and his fear, his terror, cold and unremitting, that she would die, that the darkness would enfold them all and they'd be nothing more than the blades of grass he kept forgetting to cut because he had too much to do and too much to feel.

It was a sunny day. Hot, and the heat filled with moisture. Ruth liked this kind of weather. The cicadas buzzing in the trees gave her pleasure, as did the crickets and the sound of birds in the morning. She was the kind of person who took pleasure in almost everything, and he didn't think he could bear to live without that. To see the world without her pleasure in it was too horrible a thought to contemplate, and so he decided to mow the lawn, which had gotten long and was beginning to look more gold than green in the heat of the summer.

He pulled the mower out of the shed, looked around their half acre to where he would start, put his hand down to pull the ignition, and then stopped.

His hand just stopped. He brought it up to his face and flexed it, wondering if something was wrong that it wouldn't follow his command. All the fingers seemed to be working. It bent at the wrist and at each joint, as usual. But it ached too, and he knew what that was from.

When Ruth started losing her hair, he began to dream of it. Long, pleasurable dreams of their courtship, when he would run his fingers through her hair just for the feel of it, not expecting sex, not wanting anything except the feel of her hair. He dreamed of that now, and woke with his hands aching for the feel of her hair.

It was the color of the grass when it went gold in the autumn. The color of wheat or maybe barley, which he'd never seen except in pictures.

He put the lawn mower away. He'd mow tomorrow. Right now he wanted to go inside and sit with Ruth. Put his hands on her head and see if he could help her hair to grow again. See if his touch would help. See if she needed anything at all.

Ruth died four months later, the day after Christmas, and in the long winter that followed, he dreamed that her hair grew up out of the ground and ran laughing into the house. At first he thought it was coming back to comfort him, and then he realized it was angry. Hair gone mad with rage that he hadn't saved her, hadn't been able to keep her alive. Night after night he dreamed of her hair, angry and hungry, looking for flesh to feed on. Flesh to replace the flesh he hadn't been able to keep on her in spite of his love, in spite of everything.

Her hair surrounded him, smothered him, consumed him, and he woke choking and clutching at the blanket, pushing it away. He couldn't find his way back into sleep after these dreams, and so he would wander the house and check the children and stare at late-night shows he never knew the names of. He endured them as his just punishment through months of shivering emptiness as he watched the long winter nights shorten into early spring.

Then, one night when the crocuses had already given way to daffodils, he woke from a dream, got up, put on his pants and went out into the yard, sat down under the oak tree and stared at nothing.

The night was warm, though it was only late April. He was thirty-five years old, had two children, one cat, and a dead wife. He ran a hand over his face and felt the stubble of beard growing there. He ran his gaze over the lawn and saw that last year's long growth was still there, brown and gold, and new green was sprouting up around it. That it seemed to hold the moonlight in each blade. That each blade seemed to sway and sing and shine like the moon, which was full that night.

He went back into the house and got the urn that contained his wife's ashes, brought it to the yard, and scattered it across the grass. And he never mowed that part of the lawn again.

Later on, he'd get slapped with a fine for the offense the town called unrestrained growth. He'd let his grass grow in an unrestrained way, and that, apparently, was against the law. He'd pay the fine, but he wouldn't cut the lawn. Instead, in the years that followed, he'd watch the flowers that came up in the absence of restraint. Noted that under the tree, wild strawberries came up in the spring, and produced bright, tart berries in the deep summer. They would taste like no other berries he'd ever eaten. They would taste like garnets. Like stars. Later, he would fight his town ordinance and have his lawn declared a garden. A wildlife refuge. An okay place. Later, other neighbors would follow suit and throw away their fertilizers and pesticides, and the drone of mowers would be replaced by the sound of grasshoppers singing in the long grass.

Amid this unrestrained growth he planted four fig seeds in a pot of earth to see if they would grow. Years passed and his children went into high school and he got another cat. Once in a while he dated a woman, but nothing serious. Friends told him he was too fussy. They said he was too young to be alone. Life, they said, had to go on. He kept their nagging at bay by telling them none of the women he knew liked the taste of wild strawberries.

His friends didn't have an answer for that, but among themselves they said he'd been too shaken by his loss. The bigness of grief got into him when Ruth died, and he learned not only how hard it is to bear loss, but also how inevitable all loss actually is.

But that was also how he knew that only a woman who loved the taste of wild strawberries would be able to understand the lesson with him, appreciate how much larger life is than any human being. To eat of wildness is to eat of grief, and to eat of grief is to know that all grief is merely another song of praise.

Last summer, when Rowan was packing up his last child for college and wondering how he felt about being forty-seven, Teresa DiRosa came to his nursery looking for a special order. She had been there before, many times, and he liked her well enough, but that day he noticed her in a different way. He wasn't sure if his eyes had become ready to see her, or if something about her had changed, or both. But after she told him what she wanted, he paid attention even more. She had a strawberry patch, she said, but she wanted to find out where she could get some wild strawberries to transplant into her lawn. They had a taste, she said, like no domestic strawberry anywhere. Her grandmother used to pick them and bring them to her for breakfast when they were in season. She'd been missing her grandmother, and she wanted to taste the wild strawberries again and think of her.

Rowan dug up some plants from his lawn and put them in pots for her. When she came to get them, she stayed long enough to show him how to make fried squash blossoms, bringing in a basket of the golden flowers and cooking them for him, their golden cups emitting the same light as the westering sun.

After she left, he went and sat in the long grass for a long time. Evening became night, and he listened to the grasshoppers go to sleep, the crickets wake up and start their song. He saw a neighbor pulling back the curtains and staring in his direction. Another neighbor walked by, leading a large snuffling dog on a leash. The dog lifted its head and snuffled in his direction, but the woman tugged at him to keep him away.

Rowan continued to sit in the grass, and if anyone had asked him why he did this, he would have said he was tasting the way the day passed into night, and the way night passed again into day.

ABOUT SHOPPING

TERESA CLIPPED ALONG THE BAKING GOODS AISLE, tossing items into her cart. More flour, more cornmeal, more chocolate chips, because you always needed those. Sugar and marshmallows. Evaporated milk. She stopped and picked up bags of coffee and inhaled deeply, enjoying the aroma. Amberlin trotted alongside her, silent until they reached the produce aisle.

"Teresa," Amberlin said then, "I'm concerned about you. Are you sure you aren't missing Donnie more than you say?"

Teresa put down the bunch of basil she'd been sniffing and looked at Amberlin as if she'd just noticed her presence.

"Of course I am," she said, and put the basil in the cart.

Amberlin sighed. "You know, it helps to talk about it."

"Sometimes it does," Teresa agreed. "And sometimes it helps to smell the scallions." She grabbed a half dozen bunches of these and put them in the cart too. Amberlin felt a ruffle of irritation, then gave it up. Pushing against the wall of Teresa's silence wasn't very efficient, or very much fun. It was particularly futile when Teresa was concentrating on what she needed to get, already imagining it back in the kitchen becoming the food it would be, or luxuriating in the abundance of smells and textures and colors of food around her, which represented a world of possibilities.

Amberlin wondered why she had bothered to go along. Delia would probably say she told her so. At times like this, Teresa wasn't a talker. So Amberlin wasn't doing any good, and she didn't even like to shop. The abundance of choices at grocery stores made her nervous, and deep down she was sure that shopping provided a misguided substitute for the instinct to hunt, but since it wasn't real, it never truly satisfied. That's why everyone needed so much junk.

Whenever the women went to a mall together to have a day of cat shopping, where they'd touch everything and buy nothing, Amberlin would have to go outside and pace and wish she smoked cigarettes like Christine so she could coat her lungs with something other than mall air.

"I can't stand the air," she said. "I can't stand what I'm breathing in."

She thought it was because she was breathing in what everyone else breathed out, which was a sort of hopeless wanting. Like breathing in unrequited love, only worse, because it wasn't really love. It was just hunger. She was breathing in hunger. And now, with Teresa, in the kitchenware aisle, she was breathing in loneliness. She began to feel depressed.

"Te-reesa," a voice called, and Amberlin looked up to see a woman with bouffant black hair and very red lips rolling her cart toward them.

"Hello, Karen," Teresa said, rather stiffly, Amberlin noted.

"How *are* you? Getting through the holidays?" She leaned in close. "Your first without Sam, isn't it?" she asked, oozing oily sympathy.

"No," Teresa said, stone-faced. "He left me years ago, when he started sleeping with other women. Last year he just made it official."

The woman's face lifted in shock, then came to rest again inside the lines of her heavy makeup. She made her way out of the conversation as gracefully as she could, and disappeared into the produce section of the store. Teresa pushed the cart ahead, stopping only briefly to pick up and examine a chef's knife, which she rejected after she ran her thumb along the blade.

"Teresa, what was that for? She was just being nice," Amberlin whispered.

"Karen? Not her," Teresa said. "She's a . . . a vampire. Sucks people's grief like a tit."

"A vampire?"

"You know," Teresa said. "Always looking for someone who's bleeding. They smell other people's trouble, and they lick it like it tastes good. Maybe they think if they eat yours, they won't get any of their own. They go home at night and count off how many bad things happened to other people. Then they check the statistics and figure out how safe they are."

Amberlin was surprised at the bitterness in Teresa's tone. She could be angry, but she wasn't bitter. "Teresa, maybe that's just your projection," she said hopefully. Somehow, she'd feel less depressed if that were true.

"Maybe it is," Teresa said, "and maybe she's a vampire."

Amberlin made a *tsk-tsk* sound at her. Teresa turned skeptical when psychological terminology was bantered about, much to the irritation of her friends who were in various stages of therapy. Amberlin thought that half her skepticism was fear of what would happen if she let her skin be exposed in that particular way.

The closest Teresa ever came to therapy was after her third miscarriage, when she took time off from teaching and found a nun in her parish to talk to. She was looking for spiritual guidance, but Sister Anna was more of a social activist than a contemplative. She suggested Teresa come work with her in the soup kitchen downtown. Teresa did, and Sister Anna was surprised at how knowledgeable she was about cooking. She wondered why Teresa hadn't become a cook, and suddenly, so did Teresa. Maybe it was because cooking was too easy, and a job was supposed to be work. But that fall, instead of going back to the school where her husband was principal, she went back to school as a student of the culinary arts. As it turned out, that was all the therapy she needed. By the next year she was pregnant again, and Donnie was the result.

They turned into the feminine products aisle and clipped along. Amberlin grabbed at a box of tampons and tossed them in the cart with the rest of the goods.

"You got your period?" Teresa asked.

"Yes. I feel whiny about it. And I can't even complain to Sherry, because she has hers, and she feels whiny too."

Teresa grinned. "That's what's tough about being with a woman. You get in sync and got nobody to bitch to. It'll probably get worse when you live together."

Amberlin stopped walking and frowned down at her feet. She felt suddenly and inexplicably alone. Terribly alone. She felt as if her rejection of Sherry's offer, and Teresa's rejection of her help, Teresa's bitterness at the woman who asked about Sam, James and Christine's fight, and Christine's absence were all signals of that aloneness. It was impossible, she decided, for humans to be anything but alone. Tears formed at the back of her eyes, and she stood in the aisle, waiting for the feeling to pass. It must be the holidays, she told herself. They make everyone a little crazy.

"Y'know," Teresa was saying as she walked ahead. "You oughta try liver and onions. It'll build your blood." She continued ahead about half an aisle, then realized she was alone. She stopped, turned, and looked at Amberlin, then dragged the cart backward to her.

"You okay?" Teresa asked, then ducked down to look at her face. "What is it? You don't like liver?"

Amberlin shook her head. "I'm okay. Just—gimme a minute, okay?"

"Some smart woman once told me it helps to talk about it," Teresa noted.

Amberlin picked her head up. "You don't think I should just smell the basil?"

Teresa picked it up from the cart and offered it. "If it works," she said.

Amberlin gave Teresa a weak smile. She'd come to the store to get Teresa to talk, and what she needed was someone to talk to herself. She wondered if that motive was propelling her all along. People, she thought, were peculiar.

"Sherry found an apartment," she said.

"What?" Teresa asked.

"She wants us to move in together," Amberlin concluded when she saw Teresa's uncomprehending expression.

Teresa's face curled itself into deep thought, then slowly spread into a wide smile. "Congratulations," she said, mischief making itself known in her eyes. She turned to the rack of utensils behind her and slid a turkey baster off its hanger. "Maybe you'll be needing one of these?"

Amberlin slapped it out of Teresa's hand. "Stop that. Teresa, put it back. Good God. We won't—I mean, *honestly,* Teresa. Do you have any idea how crude that is?"

Teresa laughed, and hung it back on its rack. Sherry had once told her a story about a lesbian couple who used a turkey baster for impregnation. They said it was more reliable than sex. "C'mon," she said, taking Amberlin's elbow and walking with her. "I think it's wonderful. I'm very happy for you."

Amberlin groaned and hid her face in her hands.

"What're you worried about?" Teresa asked. "Sherry's great."

Yes, Sherry was great, and Amberlin was happy with her, but was that love? And did she want to be bisexual? She thought that was a kind of cop-out, a way of not declaring your real sexuality, but she didn't see herself as a lesbian either. She felt like she did sometimes when she couldn't decide what she wanted to eat. She'd stand in a store, staring at split peas and at lentils, going back and forth between them. Split peas or lentils? Lentils or split peas? Maybe she wanted both. Maybe she wanted neither. Eventually, a clerk would ask if she needed help, and she'd say no thank you, and leave with nothing.

She wished she could come down firmly on one side or the other. Be this or that. Find a fixed spot on the horizon and follow it.

She couldn't though, and she chalked that up to a general inability to commit after her divorce, which felt like such an awesome failure. She worried that she'd picked Sherry as a way of avoiding commitment. She worried that she'd want to be with a man the minute they moved in together. She worried that she was worrying so much over something that had nothing to do with world peace or the disappearance of the Karner blue butterfly and the rain forest.

"Worried," Amberlin said, chewing on the word. "No. I'm terrified. It's not something I expected of my life, to live with a woman. I assumed I'd end up with a man and a house and a couple of children. It just seemed more likely, statistically speaking. I guess this makes me a lesbian, doesn't it?"

"What if it does?" Teresa said. "C'mon. Let's pick up some cat food."

They made their way toward the pet food, passing down the baby food aisle. Amberlin nervously handled the jars of strained peaches, strained bananas, strained peas, then put them back on the shelf. After her divorce she would buy the peaches and the custard for herself. Just for herself. Comfort food. Easy to eat, and resembling the ancient comfort of mother's milk in texture, in ease of delivery, in accessibility. She was as embarrassed to admit this as she was to face her parents after the divorce, which happened only three months after a large and costly wedding. Her parents had told her she was foolish to marry. She still had the dress, because she didn't know what to do with it. She wondered if it would be right to wear it again, for a commitment ceremony with Sherry.

"So what're you most worried about?" Teresa asked.

"I don't know," she said. "Just . . . what if it doesn't work out. I mean, I didn't expect this. I didn't plan it. And *why* do people want to live together?"

"We're social animals. We like the comfort of each other's presence. And sometimes it makes sense—for money, to raise a family, that sort of thing."

"But why would anyone want to put more people in the world? I mean, really, we should be thinking about zero population growth, not babies. I think it's pure ego."

Teresa's hand paused as she picked up a box of Cream of Wheat. Then the box went into the cart. "Maybe you're right," she said. "Or maybe we keep trying to get it right. Thinking maybe with this human, it'll be perfect."

"I think that's what my parents thought. If they just raised us absolutely right, they'd prove to the world that their stand on social issues was correct. That they had the key and knew how to use it. I remember them arranging a meeting with my kindergarten teacher to discuss ways of getting me over my confusion between yellow and green. Sometimes I think we were just social studies experiments."

Teresa chuckled. "Better than cooking experiments," she said.

Amberlin groaned. Threw her arms up in the air. "Okay," she said. "Okay, so Sherry's great. She's the best. The best I met before, during, or since my first marriage. But she wants a commitment and—hell, Teresa. Not only do I have to stop seeing myself as someone who fits in the world a particular way, but I did that once. I got married. It didn't work. I'm not good at it."

"You never tried the family part," Teresa noted.

"I was pregnant," she said flatly.

"I know. I remember. I was there when you terminated it. That's not what I meant."

"What did you mean?"

"I meant, you haven't tried living with someone just because you love them. Not because it's right, or acceptable, or because you're trying to make a political statement. Just because you love them and want to be with them."

"Awful big risk to take before you know if you'll get it right. And I don't like failure. My family didn't believe in it. My school didn't even give grades."

"Maybe," Teresa suggested, "you need more practice, to get comfortable with it."

"You think you're ever comfortable with failure?"

Teresa thought this one through. She supposed she wasn't comfortable with hers. Getting pregnant before she got married was seen as a failure by her parents. And then, when she miscarried after she and Sam were married, she saw that as a failure in herself. The subsequent miscarriages were just failure heaped on failure, but then she'd had Donnie after all, and she wondered if it was a failure that he was so angry at her right now. She wondered if her marriage was a failure because it ended in divorce. She and Sam had managed to stay married through all of the trouble of their lives, but the absence of trouble broke them apart.

He said he didn't see it as a failure. He said it was just life, moving around. She hated him for saying that, because it was just that sort of thing that made her love him to begin with, and now he was using it against her. Then, of course, there were her more recent failures. With Donnie. With Christine. All of them echoing her failure with Nan.

"Maybe you don't get comfortable," she said. "Maybe you just don't name something a failure so quick. You call it learning, or manure, or something like that."

Amberlin gaped. "Manure?"

"Yeah. It takes shit to grow good vegetables, right? Or—what's that phrase you use?—another fucking growth opportunity?"

"I suppose," Amberlin said reluctantly. "But my *parents* didn't fail. They never divorced."

Teresa rolled her eyes. "Your father lives in Maryland and your mother lives in New York. When's the last time they spent more than two weeks together in the same house?" she asked.

Amberlin's face relaxed, and then she giggled at the prospect. "They'd kill each other. Or starve from political correctness. Tuna's bad. Grapes are out. Coffee's no good. Teresa, you're not putting that slab of ham in the cart. Do you know what they feed pigs these days?"

Teresa cast her a look. "I know something about apples that don't fall far from trees," she said.

"Teresa DiRosa," a voice rasped behind them. The women turned to see a woman in a very short skirt and precarious heels under a faux fur coat and hat. "How *are* you?"

"Fine, Ann." She nodded at Amberlin. "This is Amberlin Sheffer, the baker for Bread and Roses. Amberlin, this is Ann. She teaches at Sam's school."

"So nice," Ann said, extending a hand to Amberlin. "Busy for you this time of year, isn't it?"

"Very," Teresa said. "You?"

"You know how it is. The kids're all hyped up. We're all overworked. I keep telling Sam he ought to let us out a week ahead of Christmas, and if he had any compassion at all he'd do it instead of just yapping about Penelope's pregnancy and how excited he is about it—"

The woman left her mouth open long enough to show Teresa how many fillings she had at the back, then snapped it shut and clapped a hand over it. "Gosh. Did you know? About Sam and Penelope?" she asked. "Or did I just put both feet in my mouth?"

Teresa gazed down at the woman's shoes. "No. They wouldn't fit. Not even in *your* mouth."

She turned back to the cart and shoved it furiously in front of her.

Amberlin kept up, biting her lip. She looked at Teresa and saw her face set in stoic determination not to show her emotions, which held all the way through checkout. When they left the store, Teresa set the bags down on the trunk of her car and leaned onto the roof, her shoulders shaking hard.

Amberlin patted her back, said words like "There there. We knew he'd gone nuts anyway, didn't we? There there." She wouldn't try to fix this, or cheer Teresa up. She knew better than to offer anything except the comfort of small sounds and her hand on Teresa's back. She'd been there through some of the end of Teresa's marriage, though Delia told her it had been going bad for some time before she knew Teresa.

He had his first affair a year or so after Nan's death, and Teresa was so closed in her own grief at that time, she didn't find out about it until much later. He had taken up with a woman in her twenties. And when Teresa finally put it all together, they had a screaming fight and he swore it was just a moment of craziness. He never got to shop, he said. They were married so young, he never got to look around at other women.

"You're shopping?" she screamed at him. "Get a car. Get a goddamn life."

When she found out about the second one—another woman in her twenties—she didn't say a word. She just took all the wineglasses that were a wedding present from his mother and smashed them on the kitchen floor, one by one.

"Talk to me, Teresa," he pleaded.

"I am," she replied, and smashed another glass.

He had his affairs, but he wouldn't leave. He wanted to stay with her until he got this out of his system. Donnie was in his teens and very busy, so he claimed later not to have even noticed there was trouble, but that may have been because they knew how to act when he was around. When he wasn't, they grew grim and silent in each other's presence.

Then, after all their grim silences and her even grimmer waiting, he said he wanted a divorce. Donnie's senior year of high school, and he decided to book. When she wasn't furious, she was relieved. Their home had become an absence. That's all. Just an absence. He was absent—out shopping—and she was absent because she couldn't look at him with respect or love anymore. She couldn't see him outside of what he'd done to her.

She couldn't even remember that she used to love him. She couldn't remember who he was when he was twenty-eight and she was twenty-one and he was crazy about her and she was wild for him. She couldn't remember that they both had ideals about work and life. She couldn't remember the years in between when he'd comforted her over the lost pregnancies and rejoiced with her when Donnie was born. She didn't know if they grew apart the way you do from people you live with unless you make an effort to really see them. Or if it was Nan's death, her grief, coming between them. Or if it was him. Or all of the above.

"You changed," he told her. "You closed up. I couldn't touch you anymore."

"You changed," she spit back at him. "I didn't want to touch you."

And even if there was truth in what he said, if she had turned some essential part of her inward when Nan died, he hadn't tried very hard to coax it back out. He was too busy shopping.

She hated him for becoming the stereotype of middle age, shopping for someone else's youth to replace the one he'd lost. Hated him for not rising above it. Hated him for becoming a vampire. And she was so glad it was over, like a root canal she had to live through and now could recover from.

After a while Teresa lifted her head and wiped her eyes, at which point Amberlin could see that she was grinning broadly. "Did you ever see an expression like the one on that woman's face?" she asked, choking back a laugh.

"You're . . . laughing?"

"God yes. What an asshole. What a goddamn *vampire*."

"The woman?"

"And my ex-husband." She leaned her back against the car and took a deep breath of night air. "I am so glad I'm through with him. I am so glad it's not me having that baby. God forgive me, but I am so damn glad, I can't even begin to say."

TERESA'S KITCHEN

Teresa and Amberlin didn't have time to shake the cold out of their coats before Rowan was there helping to hang them up.

"Rowan," Teresa said, "this is unexpected. Have you been here long?"

She looked to Delia, who seemed to have something like a glare stuck on her face.

"Where've you been?" she asked. "I thought you just had to pick up milk."

Amberlin knit her brows at Delia, her face asking the question What? Delia shook her head, and the gesture contained the reply of Not now.

Teresa turned this way, then that, to try to apprehend the silent conversation they were having, but Rowan took hold of her arm and led her through the kitchen, toward the living room.

As soon as she left, Delia turned to Amberlin and said, "Christine is tied up in the cellar."

Amberlin heard the words but couldn't get them to make any sense. She repeated them to herself slowly, thinking maybe they were an anagram, or some riddle she just didn't get. Nothing worked. She shook her head.

Delia put her hands on Amberlin's shoulders and got close to her face, which made Amberlin back up. Delia didn't have a very delicate sense of body space. She held on and put her face in Amberlin's. "Christine," she whispered, "is tied up in the cellar."

"What?" Amberlin asked.

"You heard me. I was down there and I saw her. She's tied to the sink."

Amberlin clutched at Delia's wrist. "My God," she said, "we have to tell Teresa."

"Shhh," Delia whispered. "Keep it down. I think maybe Teresa put her there."

Amberlin listened to the clock tick. Listened to the sound of something bubbling softly on the stove. Listened to the murmur of voices in the living room. "Delia," she said, "that's insane."

"Yeah," Delia said. She was uncomfortable as hell. Usually when problems needed solving, the teams lined up as Teresa working with Delia and Christine working with Amberlin. Each pairing had its own language, rules of order, and way of being together that made sense. Now Delia was thrown in with Amberlin, who often had a very different approach than hers. It made her nervous, not knowing what Amberlin would do. But she was angry at Teresa. Really angry. And Amberlin would understand that. "I know. What should we do?"

Amberlin chewed on her lip. "Are you sure it's Christine?" she asked.

"Yes," Delia said.

"Then, are you sure she's tied up?"

"Yes," Delia said again. "Amberlin, come on. You know about this stuff. I don't."

"Really," Amberlin said, "I don't. Not about people being tied up in cellars. Is she—I mean, could you tell if she was—you know, breathing?"

"She's alive. She talked to me."

"Then," Amberlin asked, "why didn't you untie her?"

Delia shook her head. That wasn't the kind of question she could answer just then. She could answer only simple questions that needed a yes or a no. "No. We have to talk to Teresa about it. We have to find out what's going on."

"Don't be silly. I'll just go and—" She moved forward as she spoke, but Delia clutched at her arm. Amberlin stopped. "Okay, then. Let's go and talk to Teresa."

"No," Delia whispered hoarsely. "Not yet."

Amberlin clucked her tongue at her impatiently. Sometimes Delia just didn't make any sense. "Why not?"

"Because she's in there with Rowan, and I don't want to interrupt anything."

"Delia, really. Either you want to do something about this, or you want to foster a romance. Which is it?"

Delia frowned. "Shit," she said. "Gimme a minute on that, would you?"

Amberlin raised an eyebrow at her.

"Okay," Delia compromised, "let's just maybe peek through the door and take a look."

WHEN ROWAN LED TERESA INTO THE LIVING ROOM, HE walked her to the window where he had set the fig tree down, his hands over her eyes as he led her toward it. She felt a sudden warmth, and wondered if someone had put too much wood on the fire.

"No peeking until I say," he told her.

"I feel silly," she said, laughing nervously.

"You look silly," he replied. "Almost there." He moved her forward a few more steps, then stopped. "Okay. You can look."

He took his hands off her eyes and she blinked them open. The soft silver-green leaves of the fig tree greeted her like open hands after a long absence.

"Oh," she said, kneeling down in front of it. "Oh."

"It's a fig tree," he filled in.

She lifted a leaf, and a gasp of amazement escaped her when her hand touched the supple skin of a small, round fruit. Midwinter, and it was bearing fruit.

"Pretty, aren't they?" he asked, and reached down to touch the fig with her. His hand brushed hers, and stayed there.

"Your hand is cold," he said softly.

She rocked back on her heels and pulled her hand away. "It's cold out," she said, "a cold night. Rowan, this is too precious to give away, isn't it?"

"I never meant to keep it all to myself," he said. He pulled a fruit off a branch and held it out to her.

She lifted her face and saw that she could take it into her mouth from his fingers if she chose to. His eyes, which were a soft brown that resembled the color of rich earth, encouraged her to do so. Her hands were cold, but the room was very warm, and there was stillness everywhere in it.

The radio was off. The fire crackled softly in the hearth. Amberlin and Delia were talking somewhere about something, but not in this room, where everything was quiet and slow and Rowan held a fig to her mouth while she knelt looking up at it.

Magic must be happening, Teresa thought. She waited quietly to let it emerge.

She'd learned early, partly from Nan's constant battles with people, that it was best to keep the important stuff interior and quiet. Best not to make the noise Nan made, because look where it got her. But in the last year, alone in her house and her self, she had no one left to worry about. Her husband was gone. Her son was gone. Her mother had died shortly after Nan, and her father lived in Florida now, in an apartment for seniors. A woman down the hall came and cooked for him, played cards with him. Every year he sent a birthday card and a Christmas card. Once she'd visited him with Donnie and Sam, but they spent most of their time at the beach.

She was alone. And in the quiet and the dark she could hear and feel in a brand-new way. Old fears rattled their bones and walked away. Essential wants and needs spoke in voices she sometimes remembered as her own at a younger age, even while she saw herself as an adult for the first time in her life. Adult. With a life of her own. With the right to choose for herself.

There was magic happening in that. She could feel it stirring.

When she was little, she'd stay up late on Little Christmas with Nan, waiting for magic to happen. The toys would start to dance, as in the *Nutcracker Suite*. Or the animals would talk. Something. Some magic must happen, because the darkness and the quiet was the place where magic lived, and all you had to do was sit quietly and wait for it to occur.

They never saw the magic they expected, but to this day there were certain moments, in the season of darkness and miracles, when Teresa could feel it, almost in reach. As it was tonight, just inches from her. If she listened closely, she'd hear Befana, that old Epiphany witch, scraping her broom against the earth, turning the world back toward the sun after the long night. She felt at her back the whisperings of the women who birthed her—from mother to grandmother to great-grandmother and before—and how they waited for the return of warmth, how they knew the secrets of the dark, how they lived and died knowing these things and sometimes in her dreams perhaps spoke them to her to help her cook.

She had a longing to know these people, to have them return to her whatever it was that had been absent since her sister died. Something she'd lost between her sister's death and this night. Maybe just a little at a time she'd lost it, each minute corroding her attachment to those who lived on the other side of time and the world their children had left behind.

She listened to the voices as if they grew out of the fig she was staring at, and maybe they did, because the plant was of her people, older than this country they'd come to. Nan knew this. Nan, who lived half in a world of magic, where anything was possible, and half in a world of despair, where nothing was the ruling force of the world.

Maybe, she thought, here, in this fig, she would have found the right food. Maybe here, in this fruit as old as their people, there might even be an answer for Christine, if she could hear it.

The room was very quiet and warm, and the moment was very long, but not too long for Rowan to remain patiently holding a fig out to her. Behind the whisperings of her ancestors, she thought she heard his voice, speaking softly.

"You're a very beautiful woman, Teresa," she thought he said. "Very beautiful."

Teresa brought her gaze from the fig to his face, to see if he had really said this.

"Wait," a voice said crisply, and the kitchen door swung open as Amberlin entered the common space of the living and dining rooms, Delia at her heels.

They stopped short and stared at the tableau Teresa and Rowan made.

Teresa scrambled to her feet, and Rowan took a step back.

"Teresa," Amberlin started to say, and Delia stepped in front of her.

"We were going to—um—start moving furniture around," Delia said. "It was so quiet, we thought you were alone. We could—um—do it later?"

"No," Teresa said. "That's fine. There's no . . . I mean, now is fine."

Amberlin's mouth opened, then closed tight, then opened again. "Great," she said. "Let's get started."

"Okay," Teresa said a little vaguely. She indicated Rowan and his gift. "Look. A fig tree. With fruit."

"I know," Delia said. "He showed me."

Rowan held out the fruit, and Teresa shook her head at him. "No," she said. "You grew it. You should eat it."

"And all the food you make—how much of it do you eat?" he asked.

She saw his eyes scan her slim body from top to bottom, and felt herself flush as if his eyes could brush the surface of her skin under her clothes. She laughed it off. "If I ate everything I cooked, I'd be big as the national debt, Rowan."

He lifted her hand and placed the fig in it, closing her fingers over it. "When you're hungry, have it and think of me." He turned to Amberlin and Delia. "You want help with the furniture?"

"Actually, just a few boxes that need shifting, and maybe that chair should go over there, and the couch shifted ever so slightly toward the fireplace."

Teresa left them to it, Delia being well in charge of this part of things, and went back to the kitchen. She unpacked her bags to the comfortable sound of laughter and scraping chairs and idle talk. While it was going on, she went to the cellar door and listened, heard nothing. She thought about opening it and going down, then changed her mind.

Instead, she looked at the fig in her hand and listened to its small song. Her listening was so intent, so filled with conscious longing, she didn't even hear Rowan shout out a good-bye before he left, and she didn't hear Amberlin and Delia walk up close behind her. They had to clear their throats before she turned to face them.

"What?" she asked when she saw them staring at her.

"Well," Delia said, "when were you going to tell us about Christine?"

TERESA'S KITCHEN

WHAT WAS I SUPPOSED TO DO—LET HER SHOOT herself?" Teresa demanded. "Call the cops? Put her in rehab the way . . ." She tugged at the back of her hair, and her barrette snapped out and hit the floor. She ignored it and went to the chopping block, picked up a carrot and a peeler, and began to peel.

"But, Teresa—the frying pan?" Delia gestured toward the heavy black cast iron that always sat on the stove, ready to be used.

"Not the cast iron," Teresa said, aghast at the notion. "Jesus, Mary, and Joseph, no. Just an old Teflon." She waved at it with the carrot.

"God," Delia said. "God and Jesus and all the Apostles."

The three women stood gaping, suddenly strangers to one another. They'd had fights, tensions that came and went with a quick argument or laughter, but this was a situation so far out of their ken, they couldn't even bless it with argument or words. Minutes passed while each woman waited to know herself and her relationship to this time and place.

Teresa stayed in her stubbornness. She had done this, and she would keep it up until she thought it was time to stop. Amberlin found her way back through logic. She thought Teresa was overwrought by the holidays. She'd acted impulsively and needed someone to show her reason. Delia centered herself firmly on the ground of denial. This couldn't be, and therefore she didn't have to acknowledge it. Not in any deep emotional way.

Amberlin was the first to speak.

"Teresa, you must see now that it wasn't such a good choice," she said reasonably and calmly.

"My options were limited," Teresa replied.

"Yes, but *now* you see, don't you?"

Teresa's shoulders lifted and fell.

"At any rate," Amberlin continued, taking that gesture as the beginning of wisdom, "I wish you'd told us sooner. Why didn't you?"

"Maybe," Delia said, "she thought we wouldn't notice."

"Well," Teresa admitted, "I was hoping. Look, I figured I'd have to take it about a minute at a time," she amended when she saw anger begin to form in Amberlin's stance. "I didn't know what to do, to be honest."

"Then, why," Amberlin said, "didn't you ask?"

Teresa gestured with the peeler and was still. "I don't know," she said. "Maybe I didn't want to make a fuss."

Amberlin groaned. "What will you do now?"

"I don't know. I don't know," Teresa said, getting another carrot. "I just wanted to keep her from leaving, I guess. Keep her there until she seems better."

"But you can't," Amberlin declared. "You can't leave her there all tied up in the cellar while we have a party and pretend nothing's wrong."

Delia made a strangled sound at the back of her throat, and the other women looked at her. "You should peel away from yourself," she said, and the other women looked at her. "You can cut yourself the way you do it."

Teresa looked down at what she was doing. "I was taught to work toward myself. It's safe." She turned her hand and tried to peel away from herself, but felt the motions clumsy. She dropped the carrot, cursed, picked it up, and went back to her own way of doing the task. "I can't," she said. "I just can't."

Delia walked around the kitchen, straightening up knives left on the counter. Pushing them away from the edge. Folding dish towels.

Amberlin watched her, frowned, and turned her attention back to Teresa. "It's cruel," she said, "and I don't know how hard you hit her, but she might be hurt."

"She's not," Teresa said. "I didn't even knock her out. She just stopped fighting."

Delia fiddled with the radio, and found a station that played barking dogs doing "Jingle Bells." She let it play.

"Teresa," Amberlin said seriously, "don't you think we should call a doctor? Or how about James? He'll know what to do."

Teresa snorted, and Amberlin clenched her teeth. "He's a professional, Teresa, and she needs professional help."

"Where'd it get her mother?" Teresa asked. "Could you turn that off, Delia?"

"Why? I think it adds just the right gothic touch." She didn't want to admit that there was something oddly comforting about the sound. She stood at the radio and didn't move.

"Will you turn it *off,* please?" Teresa repeated.

"Shit. Okay." She fiddled with the knob some more, until she came up with a choir singing "Silent Night" in German. "That better?"

Nobody answered. Amberlin sat on a chair at the table, her knees drawn up to her chin. Delia turned her attention back to the knives, which she pressed even farther back toward the wall behind the counter. Teresa peeled furiously at a carrot, orange shavings flying out from her hands onto the cutting board and the floor.

"Delia," Amberlin asked after a while. "What're you doing?"

"The knives," she said. "They're right at the edge of the counter. It's not safe. What if one fell?"

"It would bounce on the floor, and then somebody would pick it up," Amberlin said. "Jesus, don't we have more important things to worry about than what might happen? I mean, the knife *could* fall and hurt someone, but Christine *is* tied up in the cellar, and I think you're remaining grotesquely calm about it. I'd think you'd be worried, at least."

"Of course I'm worried," Delia said dully. "I found her. I told you about it, didn't I? And I mean, what if she makes noise? What if someone finds out what we—what Teresa did. It's illegal, isn't it? Keeping someone tied up in the cellar? Like not reporting a death right away."

She pushed the knife back a little farther. "And . . . and we're having a party and if something . . . happens . . ." Delia's voice trailed into silence, and she chewed on the end of her thumbnail as she stared out the window.

"Illegal?" Amberlin said, her voice creeping into the higher ranges. "What about Christine's pain? She must be in pain. Teresa, didn't you think of that?"

"Could we just get through tomorrow and decide what to do then?" she said grimly as she peeled the carrots. "And could somebody wash the celery and get it cut up and onto platters? The peppers too. I'm making a *bagna cauda*."

"You're as bad as Delia. Worrying about a *bagna cauda* when she's down there tied up," Amberlin said. She unfolded herself and stood. "I'm trained to deal with suicidal impulses. I'm going down to talk to her."

Teresa put down the carrot, and then the peeler. She rubbed her hand through her dark hair, causing it to stand up at the front of her forehead. A sliver of carrot stuck in her bangs. She shook it down onto the floor.

"Okay," she said. "Okay. You try. But bring her some food. She's gotta be hungry. Maybe if we can get her blood sugar up a little, she'll feel better."

She grabbed one of the brown paper bags Amberlin had brought in and pulled out a round loaf of five-grain bread. It was heavy and thick. She started cutting off slices, holding the bread at her belly, pulling the knife in toward her.

"God," Delia said, "I hate it when you do that."

Teresa stopped cutting. "Do what?"

"Cut bread that way."

She looked down at her belly. "I always cut it that way and you've never said anything."

"I am now. Look what you're doing. Cutting right into your own belly."

"That's the way my grandmother cut bread, and she was ninety-seven when she died."

"And you lick knives. I've seen you. Y'know, my grandmother told me you could bleed to death if you cut your tongue."

"Maybe," Teresa said, "she confused blood with words."

Delia raised her hands toward the ceiling in a gesture of surrender. "I give up. Do it your way."

"Jesus, Delia," Teresa said, gawking at her. "Get a grip."

Delia had watched her for years using knives casually, leaving them leaning off the edges of counters, licking them, drawing them to herself, and each time she shuddered, though she never said anything because she was embarrassed by her own reaction.

After her father died and her mother had gone to work, they would cook together when she got home from her job, and Delia always had the job of cutting the vegetables. One day, she was slicing broccoli on the cutting board at the kitchen table, her mother's back to her. Delia finished her task and brought the knife to the sink just as her mother took a step back. Delia gasped and pulled away, but she saw how close the point came to her mother's back. She thought about the place that it could've slid so easily into her. She was horrified at the catastrophe that might have happened if she were less careful. All of life balanced on an edge as thin as that blade pointed unintentionally toward her mother's back. All of life was a thin blade waiting to enter the heart.

"A grip?" she said truculently. "A grip on what? You have your niece tied up in the cellar. I don't think you can make any great claims to having a grip on anything."

"Well," Teresa said, "why didn't you untie her?"

Delia sputtered on the edge of words, then retreated. Why didn't she? Something in Christine's eyes. They were bright, but if you looked behind the brightness you'd see something awful, like sudden death. Or maybe it was because she was so authoritatively tied, with such reality and firmness, Delia just didn't feel she could.

"My father died during the holidays, y'know," she said, surprising herself. The other two women were still, waiting for more, but Delia had nothing to add on the subject.

"I know," Teresa said quietly after a while. "I know that, Delia."

"Goddamn holidays," Amberlin groaned.

"Look," Delia said weakly. "If you're sending Amberlin down, maybe you should send a chamber pot or something. What if she's gotta pee?"

"She hasn't eaten anything all day that I know of. Or had anything to drink." As Teresa spoke, she put the chunks of bread on a plate with cheese and an orange, got down a glass, and filled it with juice from the refrigerator. "When she's gotta go, I'll help her."

"God," Delia said. "God almighty."

She turned away and pressed her hands against the sink, stared out the window while Teresa gave Amberlin her burden of food. Amberlin took it and walked toward the cellar door. She gave one last look over her shoulder at the other two women before she opened the door, went through it, and made her way slowly down the stairs. When she looked back, she could see a crack of light still at the top where they'd left the door open for her.

CHRISTINE LOOKED LIKE A SMALL, TIRED BIRD IN HER nest of blankets and ropes. Amberlin took a good look, and saw a bruise on her cheek, which must have been where the frying pan caught her. She could also see that Teresa had tied her securely but given the ropes enough play that she could move her arms and legs, lie down or sit up. She supposed that if Christine made enough effort, she'd be able to make her way out of the bonds. Probably, Amberlin thought clinically, she was too depressed to try.

Amberlin went and stood in front of her. Christine opened her eyes, but said nothing.

"I brought you some food," she said, showing her the plate with the slices of bread and cheese. "Teresa was worried you were hungry."

Christine didn't look at the plate, but kept her gaze on Amberlin's face. Her eyes were circles of light, or perhaps circles that absorbed the light from the room, making it even darker than it already was.

Amberlin felt herself drawn into that darkness, and had to work hard to remember that this was her friend, a woman she'd recently seen trying on wedding gowns and laughing, a woman who listened to her when she was trying to figure out if she was bisexual, lesbian, or just crazy, a woman whose friendship delighted her. But once she did remember it, she felt even worse, because to see a friend in this state was something horrible, and something she knew neither of them would ever be able to forget. Best, she thought, to try to remain clinical and objective. Think of her as a hotline caller.

She took a moment and gathered her thoughts, seeking the right words. "I just want you to know that you're a good person, Christine," she said carefully and calmly. "We all want you to know that. You deserve to be alive, and to be well and happy, no matter what."

A slow smile spread itself across Christine's face. The tips of her teeth showed, giving her a wolflike aspect in the dark. "Is that from the manual, Amberlin?" she asked.

"I . . . well, what if it is? It's not less true because of that."

"I suppose not. It just doesn't seem to have anything to do with me. Has James tried to find me?"

"Yes. He keeps calling. Teresa's been lying to him. Do you want to see him?"

She shook her head. "Keep him away from me."

Amberlin stared at the plate of food just to give her eyes a break from Christine's face. She'd talked with any number of desperate, grief-stricken, or plain depressed people on the hotline. She knew just what to say to all of them. But she'd never seen their faces. Never sat in a room with any of them. She always had her eyes on the list of top ten successful responses taped to the wall in front of her desk. Somehow, standing here in front of Christine was different from being on the phone. Her eyes kept sucking the light out of the room. And her teeth looked so primal, so ready to rend flesh. Amberlin wasn't exactly afraid. Not exactly. Just aware that she was in the presence of a power greater than her understanding. She knew it was important to sound calm and in command of herself as well as compassionate. Her tone of voice could do as much as her words to reassure Christine that she was safe and loved. That was what her training taught her, and it had worked in the past. She had a good record on the hotline for talking people down, and had been called out on emergencies because of her reputation in that area.

"Would you like me to untie you?" she asked gently.

Christine's smile broadened, teeth glinting white. She held her wrists up as far as they would reach.

Amberlin nodded encouragement. "Okay. I will, if you'll sign a contract with me not to attempt suicide unless you talk to me first."

Christine looked confused, then lowered her arms and shook her head. "What's the point in that?"

Amberlin felt anger sting at her. To keep her from doing it, of course, but she couldn't say that. The idea was to give the person a sense of control over the situation. The illusion of control at least. And give the other party in the contract time to call the medics in case their friend decided to go ahead and attempt suicide.

"It's so you'll take time before you do anything you can't undo," she said, keeping her tone quiet and even. "I mean, you have the right to take your life—it's yours, after all—but it's a big decision, and you get only one chance at it. I can't untie you unless you sign a contract, Christine."

Christine sank back into her blankets, closed her eyes.

"Christine?" Amberlin asked. "Christine?"

She got no answer. "Think about it at least," she said, and put the plate of food down on the floor. "Have something to eat. It'll clear your head."

Great, she thought. Now she sounded like Teresa, who thought a chicken sandwich could cure any ill.

Christine's voice spoke from the depths of the blankets. "I want to shoot myself, Amberlin. What makes you think I'd have any interest in being fed?"

Amberlin thought hard. Nothing helpful came into her mind. She wished James were there, thought James shouldn't wait to ask permission to be there, he should just be there, taking the situation in hand. He was the professional. He was her fiancé. He should know how to solve this, because Amberlin certainly didn't.

She couldn't think of any words that would be the exact right words. The effective words that would bring Christine up from this place. Words. The right words. She began toying with sentences, remembering words she'd said on the hotline that worked, words her mother said to her. She wanted to place the words in such a way that they had the greatest significance to communicate, to get through, just for once, finally breach that gap between intent and meaning. But Christine's eyes, sucking the light out of the room, disturbed her concentration.

They reminded her of being a child and looking up into the incredible darkness of her mother's eyes against the impermeable whiteness of her skin. She thought of how impermeable her mother was even though she always had the right answer for every question Amberlin asked. Yes, the conflict in Vietnam was bad. Yes, it is wrong to buy products created from the oppression of women and children. Yes, it is better to eat whole wheat bread and avoid red meat. Yes, there are starving people everywhere and you should always be grateful that you have a home, two parents, an education. Yes, a good meal is a balanced meal, consisting of one protein, one starch, and two vegetables—one raw and one cooked.

Yes, I am a happy woman. Yes, your father loves you. Yes, I love you. Of course I love you. I'm your mother. We're a family—your father, your brother, and you and I.

All the words were the right ones, and yet some emotion stopped on its way to her heart. Some essential step was missing. Some gap existed between the human capacity to speak and the human capacity to hear. In this place, in the dark with Christine, she was the daughter of words spoken by rote, the sure utterance of what occurs between capital letter and period. She felt, suddenly, as if she could see above and underneath and all around the words she was made of, the words her mother said. That she could see a more real reality, though she didn't know what would happen to her if she chose that reality over the one she'd been given.

She couldn't think of any words. Instead, she thought of her father cooking supper on the nights her mother taught a class.

His specialty was a curry vegetable dish. Slices of sweet potatoes and onions sautéed in thick green olive oil and covered in curry powder. He made it every Tuesday when she taught her women's history class, but one night, it burned. He left it in the oven for too long and it burned black, so he had to come up with something else to feed his children.

Dinner that night was the only one of its kind she'd ever had. He ran out to the store and came back with fried veal patties, sliced American cheese and ketchup and white bread. And green beans from a can. Del Monte. She and her brother, astonished at this radical departure from good health and good politics, were further stunned when they were allowed to watch TV while eating. *Get Smart* was on, and she remembered laughing around the tasteless compressed veal bits and crunchy, greasy coating. The squish of the cheese, the bite of the ketchup, and the saltiness of the canned beans.

While they were eating, he told them that he might go live in the city for a while. He and their mother had talked about it, because it seemed like a good idea for them to spend some time apart, learning and growing, but they wanted to know how Amberlin and her brother felt about it. After all, they were a family and it affected all of them, so they had a right to be part of the decision.

She remembered not knowing what this meant, and not having the words to ask. She knew what divorce was, because she had friends whose parents had divorced. Sometimes it meant they were poor for a long time. Other times it meant they got extra presents at Christmas and two houses to live in. But her father didn't use the word *divorce,* so what did he mean?

She looked at her brother. He looked at her. Each face was blank. She remembered the blend of tastes in her mouth, and her sudden certainty that she'd done something wrong.

"I think," she said, "I'm going to be sick."

She retched violently over the carpet, and her father fixed her a good cup of vegetable broth and sat with her all night. He didn't move to the city. Not really. He just went away for conferences a lot. He bought something he called a summer home and spent a lot of time there. He took the office and made it into a bedroom for himself. But whenever Amberlin felt sick, he made vegetable broth for her and stayed with her while she ate it, talking to her about politics and the news. She didn't like the broth, but it seemed a necessary prerequisite for his presence, so she drank it all.

Christine opened her eyes and looked at Amberlin as if she were surprised to see her still standing there.

Amberlin tried to think of words to say. "Christine," she said, at last, "I'm here for you."

"Here for me," Christine said, as if sounding the words for depth. "What makes you think you know where here is, Amberlin?"

Amberlin had nothing left to say. The words that fell out of her mouth were hollow and unimportant at this moment, in the dark, in the cellar.

She turned away and went back upstairs.

When she entered the kitchen the women could see that she, too, had looked into the pooled darkness Christine's eyes had become. Teresa's face creased into a frown, and she held out a hand, which

Amberlin didn't take as she made her way to the refrigerator to get out the heavy cream for the cake roll.

Delia looked from one woman to the other, her face pale and brittle as glass in the sun. "Well," she said. "And now, of course, we've got a party to run."

ABOUT ENTERTAINING

When Teresa was growing up, entertaining had been an informal affair. Family and friends gathered for birthdays, christenings, funerals, weddings, and graduations at someone's home or, if the occasion was very special, in a church hall. Everyone would bring pots of sausage or meatballs, pasta, soup, bread, fruit, and cakes. Odd assortments of bottles with homemade wine and grappa would be plunked down on a table with an even odder assortment of glasses. The children would eat enormously and sneak sips of wine. The adults would eat and drink enormously, talk and sing loudly, and play boccie badly in the yard. Sometimes money would be gathered for a band, as at a wedding, and food would actually be purchased.

Zia Umberta made three-tiered cakes for weddings, but she had to be paid. Uncle Laborio knew where to get the best veal for cutlets, but it had to be purchased. And the nougats and *torrone* likewise cost something. But if she totaled it up, Teresa figured her wedding cost about five hundred dollars, which was top dollar at the time.

Still, the importance of treating guests properly was understood. Hosting a party was a sacred privilege. Teresa's family also had the responsibilities of the *sacre famiglia*. They still kept St. Joseph's Day in honor of the forgotten miracle they'd once been blessed with, though most of their Irish friends thought of it as a belated St. Patrick's Day celebration, since it occurred on March nineteenth.

For this occasion, nobody could be turned away. Teresa's mother told her that when she was a child during the Depression, even the bums who lived in boxcars knew about it and would stop by for food. She remembered having to sieve the chickpeas by hand and how it scraped her knuckles. Teresa still did this for her open house and for funerals, giving the ceci cookies to bereaved families as an amulet for peaceful mourning.

Amberlin's family entertained guests at dinner parties with cloth napkins, good local wine, and the right combination of vegetable—one cooked, one raw—protein—fish or chicken since they didn't eat red meat—and carbohydrate. Nothing was fancy, but it was all quality. They didn't have cocktail parties because that was capitalist debauchery, and they didn't like loud parties with music and dancing. They made a space where a good discussion could occur over good food that was not too extravagant.

Of the three women, Delia's family was the one most inclined to entertain in a variety of ways, and Delia could remember her mother poring over menus in *The Joy of Cooking* for dinner parties, cocktail parties, luncheons. Although she ascribed to the policy in that book—that it was best for a hostess just to be herself—she wanted that self to be the best one possible. The one most appropriate for public consumption, as it were.

To that end, she had crystal suitable for wine, champagne, and cocktails, tiny forks for hors d'oeuvres, a table with a heat- and stain-resistant top, and a number of linen cloths with matching napkins suitable for every occasion. There was the yellow with pale blue forget-me-nots embroidered onto it for Easter or any spring event, the casual summertime plaid, the autumnal gold and green, and, of course, the red with gold trim for the holidays.

Her true Irish lace she reserved for very special and solemn occasions such as Delia's first holy communion, her brother's engagement party, the christening of Delia's first baby. Candles in silver candlesticks and vases of cut flowers decorated buffets and formal dinners, which her mother knew how to conduct properly from alternating entrees and *relevées* to entremets. She also knew exactly the right dress for a cocktail party, and a vast number of easy and reliable hors d'oeuvres to serve at it, and how to pack a good picnic basket for a day at the races.

Delia didn't imagine her mother was born knowing this, and to be sure, most of their everyday food was rather bland, but having married a man who had a public position—Delia's father was a bank president in Aurora Falls—she had learned.

Her parents would get a baby-sitter for her, but she was allowed down to some parties for as long as an hour if she behaved and didn't trip on anything or annoy people. Even as a child she was big for her age, a little clumsy, and a little inclined to talk too loud.

"You must learn to restrain your natural voice," her mother told her. "A little stillness won't hurt you at all."

Her father would always greet her entrance joyously, scoop her up in his arms and say, "Look who's here. The queen bee." Then he'd turn to whoever stood nearby and ask them seriously if they didn't think she was beautiful. "Cut from a queen's cloth," he'd say. "That's my girl."

Delia, who was naturally gregarious and pleasure-seeking, loved the parties. She liked the hustle and bustle of preparation, the feeling of life in motion. She liked the pretty candles and flowers and the swirl of people in their colorful clothes, who patted her head absentmindedly and said nice things about her. And the bowls of candy, the platters of odd little foods—stuffed mushrooms, tiny hot dogs wrapped in puffs of crisp dough, celery sticks with cream cheese, and the little triangle sandwiches filled with all manner of interesting tastes.

She liked to get a plate and take one of each, then just look at them for a while. The many foods reminded her of times she would go to the beach and collect small colored stones. There was an infinite variety of shapes and colors and textures for her to choose from, and each one felt good to her hand.

When they left Aurora Falls and moved to Poughkeepsie to be closer to her grandmother, there weren't any more parties, and she missed them. She was glad to meet Teresa and at least have her family's parties to go to. Though they didn't have candles and flowers and the people didn't dress up, there was a lot of laughing and a lot of food.

Of course, they had fewer parties even in Aurora Falls when her father started getting sick. He showed the first signs of illness right after New Year's, and then he stayed sick through the rest of that year. They still had their Easter party and their Fourth of July picnic the way they always did, but a lot of the in-between parties stopped. Before Thanksgiving they had a cocktail party, and Delia remembered that nobody talked about how thin and tired her father looked. If anyone asked, he said he had a blood condition and it was being treated. She'd heard the name of it—leukemia—and she knew it was bad, but she didn't want to think about it too much.

By Christmas he was much worse, and it was hard for him to get up and down the stairs. Delia's mother wanted him to go to the hospital, but he wouldn't, so they had a nurse come in to the house every day. And he insisted they have their usual New Year's Day open house, saying their friends and business associates would expect it. But then he was too sick to come downstairs for it. He stayed up in his room, in bed. People who came to the party asked how he was, and her mother always said the same thing. He was doing well. Today his medication had gone awry, but he might be able to come down later and say hello. Only Delia and her mother knew he hadn't left his bed in three days.

Right around dusk Delia decided to go to see her father. She didn't like the medicine smell in his room and was sometimes frightened of how he looked, not really sure this was still her father at all, but she knew he liked to see her, and when he couldn't get up she went to visit around suppertime. All the adults were busy talking, twirling little paper umbrellas in glasses of pink drinks, eating the small and pretty foods on the platters around the living room. Delia ascended the stairs and went to the end of the hall, where her father had his own room. She brought a plate of little lemon meringue tarts with her, and a small plastic knife which she thought couldn't hurt anyone.

She knocked on the door, but he didn't answer. She waited, and while she waited she noticed that the little plastic knife had its tip stuck in the meringue. She picked it up and licked it, remembering her grandmother's warning about licking knives, but decided she must be safe with a plastic knife. She knocked on the door again, then pushed it open and looked inside, and saw him, still propped up on his pillows, his eyes closed.

He was sleeping. She could go tiptoe in and kiss him, then feel as if she'd completed the ritual properly. But when she got to his side, she thought something was wrong. There was something that looked like vegetable soup coming out of his mouth. When she touched his hand, which hung down over the side of the bed, it felt cold. She stood at the side of the bed, staring at him. Nothing happened at all for a long time.

Then the door creaked open, and her mother was in the room. Delia saw her eyes get big. She put her hand to her mouth and made a sound Delia had never heard her make before. It was a sound that went into her sharply. Like what she imagined it would feel like to lick a real knife.

Her mother walked over to the bed, and then she jumped when she saw Delia.

"Dee," she said, "what're you doing here?" She put a smile on her face in just the same way she sometimes put lipstick on. Carefully drawing it onto her mouth.

"I came to visit Daddy," she whispered.

Her mother took her hand. "Come outside, honey. Daddy's resting."

Delia looked up at her smile, which was red as the candy hearts they put on sugar cookies and white cupcakes for Valentine's Day. She looked down at the plate of lemon meringue tarts in her hand. "Should I leave these for when he wakes up?"

It was her way of asking a question she didn't know how to ask. Her mother frowned and her red lips moved around some without making any sound. "No, honey," she said. "That's okay. Let's go now."

That was how Delia knew he was dead. She stared at him, trying to understand, and failing. Her mother tugged at her, but her feet were planted on the floor and wouldn't move. She wasn't being stubborn or bad. She just couldn't get her feet to move. Her mother sighed and knelt down in front of her.

"Listen, honey," she said. "Your father would want us to go back to the people downstairs. He . . . he wouldn't want any fuss. I know this doesn't make any sense to you at all, but you'll have to trust me on it."

Delia stared at her and said nothing.

"Trust me," her mother repeated. "We need to go back downstairs and talk to all the people. When they leave, I'll take care of everything. You just—know that I love you, and so does your daddy."

Delia looked down at her feet and told them to move. They

listened to her at last, and she followed her mother downstairs, where people laughed and talked and the soft Christmas lights and candles were everywhere, and crystal bowls filled with hard candies of all colors looked like bowls of jewels piled deep, ready for the taking.

The party went on into the late evening, and she fell asleep on the couch long before the doctor came to take her father's body away.

TERESA'S KITCHEN

ON THE FRIDAY NIGHT BEFORE THE ANNUAL BREAD and Roses open house, it was no easy task to be Dr. James Tyrol. He picked up the phone, dialed Teresa's number, listened until the answering machine picked up, then pressed a finger against the receiver.

He wouldn't leave another message. They could pick up the damn phone and talk, or they could do the right thing and call him. They ought to be worried, he thought. They ought to be frantic. He was.

Sitting in the bedroom of his apartment, he could see his face in the mirror and recognized it as the face of someone who was under stress. His mouth was pinched. His pupils were dilated. He had a slight twitch in the muscle of his jaw. He wondered if this was what married life with Christine would be like: one crisis after another. For the first time in their relationship, he thought maybe he should postpone the wedding. It was such a big commitment to make to someone who might not be the kind of woman he wanted to marry. Maybe she was too . . . something. Too full of the past and all its baggage. Too unpredictable. Too heavy with emotions.

It might be best not to call it off, but to postpone it until he knew it was right. He thought of his mother, who had already sent out invitations to the engagement party. She would be upset, and that would upset his father, who liked to put everything right for her. No. He wouldn't postpone. But he had to find Christine and make sure she was okay. That was his responsibility not only as her fiancé, but also as a psychiatrist.

He used two fingers to massage his temples while he thought about his next move. He had returned to his apartment after a long day of meetings, in which he had to use the force of his charm and will to get the arts project moving against the human tendency for inertia. He'd dealt with the patients who preferred their visions to medication, or the familiarity of depression to the unknown world of wellness, or the magnificent highs of their mania to the colorlessness of normalcy. It was all a tug-of-war, with them bunched on one side of the rope and him on the other, alone.

Christine sometimes accused him of ego, but in his job if he didn't have a reliable ego, he'd collapse, and nothing would ever get done. No change would ever occur. Her own family was living proof of that.

There was, first and always, Teresa, who insisted on seeing him as a villain of some kind. She was just set in her ways, and her ways harked back to before her grandmother. Somehow, her mother's generation had skipped having any influence on her altogether. An entire century had slipped by without her noticing. James thought that if she had her way, exorcisms would be the treatment of choice for mental illness.

Christine told him she'd come around. She was just raw. Often she didn't have the words to put to what she was feeling. She had to say it with actions or food, and you had to learn to read it that way.

James had pointed out that she kept giving him cold fish. Every time he came for dinner, she'd offer him a dish of cold fish. Cold salt cod. Cold anchovies. Cold jellied squid. How was he supposed to read that?

They'd had a pretty good blow-up over that one. Christine had gotten all Italian on him and started in on how Teresa had helped her and how Teresa loved Nan. She was family, so he'd better learn to deal. James finally relented and suggested that maybe Teresa was a little jealous. Maybe she saw James as taking Christine away from her. Christine would grant that. Teresa's passions, though inarticulate, ran deep in all areas. James didn't really believe jealousy was the problem though. Teresa was just old world. She was a raving individualist, stuck in the Western European model of thought, and she never learned to trust shrinks. Fearful and controlling, that's what she was.

But he wasn't about to let her run this show. She wasn't in charge anymore.

He picked up the phone again and dialed the number for the police. He had considered calling the suicide hotline, but he felt foolish—a professional calling an amateur volunteer outfit. And what if he got Amberlin's girlfriend and she recognized his voice?

A mechanical nasal voice asked him to punch in the number for the division he wanted or dial 911 for emergency assistance. He debated briefly between six for missing persons and seven for domestic violence reports, then chose six. He didn't have proof of any violence against Christine, and he hadn't killed Teresa. Yet.

After he listened to a few verses of Jose Feliciano singing "Feliz Navidad," a gruff male voice came on the line.

"Detective Foster. How may I help you?"

James cleared his throat. "Hello. This is Dr. James Tyrol, and I'm psychiatric director of the Upstate Institute for Mental Disorders, and I want to report a missing person."

"Yeah," Detective Foster said blandly, his undertone indicating that he didn't like people who stated the obvious. "Go ahead."

"Well, Dectective," James continued, "this is by way of a special case, and I think it qualifies as an emergency. The missing person is my fiancée, Christine DiRosa, and I have a note indicating suicidal intent. I really need to make sure—"

"What's the note say?" the detective cut in.

"Say?"

"Yeah. Like, what she wrote."

"Oh. Of course." He reached for it in his jacket pocket and read it. When he was finished, there was a pause. James let it go for half a minute before he spoke.

"So you see," he said, "I think this is beyond the usual missing person situation and calls for immediate action. Now, I can give you her history and photos, and she has family in the area you can talk to. I particularly recommend that you contact her aunt, a Teresa DiRosa, and I'll give you her address as well. Should I come down and do that, or will you send someone to me?"

The pause came again.

"Detective?" he asked. "Hello?"

"Yeah," Foster said. "I'm here. Look, sir—um—Doctor, how old is the person in question?"

"She's twenty-eight, but I don't see—"

"Well, Doctor, that note you read doesn't sound like suicide to me."

"What?"

"No, sir. She says she's sorry to leave you and it's not your fault. That's all."

James felt sudden confusion. How could he see it as not a suicide note? What else could it be? "You don't understand," he said patiently. "Her mother killed herself. Right around this time of year. She has a family history of—of history, I mean, hysteria and possibly mania and her aunt is a cook."

When the detective let out a long sigh, he became aware that he was babbling and shut up.

"Sir," the detective said, "I'm sorry, but it doesn't read like suicide to me. It sounds more like she might be dumping you."

"What?" James asked.

"Like maybe she wants to break up with you."

James hung up the phone.

He stared at it for a while, wondering why he had picked a forest-green phone. He remembered liking a beige one much better. Probably it was something Christine suggested, to put more color in the room. She was always looking for more color.

No other thought would occur to him. When he looked for any, he pulled a blank.

After some time had passed and he decided that the police were as stupid as everyone always told him they were, he picked up the phone, dialed Teresa's number, waited until her answering machine picked up, then hung up.

THE PHONE RANG IN TERESA'S KITCHEN. THEY ALL STARED at it and waited. When Teresa's voice on the answering machine said "Hi, you've reached—" the caller hung up.

"Is that the fourth time?" Amberlin asked.

Delia shook her head. "Third. Just the third."

"James," Amberlin said.

The women sighed in unison, and turned back to their various tasks.

Teresa surveyed the counters lined with trays of food that was ready and wrapped for the big refrigerator. "The cold plates are all set?" she asked.

"Set," Delia replied as she finished loading up the dishwasher and set it to running. Then she went to the cupboard and got out a box of Cream of Wheat, poured some into a bowl, added water, and put it in the microwave.

"Antipasto?"

"In the refrigerator, minus the lettuce, which we'll add tomorrow. You sure you don't want tomatoes?"

Teresa wrinkled her nose. "In December? Like eating Styrofoam. What's the cookie count?"

"The ceci and the dadaluce and the pizzelle are done," Amberlin said. "I've got those cakes left to do."

"The Parozzo Abruzzese?" Teresa asked.

"Those," Amberlin said, and pushed herself up from the table a little unsteadily. She'd been drinking brandy, which Teresa gave her when she came up from the cellar. She swore she was fine, but the glass had emptied rapidly, and Teresa had refilled it, and now it was empty again.

"Where're the almonds?" she asked. "I'll crush them."

"On the table. In front of you," Teresa said, pointing at them before she went back to checking off points on a notebook while Amberlin made her way to the counter, where she poured the bag of almonds into the food processor and started it whirring.

Delia took her Cream of Wheat to the kitchen table and twirled a spoon around the bowl, making brown sugar circles around the bananas she'd cut into it. She lifted the spoon to her mouth and sucked some of the gooey mixture onto her tongue, closing her eyes and enjoying the combined sensation of smoothness and grittiness.

When she opened her eyes and swallowed, she saw that Amberlin was studying her without anything like sympathy.

"How can you eat that stuff?" she asked.

Delia shrugged. "Like this." She lifted the spoon again, then took a sip from a mug of hot chocolate, which had been laced gently with more of the brandy. "Some people stop eating when they're terrified. Other people seek comfort in food."

Amberlin shook her head. "Comfort food is graham cracker mush. And it has to be really mushy, because that's the thing about comfort food. You can't have to work to eat it. No chewing allowed. It has to just slide down your throat like mother's milk, because that's why it's comforting. Right?"

"My mother's milk was liver," Teresa said, "and onions."

Delia made gagging noises.

"I can't help it. When I was little, my mother used to make it for me and Nan. She said we were anemic and needed the liver to build our blood. She never made it for anyone else, so I figured it was something special. Nan loved it too."

"That seems to be your cure-all," Amberlin said a little sharply. She went to the refrigerator and got out eggs, then closed the door hard. "Maybe we should make some for Christine?"

Delia dug her spoon back into the Cream of Wheat and twirled it more. Teresa opened a drawer and started counting out spoons.

"We can't just pretend she's not here, and we can't leave her there forever. She'll get . . . damp. We have to talk about this, and see if we can come up with a plan to help her."

"Talking to her didn't work, did it?" Delia pointed out.

"These things take time," Amberlin said. "You can't expect just one little talk would do more than lay the groundwork."

"But you did, didn't you?"

Amberlin glared at Delia. "Got any better ideas?"

"I have no ideas. None at all. Except that maybe if we give her time, she might come around on her own. I mean, people do that, don't they?"

Teresa didn't look up from her notebook. "Not in my family."

"Well, does she have a therapist or anything?" Delia asked. "She was seeing one for a while, wasn't she?"

"I know a really good psychiatrist who consults for the hotline," Amberlin said. "Dr. Lilli. We could call her."

"No," Teresa said adamantly. "No and no again."

"Well, why not?" Amberlin asked. "Someone who knows what they're doing might be helpful about now."

"Look," Teresa said reasonably, "no matter how good she is, if we call her in, she has to do her job, which is to get Christine into a hospital. Now, how do you think that'd make Christine feel about herself?"

Delia licked her spoon and nodded. "Teresa's right. We don't want to call someone who'd just cart her away to the nuthouse. That's no answer either."

"But she needs a doctor," Amberlin insisted.

"She can see a doctor when she's ready to walk to one on her own two feet. Right now she needs time," Teresa said. "Time and . . . and love."

"Hitting her with a frying pan? Tying her up in the cellar? That's love?"

"She's alive," Teresa said, and began unloading the dishwasher.

Delia groaned and stood up. "That's my job," she said, and went to it, putting Teresa firmly out of her way.

The women were silent, each tucked into herself and either guarding or examining her own stance. Teresa, beating eggs for the cake, held to her inarticulate instinct that Christine must stay where she was. Something would happen, and then they'd know what to do next. Delia, at the dishwasher, tried to nurture a flagging denial, sticking firmly to the surface of the situation, which was that they had to run a party and keep Christine somehow intact. And as Amberlin worked the almonds through the food processor, she kept feeling that the only answer was to give Christine to the person who might best help her. To James.

Though Delia stood up for James when Teresa took against him, that was just to help Teresa move more toward the middle in her attitude. Delia neither liked nor disliked him intensely, because she felt she didn't have to. That was Christine's choice, and all she wanted to do was make sure Christine got all the support she needed for that choice. She figured with enough encouragement, Teresa and James would eventually learn to get along.

But Amberlin liked James. The vagaries of human action and interaction were a constant source of interest to her, and so she enjoyed talking to James about his work. She recognized that she had a tendency to elevate him because of what he did, but she didn't see anything wrong in that. He'd chosen to become a healer, and that was a special calling that took devotion and sacrifice. He deserved a certain amount of praise for making that choice. And in spite of his current argument with Christine, he seemed to truly want to take care of her. He would know what to do. And he must be suffering terribly at not knowing where she was, or even if she was alive. He must be feeling horribly abandoned. Amberlin could feel that as if it pierced her own heart.

When the almonds were crushed and in a bowl, Amberlin turned to the other women. "I think," she said, "we should call James."

Teresa raised her head and stared at Amberlin as if she'd said something in a different language.

"He wouldn't put her into a hospital," Amberlin noted.

"You think because he went to school and memorized the rules of insanity he's got the answers? Amberlin, that's why she's down there in the first place."

"What's that mean?"

"It means he's a jerk."

"He's a professional," Amberlin said. "And just because your sister wasn't helped and you can't face that doesn't mean psychiatry is a bad thing."

"He's a professional jerk," Teresa shot back.

"And what're you—an amateur?"

Teresa smoldered briefly, then opened a cupboard and started counting glasses. "An amateur is someone who works for love rather than money. So maybe I am," she said pointedly.

"Great," Delia said. "Just great. Merry fucking Christmas, everybody. Amberlin said it was a stupid holiday and I'm beginning to reach agreement with her."

"Look, all I'm saying is we can't do this. Leave her there alone during the party. We've got to help her, and Teresa's being stubborn about it."

"I'm not stubborn," Teresa said, slamming a cupboard door shut. "I'm right."

"What?"

"You never accuse me of being stubborn unless I'm right," Teresa said. "So I must be right."

Amberlin groaned, and Delia held her hand up to try to smother a laugh.

"And what, may I ask, is so funny?" Amberlin asked with excessive politeness.

"Nothing. Only you have this fight every year. At right about this time. Usually it's about flour though. You know—white flour versus whole wheat? Teresa's stubborn and inflexible, and you're unwilling to let people just be. Teresa won't ever talk about anything. You always insist on talking everything to death. The usual."

Teresa's face loosened into a smile. "Maybe I am a little stubborn sometimes."

Amberlin chewed on her bottom lip, then let her chin come down from regal height to everyday level. "Maybe you are," she agreed.

Teresa would have added to the conversation, which would probably last as long as their friendship, but the ringing phone cut off any comment she might have made.

The three women stopped and waited.

"This is ridiculous," Amberlin said, and took a step toward the phone.

"Don't answer it," Delia said, clutching at her arm. "Don't."

"Why not?"

"What if it's James?"

"What if it is? The poor man deserves to know his fiancée is still alive."

"What if it's the police?"

"The police? Delia, really—"

The machine clicked in, and they heard Teresa's voice asking for a message, then the beep, then not James at all, but Rowan.

"Hi," he said. "I just wanted to let you know I'm available after noon tomorrow, if you need anything. Um—sleep well. Or, maybe sleep fast, right?"

The three women all let out their breath at once.

"Well," Delia said, "that wasn't so bad after all."

ABOUT TIME AND LOVE

AT LAST YEAR'S OPEN HOUSE, AFTER TASTING TERESA'S sauce, Rowan asked her what the main ingredients were so he could try to make it at home. Teresa told him there were two. Love and time, in that order. And that was true, she said, for all good food.

It took time as well as heat, she would say, to create the special effects necessary. Time had to pass for the miracle to occur. Subtle changes occurred in time, and there was a small margin between done, not done, and burned beyond repair.

Delia had laughed raucously and said that sounded like sex, not food. Rowan bit back a smile, and seeing that Teresa was blushing, he changed the subject.

Teresa wanted to kick Delia but covered the impulse with handing her another plate of food. She understood time, though sometimes she was confused about love. And sex? Well, why drag that into it when it had been so long since she had any?

One Christmas while they were preparing for an open house, the women got into conversation about foods that were sexy. Teresa said she always liked to eat light before sex, and heavy afterward. She found the piney spice flavor and slick orange color of mangoes an inspiration to passion and pleasure, if not love. Amberlin thought that any food that was slippery and required a great deal of licking was sensual. Ice cream and whipped cream, or fried chicken, where you lick your fingers again and again, were sensual experiences in and of themselves.

Delia asked her if that was a girl thing, and before Amberlin could take offense, Delia amended her question. "I mean, I guess—well, what's it like being with another woman?"

Amberlin thought about it and said it was slower. More sensual. And very powerful. There was something very powerful and beautiful about the bodies of two women together, which was probably why it was such a popular male fantasy. Two wombs. Two vaginas. Two beings capable of that dark and fertile mystery. It could be disconcerting, dragging you down into a swirling eddy of depth that made you long for something clear and crisp and rational. Something with sharp and well-defined edges. Or it could just be warm and fun. Especially with whipped cream. Amberlin said she tried Fluffernutter once as a substitute, but it was too sticky. Too much like work.

The women made a distinction between food that was sexy and food that was sexual. Christine had read in *The Joy of Cooking* about lamb fries, which she thought was a strange version of French fries, until she got to the description of how to prepare them for cooking. She wondered if the authors meant to be provocative when they wrote about cutting into the loose outer skin for the length of the swelled surface. She wondered what they meant when they said it was best to disturb the flesh as little as possible. How, she asked, do you cook testicles and not disturb the flesh? Teresa said she didn't know. It was probably the one food she'd never cooked.

Lamb fries, they all decided, were sexual without being sexy. Like zucchini and sausage and cocktail weiners. They made you think about sex, but they didn't inspire you to feel sexual. Especially cocktail weiners, which always reminded Delia of a certain ex-boyfriend who was a big talker, and not much action.

The women found that different foods were sexy to each of them. Lobster was sexy for Delia, not so much because of the animal itself, red and covered in a hard shell, but the act of eating one. Cracking the claws and back was such a predatory gesture, followed by the slow dipping of the slippery meat in butter and the savoring of the delicate flesh.

For Christine the sexiest food was champagne, licked from all the appropriate places. It bubbled and frothed against the skin, making the most delicious frissons along the surface. Even James, who was not very adventurous in these matters, enjoyed champagne.

Teresa thought of honey, which, like sperm, was supposed to be good for the skin. She had a very vivid memory of watching her grandmother getting ready for her bath, wrapped in a thick terry-cloth bathrobe, mixing honey and milk in a ceramic bowl. She'd take this mixture and, as the water ran hot and steaming into the tub, slather it on the deeply wrinkled skin of her face and neck. Teresa could still hear the deep sigh of pleasure she'd give, and could still see her grandfather standing in the doorway, watching his wife do this. He had laughed at her and said something in Italian. Grandma had laughed right back, but there had been a look in her eyes that Teresa never saw before, and she knew it had something to do with being married and in love.

At the time it had surprised and embarrassed her to think that old people could still be in love, but she never forgot it. When Sam left her, she went and got herself a jar of raw honey from a woman who kept hives outside of town, and before her bath she would make herself a mixture of honey and milk to slather on her face and neck.

What they all agreed on was that sexy food involved time and love. Time to eat or lick or look at or enjoy, and the love necessary to think about making it right.

If they had asked Rowan Bancroft, he would have agreed. When he went to Teresa's house and saw her stirring the sauce, slowly and meditatively, focused on her task, he thought he'd never seen a sexier sight. It had been years since he'd had time to cook in that slow, conscious way, or think of food as anything except a task to be done for his children. He'd almost forgotten that food was a pleasure as well as necessity.

Grief and time had erased his memory of desire, but now Teresa was reminding him that it still existed, and he could still feel it.

After he dropped off the fig plant at Teresa's, when he got back in his car he saw that his hand was shaking. He pressed it into the steering wheel to stop it, and the tremor moved up his arm. He hoped he wasn't about to have a heart attack.

He'd waited a full year after Teresa's divorce to give her time to recover. He didn't want her to think he was the kind of man who preyed on divorcées. And maybe he'd stretched that time out a little longer than he needed to, wondering how to approach her. But now that he'd started it going, he'd like to survive to enjoy any possible benefits.

When the tremor passed, he drove down the street and at the corner turned right, headed toward home. He was hungry, he was tired, and he was a little confused in a way he hadn't been since he was a teenager and he had to ask himself questions like Will she? Won't she? How do I know which one it is?

She was a very self-contained woman, and that gave her an air of mystery and power. He was a pretty open man, and that, he thought, made him vulnerable to playing the fool. Which may have been why he had avoided all except the most casual interactions with women until now. If he was going to lay his heart out on the block, it might as well be for something that seemed worth the potential pain. He supposed he was trembling because now he was deciding whether or not this was that something.

He drove down the quiet streets, and at a red light on the corner of Vly Road, his peripheral vision was caught by a restaurant sign glowing on his left. The Little Falls Inn. He'd been driving by it for years, and knew it was one of the finest restaurants in the area, and also one of the most expensive. He had always promised himself that when he met the right woman, he'd take her there. Someday. Someday he would. Maybe Teresa would be that woman, he thought, glad to have a night off from cooking, to let someone cook for her for a change. He had a feeling that was a rare event in her life.

The light turned green and he drove forward. Then, for no apparent reason, he found he was making a left turn, turning into the parking lot of the restaurant. He was hungry.

He stopped the car and got out. "What the hell am I doing?" he asked himself.

The answer was plain. Taking himself out to an expensive dinner.

He walked up to the front door and read the menu. No prices. That was bad. But the food looked good. Duck with raspberry sauce. Salmon stuffed with rosemary and lemon. Quail stuffed with grapes. Chocolate mousse truffle cake.

He was hungry and it had been a long time since he treated himself like someone worth taking out to dinner. He felt silly, going in to a restaurant alone. Especially one like this. Would it make him look like a loser? A man who couldn't get a date?

Or would it give him courage to ask the woman out? Because maybe what he needed to know was that as lovely as she was, he had something to offer her too. He'd waited a year to make that offer. He'd waited too many years to take himself to a restaurant. It was time for him to stop confusing fear with patience.

He opened the door and went in. A subdued waiter asked quietly if he wanted a table for two.

"One," he said. "Just me. I mean, just for me."

"Very good," the waiter said.

And he supposed it did him good to sit there and eat quail with grapes, at any price, because the sprig of parsley on his plate reminded him of one more present he wanted to give Teresa. He would call her when he got home and remind her he was available to help, though he knew she wouldn't take him up on that offer.

But tomorrow night he would bring one more gift, for both of them.

Something leafy and green in the dead of winter. Something that said it was time to move forward.

TERESA'S KITCHEN

AT ONE A.M. TERESA LOOKED AT AMBERLIN AND DELIA and said, "Time to call it quits for the night. I'm gonna fall asleep in the sink if I go anymore."

Delia and Amberlin, who had been drying dishes, put down their dish towels and stretched their arms.

"Which room you want?" Delia asked Amberlin.

"I'm upstairs," Amberlin said, stretching out her full length, then reaching down to touch her toes and coming up with a large yawn.

Teresa left the kitchen, went down the hall and up the stairs, and reappeared momentarily with a pillow and an armful of quilts. "Could one of you get the door for me?" she asked, tilting her head toward the cellar.

"What're you doing?" Delia asked, her eyes growing wide.

"I'm going downstairs. I don't want to leave her alone all night."

Amberlin frowned. "It'll be cold, won't it?"

Teresa shrugged. "That's why I got blankets."

Amberlin chewed on her lip. "Do you have more blankets? I'll come too."

Delia's hand flew to her mouth, and her milk-white skin mottled over with red. "You can't. Sleep in the cellar?"

"Christine is," Teresa pointed out.

Delia felt herself sinking, like being dropped into the bottom of the lake. "But—what about me?" she asked.

"You can stay upstairs," Teresa said matter-of-factly. "We don't all need to go. Amberlin, you can stay upstairs too."

"No. I'll come down. Maybe she'll talk if we're both there."

"I don't feel good about this," Delia said, the red leaving her face and her lips going a little pale around the edge. "I just don't feel right."

"It's okay, Delia," Teresa said. "Really. Stay upstairs."

"No. It's not okay. None of it is okay," she said, and her voice worked its way up the scale toward soprano range. "You've got her tied to a sink, for chrissake. In the cellar. And here we are cooking and pretending she's not here, just like Amberlin says, and we're gonna have a party on top of her tomorrow. Right on *top* of her."

Something churned up inside her that she hadn't expected. Feelings like the hum of electricity rising into its most highly charged state. Feelings like she would scream. Like she would explode. She pulled at a piece of her hair and twisted it around her finger, untwisted it, and twisted it again as she looked from Teresa's shocked face to Amberlin's.

"I can't," she said, shaking her head back and forth. "I can't. I can't. You've got to do something about it, because I can't."

Amberlin and Teresa gaped at her. She was shaking now, her arms trembling lightly. Amberlin reached out and put a hand on her shoulder, but Delia pushed it off. "No. I can't," she said again, her wide eyes moving from one woman to the other. "I have to—I have to go. I have to go home. I have to leave. Now."

And she twisted around on her heel and clipped down the hall.

Teresa and Amberlin stared at the space she'd just occupied. Looked hard at her absence. "Should we go after her?" Amberlin asked.

"I don't know," Teresa mused. "I think she's in some kind of shock."

"Then maybe we should."

"No. It's just too deep. It's too far down for her. It goes too deep, and she's afraid, that's all. She'll be better in the morning."

"Now you sound like her," Amberlin replied.

Teresa shook her head. She'd known Delia a long time. She was a big woman, and so everybody assumed she was stronger than normal too. But Teresa knew better. Knew she was permeable, like her skin. Sometimes she had to keep happy because unhappiness was too much for her to take. It pulled her down too far.

"I think we should go after her," Amberlin suggested, but before they could move, Delia returned and stood looking at them with resolve.

"Delia," Teresa said, "are you okay?"

"No," she said. "I'm not. And you shouldn't be either. If you thought about it, you wouldn't be. Anything could happen tomorrow. She could get out of her ropes and break one of your glass jars and slit her wrists. Then we'd find her bloody and dead after giving a party. A damn party."

"She won't," Teresa said.

"How the hell do you know? Those ropes didn't look too secure to me."

"She knows," Teresa said, struggling for an explanation she couldn't quite articulate. "She knows it's not time. I put a . . . sort of a spell on the ropes."

"A—what?"

Amberlin joined in at this point. "Teresa's speaking metaphorically, Delia. She didn't put a spell on the ropes. She doesn't believe in that."

"Yes I do," Teresa said crisply. "It's a family thing. Delia understands. And Christine knows. It's not time."

As Teresa spoke, she kept her face to Delia's, and Delia searched it, biting on her lip, her own face tight with anxiety. Teresa said nothing, but after a moment she nodded, and Delia sighed. Amberlin shook her head, wondering what it was Delia understood. What Teresa said, and what she didn't say, made little sense to Amberlin. Of course, Delia had known Teresa longer, and maybe that's what it took. Listening over time, like listening to a new language, until at some unfathomable point, it began to make sense.

"You're sure it's a good spell?" Delia asked. "Better than the one you put on Peter Hawley in eighth grade?"

"Yeah. Better than that."

"I hope so. He never even looked at you."

Teresa's mouth turned up in a grin.

Delia ran her fingers through her hair. "You're really gonna sleep down there?"

"Yeah," Teresa said, "but you don't have to."

"I'm sorry," Delia said. "I'm sorry if that's not good enough."

"It's good enough, Delia," Teresa said. "It's fine. Why not?"

Delia turned a pained face toward her. "I'm supposed to be good in a crisis. Especially with people. You know. I get people together. Make sure everyone's happy. But this—I can't organize it."

Teresa shook her head slowly back and forth. "You think I didn't know that already?" she asked. "You think anyone can?"

Delia chewed on her lower lip, and the rims of her eyes filled up with tears. "I wish Michael were here. He's better at this sort of thing than I am."

He didn't mind the progress of life toward chaos. Didn't tell her to be quiet or small or anything. He just let things in. Easygoing, people said. But they said that about her too. Only they didn't know squat. He wasn't easygoing. He was just strong enough to take it. And she wasn't easygoing either. She was just lucky for the most part, and knew how to hide it when she wasn't.

"You can go home if you want," Teresa said. "Come back in the morning."

Delia shook her head. "I don't want to be a wimp."

"You're not. But if you stay, you're stuck with just us."

Delia looked at Teresa. So small. When they were in junior high, Delia could pick Teresa up and throw her over her shoulders like a sack of potatoes. When they got in fights, Delia knew she had the advantage of size and strength, though she found there was no accounting for sheer stubbornness. Teresa was small and chaotic but durable as flame.

Delia opened her broad arms wide and engulfed Teresa in them. Squeezed her hard, then let her go.

"Maybe," she said, "I could try it for a while, if you bring candles."

"Candles," Teresa said. "Sure. That'd be nice."

"I'll get them," Amberlin said, and trotted off to the living room to gather them up.

They got blankets and pillows and candles and headed for the cellar, which was dark except for the candle Teresa brought down to light their way. It was a small and fluttering circle of light in their faces, and did little to illuminate the stairs.

Once they were in the cellar, light from the street came through the window, enough to allow them to see, and Teresa walked over to Christine and knelt down, peering at her through the semidarkness.

"Christine?" she whispered.

There was no answer.

"She's asleep?" Amberlin asked.

Teresa nodded. "Let her sleep. Might do her more good than anything else."

The women worked in silence, creating human-size nests for themselves on the cold and hard cellar floor. Teresa found a workout mat of Donnie's and gave it to Delia, who wanted to insist on Amberlin using it, who wanted to insist on Teresa using it, who wouldn't take it because somebody else should. They went on like that for a while, then with deep sighs, Delia gave in. She was too tired to keep it up.

They lay down and stared at the ceiling, at the wooden planks and the intricate design of cobwebs that ran across them. Amberlin hoped no spiders would drop from them onto her face in the night. Behind them, the furnace hummed and made some heat. In a very little while, Delia's breathing slowed. Amberlin sighed and rolled over onto her back.

"Amberlin," Teresa whispered. "You asleep?"

"No," she said, "I can't yet. Too wound up."

"Do you really not believe in ghosts?" Teresa asked unexpectedly.

Amberlin rolled onto her side and leaned up on an elbow. "What?"

"Do you really not believe in ghosts?" Teresa asked again.

She considered. "I told you. I think there's some kind of spirit things we can't explain yet. Energy bundles, or something. Why?"

"I was thinking about Nan. Wondering if she can see this. Wondering what she thinks."

"Don't start," Delia's voice muttered. "I'll go upstairs."

Teresa lifted her head and looked at Delia. "You like ghost stories," she said.

"Not tonight." She shoved her head under her pillow. Teresa shrugged and turned back to Amberlin.

Amberlin shook her head. "I don't know that I believe in ghosts that watch us, or any of that," she said.

"My grandmother used to sing this song to us," Teresa said. She sang, in Italian, a line or two, her voice carrying the tones easy and true. Although Amberlin didn't know what the words meant, the sound filled her with warmth, a soft, protective blanket.

"Pretty," Amberlin murmured when she stopped. "What's it say?"

"It says that a thousand angels sang the day you were born, and they smile on you and watch over you all your life as you go on your way. So sleep and listen to the angels. Sleep and dream. Sleep and dream."

She sang a little more. *Dormi, dormi, sogna piccola amor.*

Amberlin found herself floating away on the song as if it were a boat to carry her to her own dreams. She lowered herself into her bundle of blankets and felt warm and drowsy and good.

"That's nice," Delia muttered. "Sing more."

Teresa sang the song through. Then she sighed and spoke, her voice as sweet in speaking as it was in singing. Not her usual clipped speech that seemed so definite, so sure of itself.

"Grandma told us the angels were watching," Teresa said. "Then she told us about Befana. The Christmas witch, she's called, but she was around long before there was Christmas. She was an old *strega,* and every year she swept the earth until it turned away from the winter and back to the sun. She'd sweep in the new year, sweep away the old. Always sweeping, sweeping."

"Hmm," Amberlin mumbled, letting Teresa's voice carry her where it would. At the back of her eyelids she could see the old woman, hunched over a broom and muttering to herself, her gray hair thick and a little unkempt. She saw herself going over to her and patting at her hair, trying to comb it while the old lady laughed at her. Delia, falling into dreams, saw the same.

"*Befana* means 'epiphany,' " Teresa said, "and she brings her gifts on January sixth, when her sweeping job is done. Did I tell you about that before?"

"Hmm," Delia said.

"I don't think so. Anyway, the story is that she was late the year Jesus was born. She wanted to bring him a gift, because everyone told her this was the child who would save the world, but she had work to do, so she couldn't get there when all the angels and the three kings and everyone else did."

Amberlin saw the great line of people approaching the small house on the small, dusty street where she stood with Befana. Some were on elephants, some walking, some riding donkeys. They wore robes of red and gold and purple, or tunics and pants in the roughest of brown cloth. Goats and sheep trotted alongside camels and even a few chickens with great colorful feathers on their feet like slippers.

Above her she heard a sound like bells, only not like bells. She looked up and realized it was a sound she'd never actually heard before: the sound of angels' wings moving the air. Something like feathers, or maybe more like silver frost, fluttered down off the wingtips, making the bell-like sound, almost singing, almost speaking, almost laughing.

"Angels," Delia muttered, "we have herds on high."

"That's right," Teresa said. "Herds and herds of angels."

Befana looked up at the angels who rode the sky over her head, beating their wings and singing their heavenly songs. *We are going to Bethlehem, Befana. Come with us to greet the divine child. The magic child. The child who will save the world.*

Their voices were almost as beautiful as Teresa's, as if gold fell from their lips when they spoke. Their voices had the richness of gold. But Befana didn't go. Not right away. She had her work to do, though Amberlin was eager that she should get it right and Delia was worried she would miss the party. The old lady patted Amberlin's arm. She'd go in her own sweet time.

"A few days later, she was ready," Teresa said. "Her sweeping was done, and the world was back to the light. So she packed up her gift—which was ceci cookies, our grandmother always told us—and headed down the road with her broom, in case the baby's house needed a good sweeping. She went as fast as she could, but she was old. Old as the earth. So she was slow, and time was different for her. When she finally made it to the manger, nobody was there."

Amberlin looked over the old woman's shoulder as she stood scratching her head amid the leftovers of what looked like a party. There were bits of bones and gristle left from a chicken someone had cooked. There, a shawl someone forgot. Over there, the manger where the new baby had slept. It was so sad, Delia thought. So horrible to miss such a moment and not ever be able to retrieve it. What a horrible mistake, Amberlin thought.

Befana scratched at her behind, and shrugged.

"That's okay," she said. "There's lots of babies in the village. I'll bet any one of them could be a divine child. Maybe even they *all* are."

"That's just what Befana said," Teresa continued. "She didn't feel bad at all about missing the other baby. Grandma DiRosa told us she just went to the village with the ceci cookies, and found some babies to give them to, because any one of them could be divine. Any one could save the world."

Befana went from house to house, delivering cookies, saying to each child, "It could be you. It could be you. It could be you," until finally she turned and put a ceci cookie in Amberlin's hand, one more into Delia's, her old, rheumy eyes looking straight into theirs as she said, "And it could be you."

"Ever since then, Befana brings cookies and gifts to children every year," Teresa said, "because she knows the divine child could be any child, anytime, anywhere."

She sat up in her nest of blankets and lifted a napkin from her lap. She unwrapped a ceci cookie, stood, and brought it to Christine, put it on the plate at her feet.

Christine's eyes were closed, and Teresa reached over and touched her head. "It could be you," she said to her. "It could certainly be you."

Delia, falling quickly into dreams, felt herself surrounded by a celebration that seemed to be about her. She had stayed in the cellar, in the dark, and that was something to rejoice in. Amberlin dreamed of a thousand angels singing something beautiful, each sound created to welcome her and Christine and Delia and her children and Teresa and hers into the coming day.

And Christine, who was not asleep at all, had heard every word Teresa said, and many that she didn't.

ABOUT WITCHES AND ANGELS

ALTHOUGH DELIA AND AMBERLIN AND EVEN CHRISTINE all had their doubts about witches and angels, Teresa and Nan had been raised on them. These beings were part of their deepest consciousness of the world and how it worked. But Teresa was often confused about the difference between the two.

As a child, she knew that both had power, and both could fly. And although angels seemed to have boys' names, they looked very much like girls. While witches, who were apparently all female, didn't look it.

She found the prospect of meeting either a witch or an angel daunting, since the stories she heard about witches often had to do with them eating children, and the stories she heard about angels had to do with them carrying children up to Jesus. Either way, she figured you ended up dead, and while it might be nice to be in heaven and live on clouds with God, she thought it would be better to go there when she was old.

She asked Grandma DiRosa what the difference was, and Grandma told her a long story about a Mama Strega, who lived in a garbage dump. Two girls came to visit her, and the first one helped her clean her house, which was filthy, and her hair, which had fleas, and was given gold and silk dresses and magic. The other girl didn't help, and so sausage grew out of her head. Teresa wasn't sure that answered her question, but it was a good story.

Nan told her Grandma was clearly a witch. She wore black, and angels always wore white. Also, witches liked to cook—they always had a stove or cauldron going—and angels didn't eat anything except clouds, which they swallowed in great quantities, and when they had to go to the bathroom, it rained.

Teresa thought if Grandma was a witch, she might be Befana, since she was the one who snuck cookies and oranges into their rooms at the Feast of the Epiphany, and since she told the story of Befana as if she knew it from personal experience. Nan said she was just an ordinary *strega*. But she was a witch. No doubt about it.

She gave them tea that tasted very unlike the Lipton's they drank with their mother, and she hung strings of garlic and curling, strangely formed crosses of herbs around the house. She burned candles on top of her bureau, which was lined with tiny statues of magic people who carried bolts of lightning or had holes in their hearts or their heads, blood pouring down their faces, which looked sad and loving.

Her arms were the broad branches of an oak tree straining only slightly under the weight of the iron kettle she hefted to the outdoor stove they used to boil down the tomatoes for canning. Sweat poured down her face as she stirred and stirred, all the while mumbling words or singing songs that Teresa and Nan understood only parts of.

Once Teresa asked her what the words meant, and she raised her dark, arched eyebrows until folds of skin made deep grooves on her forehead.

"It's a prayer," she said a little tersely. That was all.

Grandma was like that. She could have the softest voice, and the softest lap to crawl into because she was cushioned all over with a good soft layer of fat. If they slept at her house in the big middle room, which they often did in the summer, she would tell them stories as she tucked them in, about living in Italy and the chickens that chased her in the yard. About how Great-grandma Emilia stood in front of the house, shouting to her children to come home for supper. She'd shout so loud, her voice bounced clear over the village. About how she and her sisters, whom the girls called Zizi Zum and Zizi Em, stood on the hill and looked toward Rome and dreamed and dreamed what it must be like. Golden-domed and full of life. All the great buildings and people in beautiful clothes.

She called Italy the old country, and Teresa thought the word covered everything there—the people, the trees, the earth itself.

And then, sometimes, Grandma's eyes would turn into iron and her voice would be sharp as the edge of the knives she used to cut the bread as she held it against her belly. Teresa thought she was the most powerful woman in the world except for Nan, and she loved the food that seemed to roll from her very body onto the kitchen table, where she and her siblings and her children and their children shared meals.

It was a big table. It had to be to accommodate everybody in the family and the occasional stray priest, nun, or out-of-work acquaintance who sat at it. And before every meal, her grandmother would mutter more of those strange words, kiss the palm of her hand, and then press the kiss into the table.

Another prayer, Teresa thought. But somehow, she didn't think it was the same god Mom spoke to in church.

Later, when Teresa was in school, she took a class called Cultural Practices and Food and learned that the Abruzzi people were known for the spells they said over their food. The spells were apparently potent. There was a saying in Italy: If an Abruzzese is in the kitchen, the restaurant will prosper. Teresa still kissed the table before a meal. And sometimes when she cooked she sang words that seemed to be drawn out of her with the heat of the stove. Her hands would move over the bubbling sauce, and if her son asked her what she was singing, she would arch her eyebrows and say, "It's a prayer."

SHE'S MAKING MAGIC," NAN WHISPERED TO TERESA AS they rocked on the glider in the yard, sucking on candy-covered almonds and watching her put the tomatoes into the great iron kettle on the backyard stove. "It's a spell. She's a witch."

A delightful shiver ran through them both, and they rocked the glider back and forth in silent reverence, watching their grandmother the witch at work.

Nan listened, closely, and Teresa sucked hard on an almond nougat as she wondered what the spells would do.

Nan was on a campaign to learn Grandma's spells and use them. She wanted to make spells for money and happiness and love. Especially love. Teresa wasn't interested in that, except in the ways her sister talked about it. Nan was twelve, and so wise. She knew so much and could do so many things Teresa hoped someday to do.

She could ride her bike all the way downtown and meet her friends at the music store where they hung out, and come back with records that were very unlike the opera and jazz her parents and grandparents played. She could even play some on her guitar, and her voice sounded almost like the people on the records. She was going to be a star someday, she told Teresa in secret one night when they stayed up late talking. Teresa looked out her window at the night sky, which was studded with bright points of light, and imagined Nan flying up to the darkness and waving at her from that height. She felt privileged that Nan shared these secrets with her, even if she was so much younger and, as Nan reminded her, couldn't possibly understand most of it.

Nan told her that as soon as they figured out the spells, she was going to write them down so they could use them when they needed them. It would be their family magic, and they couldn't share it with anyone who wasn't a DiRosa.

As Grandma DiRosa stirred and muttered, Zizi Em and Zizi Zum arrived with a basket filled with flowers from their own gardens. They put the basket down, and the three women with their silver hair and broad backs stood over the kettle with their eyes closed, humming some long-ago tune while the tomatoes bubbled red and redolent in the pot.

Nan's eyes grew wide. "Listen," she hissed, her feet crunching on the earth as she halted the glider's motion. "They're doing it."

Teresa went still, suddenly frightened of what might happen next, though she'd seen her grandmother stir tomatoes every August for as long as she could remember. But what if she were a witch and could make spells? What would that power do? Would things burn? Would there be noise? Would anyone be hurt?

"Nan," she started to say, "maybe we shouldn't." But Nan pushed an elbow into her side to keep her quiet. Teresa breathed in hard and the almond she was sucking on went down her throat. She started to choke, then couldn't choke anymore, so she stood up and flailed, then fell face-first into the warm earth.

At the sound of her choking and the sight of her flailing and falling, all three women turned from their work and lumbered to them as quickly as their bulk allowed, chattering in Italian. Zizi Zum pounded Teresa on the back and Grandma shouted imprecations in a mix of Italian and English as Teresa struggled for breath and couldn't find it. Their noise brought Uncle Henry dashing in from the garden and Grandpa Donato from the kitchen. Uncle Laborio, who was watching a baseball game in the living room, never heard a thing.

"Mí Dio, oh, Di, Maledizione," Zizi Em sobbed as Teresa turned various shades of red.

"Turn her upside down," Uncle Henry suggested, making a grab for her ankles.

Sharp light bounced off the silver of Zizi Zum's rosary, which she clutched in front of her as she said a frantic prayer to the Virgin for succor.

Nan got into the fray, shaking Teresa hard and shouting. "You broke the spell. You broke the damn spell. Now we'll never know it."

Teresa, water rolling from her eyes, coughed up a chunk of almond and sucked in a deep drink of air.

"Aah," the women sighed.

Henry took out a red cloth and wiped his forehead. Donato made the sign of the cross on his chest and kissed his thumb. Everyone went back to work.

Nan scowled at Teresa. "You ruined it."

"No I didn't," Teresa said, not sure what she was denying, but knowing it was important to do so.

"Yes you did."

"We shouldn't anyway," Teresa said.

Nan scowled harder, but was listening. "Shouldn't what?"

"Try to get the spells. It's dangerous."

Nan bent her face down to Teresa's, her dark eyes like the night sky without stars. "So what?" she said. "So what?"

She stomped away, and Teresa made her way across the long yard to her own house, where her mother was cooking dinner. She felt shaky inside. Maybe Grandma and the Zizis had made a spell to save her and this was what you felt like after someone put a spell on you. If so, she wondered what it felt like to be the person making the spell.

Teresa stopped and stood under the grape arbor, the gravel warm and crunchy under her feet, the bees sucking at the ripening fruit above her head. For the first time, she wondered what it was like to be a witch. To have that power.

Would it make people angry at you, the way they got angry at Nan when she was disrespectful to their father? Would you feel lonely? Would you be afraid of what you could do? Nan often seemed lonely, she thought. Maybe it was like that, to be a witch.

She walked thoughtfully up the drive to her house, ascended the steps, and opened the door. Once inside the clean, bright kitchen, Teresa stared at her mother, who was putting a chicken in the oven. She had missed the whole thing. Hadn't heard the shouting. She worked to the sound of the television that blared a game show from the living room.

Grandma might be a witch, but her mother definitely was not. And maybe her mother's world was safer. More certain.

"Mom?" she asked.

Her mother turned to her and smiled. "Supper in an hour," she said brightly. The sound of the TV caught her attention, and she spoke to it.

"Andrew Jackson. No, you idiot. Not Jefferson, Jackson." She shook her head. "Why are the people on TV so stupid? I oughta sign up for one of these shows."

"Mom?" Teresa asked again.

Her mother blinked at her, stood with a hand on her hip, head crooked to one side.

Teresa paused. She thought her mother had something she wanted to say.

"Honey, I've gotta get the potatoes started," her mother said.

"Is Grandma a witch?" Teresa asked.

Her mother's laughter was soft and silver, like music falling into the room from an open window. "Of course not," she said. "There's no such thing as witches. Whatever gave you that idea?"

Saturday

TERESA'S CELLAR

DELIA SAT UP AND LOOKED AROUND AT THE GRAY morning light. After a moment, she remembered where she was and why.

"Wow," she said. "I did it."

She heard a moan emanate from the bundle of blankets that Amberlin occupied near her.

"I mean, I stayed all night," Delia said. She rubbed at her eyes to get the sleep out, and looked around. Only the top of Amberlin's head was visible, the rest hidden under blankets. Christine seemed to be still asleep. Teresa was gone.

"Holy shit," Delia exclaimed. "What time is it?" She untangled herself from her covers and leaned over Amberlin, poking at her. All she got in response was another groan.

"C'mon, girl. We've got a day ahead of us. I have to go home and get my stuff and—and there's all those phone calls I didn't make last night. You getting up?"

Amberlin said something, her words muffled and indistinguishable.

"Look," Delia said, "I gotta go. Don't go back to sleep. Okay?"

Delia stood up and Amberlin, trying not to be awake, could hear the clatter of her feet as she made her way up the stairs.

Amberlin tried to obey the order to wake up, but her body wanted to stay in the warmth of the blankets and the sweetness of dreams. She told herself that five more minutes wouldn't matter, and closed her eyes.

When she opened them again, the light in the cellar had shifted to brightness, and she felt something tickling her nose. She peered at it cross-eyed. A spider. She brushed it off and sat up quickly to find that she was very cold. Much colder than she wanted to be. She looked over at Christine, who seemed to be still asleep under a mound of blankets that now included the ones Teresa had used. She stood and got her bearings. She had no idea how long she'd slept, or what time it was. She listened for a moment, heard no sound of human life, and made her way groggily up to the kitchen.

"Teresa?" she asked. Nobody answered. "Delia?" she tried. No response.

Amberlin spotted the white notepad on the kitchen table and went and read it:

Out of oil, but the truck should be here soon. I'm at the store. Delia's home kissing her children and husband. Please slice the salmon.

"Great," Amberlin muttered. "Now I'll freeze to death slicing the damn salmon."

The phone rang and she didn't pick it up, but she stood and listened while the caller left a message.

"It's James," a disgruntled voice said. "I would like to speak with Christine if she's there. If she's not and you really don't know where she is, I think it's time we took measures." The voice changed from disgruntled to firm as he said, "I strongly advise that you call me back soon, or I'll be forced to take action without you."

Amberlin rolled her eyes. "What else, huh?"

She wished he *would* take action, real action like coming over and insisting on helping Christine, instead of just calling. What good did calling do, except upset everyone?

Shivering and shaking, she went to start a fire in the fireplace, and saw that Teresa had already done so. She warmed herself by it, went into the hall closet, and grabbed a wooly sweater to put over her own clothes, then went back to the kitchen, where she pulled a filleted salmon from the refrigerator and got the small knife to cut the thin slices Teresa would want.

This was one of her least favorite jobs, one that Christine usually

"You think I'm funny?" Amberlin said sharply, and immediately felt ashamed of herself. Talking sharply to suicidal friends wasn't very nice. Next she'd be taking the handicapped parking space because she was in a hurry.

"I know how to bleed a line, Amberlin," Christine said. "Untie me and I'll do it for you."

Amberlin twisted a tired face toward her. "And then what?"

"Then I'll leave," she said. "That's all."

"And after Teresa got back, how long do you think I'd be alive?" Amberlin said, shaking her head. Again, she felt a stab of shame. Her first thought was her own life, not Christine's, and it was Christine who needed help.

No. She needed help. Amberlin needed help. She was freezing.

"Why don't you just tell me how to do it," she suggested. "I can follow directions."

"No," Christine said. "Only if you let me go."

Amberlin glared at her. The hotline told them suicides could be manipulative. The ultimate manipulation. "You want to die that bad?" she spat at her. "Fine, then. Fine."

Amberlin pushed herself up and stomped up the cellar stairs. She knew where Christine's gun was, and she was tired of being manipulated. Damn tired of it. All day long she made food for people so they could eat healthily, and then she walked back to her apartment past the lines at McDonald's, because they were good at manipulating people. She talked sense to Teresa, who didn't listen. She tried compassion on Christine, who couldn't feel it. And she stood up for James, who could do nothing more effective than make stupid, vaguely threatening calls when he should be here taking care of this.

All her life she'd listened to all the right things. Did all the right things. Said the right words. Cooked the right foods. Slept with the right men, and even married one of them, and what good did it do her?

Was she happy? Was Christine better? And was she freezing, or not?

Amberlin went to Teresa's room and found Christine's purse on her bureau. Inside it was the gun. She pulled it out, felt its coldness and heaviness in her hand. She brought it downstairs with her, down to the cellar, and stood in front of Christine, pointing the gun at her.

did, and when there was a knock on the door, Amberlin
atheist parents and turned her eyes heavenward. "Thank
breathed, and went and opened the door.

The man, who wore a cap that said JOE, handed her an inv
tipped his hat, then mumbled something she could not begin t
prehend. But when he tried to walk past her into the hou
blocked his way.

"What?" she asked him. "What did you say?"

"Bleed the line, ma'am. The tank was empty and it won't run
less I bleed the air out."

"Oh," Amberlin said. "I see. Well, how do you do that?"

"I go down to the cellar and loosen the spigot until oil runs out
he said patiently.

"Oh," Amberlin said again. "That. The spigot. Well, okay. I'll take care of it."

The man lifted a foot and held it there, looking at her inquisitively. "You will?" he asked.

"Sure," she said confidently. "Done it a million times. Thanks, now. And Merry Christmas."

She closed the door on his surprised face and retreated into the chill of the kitchen, where she stomped her feet and jumped up and down and cursed.

"Bleed the damn line," she said. "Goddammit. Let him down there and explain Christine. How? An overnight guest who's into ropes? Goddamn Teresa. Goddamn fuel lines. Goddamn salmon. Delia's right. We have to do something."

She slammed around the kitchen for some time, finally getting a wrench and a screwdriver and heading back down to the cellar, where she knelt in front of the furnace as if worshipping an ancient god of heat, and tried to figure out which of the hundreds of protrusions on the metal surface was the spigot the oil man meant.

She stared for some time, trying to determine what the logical course of the oil was, where it would come out, where it would go in, where it would get hot. It was like trying to make brioche without a recipe, she thought at last. You might get it right eventually. But it would take a damn long time, and a lot of mistakes first.

To her right, she heard a low laugh. She turned to it and saw Christine, biting back a grin.

"Is this what you want?" Amberlin asked. "You want me to shoot you?"

Christine's face showed a bored anger. "Don't bullshit me, Amberlin. Untie me or go the hell away."

"No," Amberlin said, raising it and pointing it at her. "I'm going to shoot you."

Christine smiled, amused either at the prospect or at Amberlin's shaking hand. "Is this some kind of hotline trick? Something from the manual?"

"What do you think?" Amberlin said through clenched teeth. She couldn't answer because she didn't know the answer. Hadn't a clue what she was doing or why.

Christine closed her eyes and tilted her face up like the cup of a flower drinking light.

"Do it," she whispered.

Amberlin's hand shook harder. She looked at it, and realized it wasn't cold or fear, but anger that coursed through her muscles with an energy she couldn't control. This wasn't what she wanted. It wasn't supposed to work this way. She wanted to be sympathetic and helping and kind and gentle. She wanted to get it right for Christine. She wanted to help her. To save her. To make her well.

Christine was betraying her. They were supposed to be friends, but she wouldn't let Amberlin *be* her friend. She wouldn't cooperate, wouldn't be well. Delia and Teresa had abandoned her, James was a damned impotent fool, Christine was rejecting her help, and all of this raised an anger in her she didn't know she was capable of. Her shaking hand let go of the gun and she kicked it hard. It skittered across the cellar floor toward the stairs.

"Goddammit," she roared, "what the hell is wrong with you?"

She flung her arm out and it found a jar of tomatoes on the shelf to her left. She pulled back and hurled it over Christine's head and watched with satisfaction as it smashed against the wall behind her. Christine opened her eyes and ducked, covering her head with her arms.

Amberlin, another jar in her hand, stopped mid-throw. "You—ducked," she said, amazed. Christine gaped, and her face turned pink.

"You ducked," Amberlin repeated. "You got the hell out of the way."

She grabbed another jar and hurled it, and Christine ducked again.

"Go ahead." Amberlin laughed wildly. "Protect yourself. You can't help it, can you?"

She flung jars of tomatoes, jars of pickles, jars of beans, until the wall looked like a Kandinsky version of Christmas, red and green and red again. She kept throwing, and Christine finally got all the way under her blankets and cowered there, waiting for the storm to pass.

Amberlin, breathless and pleased, picked up the gun and went back upstairs.

ABOUT DIETS

TERESA HAD NEVER DIETED IN HER LIFE AND HAD NO idea what it meant to be eating either too much or too little for her body's good. She ate what her body told her to eat, and it seemed to work out okay.

Delia had tried a variety of weight-loss programs in a desultory way, and found that her weight was actually stable enough without any of them, barring pregnancy and other waistline disasters. Sometimes she'd be ten pounds up, and sometimes five down, but she could carry it. She was mostly sinew and muscle and bone because she didn't slow down long enough for fat to stick to her.

Amberlin, on the other hand, had tried everything from going vegan to all protein to a Mediterranean diet, not so much in search of the perfect body as she was in search of the perfect self. Only when she was in college did she have anything like a weight problem, which she blamed on being away from her family and tasting junk food for the first time, with nobody to tell her no. And her roommate, Sarah, was no help.

When she got to her dorm room the first day, Sarah was sitting on one of the beds with a dark-haired young man who was strumming a guitar. She wore a white balloonlike dress and had a blue headband tied around her fine short hair. Her eyes were large and her features delicate. When she stood and crossed the room to greet Amberlin, she moved as if she thought she was beautiful.

"Hi," she said. "I'm Sarah, and this is my Italian boyfriend, Tonio."

Amberlin wondered if Sarah had other boyfriends from other countries, and if tomorrow she'd see Sarah walking with another young man and be told, "This is my Irish boyfriend, Patrick."

"Nice to meet you," Amberlin said politely. "Am I interrupting you?"

"Not at all," Sarah said. "I hope you don't mind if Tonio stays with us a few days."

Tonio flashed white teeth at her. Sarah gazed with her wide eyes.

"Of course not," Amberlin said.

Tonio stayed a week, and then was replaced by a Belgian boyfriend, and then an Israeli, each of whom was very discreet in his comminglings, and each of whom had white teeth to flash in place of language.

As the semester progressed, Amberlin noticed two things. First, she noticed that her heart would pound a little harder when Sarah entered a room, and she often wished, in a vague and uncommitted way, that the boyfriends would go back to their home countries long enough for Sarah's bed to be empty and available. Available for what she didn't name to herself. She knew only that she had a sort of crush on her, and since she'd never seen herself as someone who would have a crush on another woman, she was deeply disturbed.

Not that there was anything wrong with it. Her parents had told her about homosexuality a long time ago, instructing her never to use slang words like *fag* and *dyke* because anyone might be. She wasn't sure how they'd feel about it if either she or her brother announced that they were gay, though she knew they'd put a good face on it. But this was different. She'd been attracted to boys. Now she was attracted to girls. It wasn't supposed to work that way. Her parents wouldn't like it if she couldn't make up her mind.

After she noticed this about herself, she observed that Sarah wasn't concerned about being good or civic-minded, and yet she thrived. This surprised her, since she secretly believed she would die if there wasn't a significant reason for her to take up space on the planet. That idea wasn't words, or thoughts even, but dark, faceless platelets hurtling through her veins with the nutritional diet her parents had fed her.

As an experiment, she tried bending to Sarah's ways, since Sarah was obviously happy and she was not. She'd go out to dinner with Sarah and her current nation and eat enormously of fast food, which was what the imports always craved. While Amberlin was eager to try their foods, they preferred McDonald's and Perkins Pancakes and Pizza Hut.

She wasn't happier, but she gained twenty pounds, which wasn't much to distribute on her tall frame, but when she went home for Christmas break, her parents were appalled.

"Maybe you should take up running," her mother suggested gently, the inherent criticism of the comment peeling away all levels of self-confidence Amberlin had accrued during her time away.

"A little involvement in local activities would help keep you busy," her father suggested. "Don't you have a Sanctuary group near you?"

For the month that she was home, Amberlin looked in the mirror and saw saddlebags of thick dough on her hips, her ankles, her fleshy arms. Her face was plain, her cheeks were plainly fat, and she was too tall and lumbering. She had caved to social pressure, given up all her carefully constructed moral codes, was so greedy that she craved both men and women as well as a Big Mac, and this was the inevitable punishing result.

By the time she returned to college, armed with her mother's special concoction to ward off hunger and burn calories at the same time, she had determined that her life of gluttony had to end. And by a quirk of fate, Sarah was in the same frame of mind. Her last boyfriend, from Ghana, had left her for a woman who was five foot ten and weighed about one hundred ten pounds. Sarah was determined to get him back.

Together, they formulated a plan. They stopped going to the dining halls. Stopped all trips to fast-food places. Cleaned their room of all snacks and crumbs and unplugged the small refrigerator where they stashed leftovers. And they tried diets.

The premixed milk-based diet drinks made Sarah flatulent and headachy. The diets that required real cooking were impossible, and the diets that were hinged on exercise didn't leave them time to get their work done. They finally chose the grapefruit and egg diet, which was big at the time.

It consisted of eating one small meal the first day, six eggs and two grapefruits the next day, and fasting the third day. The rules were easy to remember, the eggs could be cooked on a hot plate, and the program was easy to follow. Amberlin felt something like joy that became ecstasy hinged on the power she had to stick to these rules. She lost her extra twenty pounds within a month, and decided to keep going, since she was getting so good at this.

As she dropped the next ten pounds, people told her she was looking sick, but she chalked that up to jealousy at her transformation. Her body and face were changing, winnowing away any unnecessary baggage as she stepped into her power. It was a heavy power. She could feel the burden of it in her legs, which walked sluggishly, and her head, which sometimes pounded as if weights were sitting right on her skull, but the heaviness of it was just another indication of its strength. Like a weight lifter in training, her capacity to bear her increasing power grew with practice, so that the more the diet dragged her down, the taller she stood. She could do anything.

Her success was accented further by the fact that Sarah lasted only three weeks before she went back to what Amberlin now considered the demeaning world of real food. She was stronger than Sarah. And since her abnegation of food dissipated all sexual feelings, she felt she'd even triumphed over her sexual greed. She didn't have to worry about who or what she wanted as long as she continued not to eat. Her victory was complete, and all the sustenance she needed.

She supposed she would have starved herself to death if the planets hadn't lined up in an extraordinary way. It was called Harmonic Convergence, and she was listening to a radio show about it while she swept classroom floors late at night after classes, which was her work-study assignment that semester.

Harmonic Convergence meant that a perfect alignment of the planets had occurred, the radio announcer said, adding that many people believed this meant the world was about to end. Amberlin was pushing the broom silently along the gray linoleum floor between the metal and Formica chairs, and there was nobody in the building except for her and Jasmine, who was cleaning the bathrooms next door. Jasmine was an old yellow-skinned black woman who smoked long, bent Carlton cigarettes and had orange hair. Poverty and overwork made her thin and bent as her cigarettes. The closest she got to higher education was cleaning bathrooms for people who went to school. Amberlin felt guilty about her life in comparison to Jasmine's, but remained confused as to what she should do about it.

"Hey, Jasmine," she called. "You hear that? Radio says the world's about to end."

Amberlin heard the sound of a toilet flushing. Footsteps.

Jasmine appeared in the classroom doorway and turned her slightly wandering eye up at the heavens. "How you know it ain't?" she asked.

Amberlin couldn't find an answer.

Suddenly it seemed possible that the world would end while she was sweeping the floor. Why not? Though her exposure to the variety of religions in the world had taught her more skepticism than respect, it seemed possible now that those who believed in magic or religion or the planets could be right, and she could be wrong.

Jasmine was still standing in the doorway, and Amberlin thought that maybe her own eyes had gone transparent and this old woman knew exactly what she was thinking. Maybe she was, in fact, from another planet. One of those lined-up planets where everyone knew exactly the best way to live.

She leaned against her broom and felt the motion of the planets inside her, all of them lining up, and she was suddenly transported to the space between them. The sky sliced through her, pale and indifferent, as the absence of atmosphere sucked her away into nowhere, into that place where there were no boundaries. No rules she could read. No diet she could possibly follow.

It was a long fall to nowhere, but it felt pretty good, so she let it happen. The next thing she saw was Jasmine's face peering into hers, inverted. At first she thought it was a new planet. Then she realized she'd passed out, was flat on her back, and the old woman was leaning over her, looking scared.

"Is it over?" she asked.

"What? What?" Jasmine sputtered.

"The world. Is it over?"

Jasmine patted her shoulder. "You just lie here, and I'll call someone. You got family nearby?"

Family. Amberlin gasped in horror at the thought of her family being called. "I'm fine," she said, sitting up, finding her legs and standing. "I just . . . didn't eat enough today. Low blood sugar."

"Hey," Jasmine called after her as she made her way down the hall, but Amberlin didn't stop.

She stumbled her way back to her dorm room, where she could collapse in better form on her own bed, without her family's intervention. As soon as she got herself into her room and on her bed, Sarah's head popped up from her pillow.

"Hi," she said. "You're home early."

"I didn't feel well," Amberlin said.

"No wonder. The diet you've been on."

Amberlin lay on her bed, shaking and confused, not sure what had just happened to her. She'd heard stories about first-year students cracking up. A premed student with a 4.0 GPA who was found in the cafeteria one morning buttering all the cups. She didn't want to turn out like that.

"Sarah," she said, "is insanity hereditary, or can you make yourself crazy?"

Sarah was silent for a moment. "Have you been talking to your parents?" she asked.

"No. I just . . . want to know your opinion. Even if you do everything right, and have the right genes and know everything you need to know, can you still make yourself crazy?"

Sarah nodded and replied quietly, "Sometimes doing everything right is what pushes you over the edge. But it's a long way back, and nobody can get you there except you."

Her words went into Amberlin's bloodstream like an IV, and invaded her center. She went to the refrigerator, where Sarah had left three apples, a carton of milk, and two crusty slices of pizza.

She felt as if she were actually growing lighter with every bite. As if she had in fact become so heavy with her diet that she couldn't eat enough to lose the weight she'd gained on it. The burden of it was gravity, sucking her down into those interplanetary spaces, leaving nothing of her except the diet itself, which weighed more than any sorrow.

When she finished the pizza, it had tasted so good, she went to the phone and ordered another. And though she didn't let herself know how she felt about women until Sherry came into her life, for the first time in her life she was aware of how good it was to get something exactly wrong.

TERESA'S KITCHEN

WHEN TERESA OPENED HER BACK DOOR AND STEPPED into the kitchen, she heard the sound of crashing and of glass breaking below her. She looked down at the floor, down at her feet, and said a small but very powerful prayer.

Silence returned quickly, and she waited, staring hard at the cellar door, which was cracked open. She heard the sound of footsteps ascending. The sound of someone coughing a little, then clearing her throat. Finally, Amberlin's long arm reached out and grabbed the doorjamb as she pulled herself up and into the kitchen.

"Jesus, Mary, and Joseph," Teresa said, seeing the look on Amberlin's face and the gun that dangled carelessly in her hand. "What did you do?"

Amberlin gave a slightly hysterical laugh. She lifted her empty hand and pointed her long, elegant finger at Teresa. "How come," she said, "you think I'm rigid and foolish. That I'm wrong to try and get it right."

Teresa put her hand on her hip and tapped a foot. "How come you think I'm hell-bent on getting it wrong? Compulsively independent. Overly dramatic."

"You trust Delia more than you trust me," Amberlin said accusingly. "You like her better."

Teresa shrugged. "I've known her longer. I don't like her better. I know her better."

Amberlin dropped her arm to her side. "That's why?"

"Well, yes," Teresa said. "Of course. I mean, she's been around long enough that I know she won't scoot at the first sign of my stupidity."

Amberlin looked at Teresa's proud stance, her one hand on her hip and her chin high, and from there saw for the first time that her eyes were a little shy, and vulnerable. A new thought occurred to her. Teresa was afraid of being abandoned. Amberlin almost opened her mouth to say something, and then stopped herself. She understood suddenly how that wouldn't do any good, and wouldn't be right.

"Don't you know that about me?" she asked instead.

Teresa scanned Amberlin, and a half grin began to form on her face. "Not yet," she said, "but I will."

Amberlin started a smile in response, then dropped it. "How? How will you know?"

"How do you know when the sauce is ready? Time and love, I suppose," Teresa said. She held out a hand, conciliatory and generous. Amberlin took it and squeezed.

"You think it's okay that we think these things about each other?" Amberlin asked.

Teresa shrugged. "I still love you. And even when I think you're trying too hard, I appreciate the heart that goes into it."

Amberlin laughed. "You always appreciate heart, because you're so overly dramatic."

Teresa dropped her hand. "Yeah," she said. "Raised on opera. Grand opera." She pointed a finger at the cellar door. "You wanna tell me what happened down there?"

Amberlin nodded, held up the gun. "I should put this back. Maybe wash up."

Teresa followed her upstairs to her own room, where Amberlin put the gun down on the bureau, and then to the bathroom. Frothing over with excitement and soap, Amberlin told her what she did, what Christine did, and what she thought it meant.

"She ducked, Teresa. Don't you see what that means?" she said, beaming, wiping her face with a towel. "Don't you see?"

"Not really," Teresa said. "All I see is you threw away a lot of my good tomatoes."

"For a good cause, Teresa. What I did proves that Christine doesn't want to die. She protected herself. Instinctively. Without any thought at all. She doesn't want to die. Maybe that means we can let her go."

"No," Teresa said with finality. "Not yet." She turned and walked out of the bathroom. Amberlin followed Teresa down the stairs and into the kitchen.

"Where are you going?" Amberlin asked.

Teresa paused briefly, one hand on the cellar door.

"You want heat? I gotta bleed the line."

She disappeared down the cellar, closing the door behind her. Amberlin debated following her, but the kitchen door swung open and Delia entered, carrying a garment bag.

"Good morning," she said. "Kids're fine. Husband's fine. I've got my blue velvet and am ready to rock and roll. Where's Teresa?"

The cellar door creaked open, answering her question.

"Hey," Delia said again. "What's going on?"

"Not much," Teresa said. "We got heat, and a lot of work to do. Gotta get the rest of the vegetables chopped and the sauce for the salmon done."

"Wait a minute," Amberlin said. "What about Christine?"

Teresa went to the refrigerator and got out vegetables, flung them on the chopping block. "She's sleeping," Teresa said. "I gave her a towel to wipe off the tomatoes."

"Tomatoes?" Delia asked, looking now from Amberlin's agitated face to Teresa's back, which expressed stubbornness with eloquence.

The phone rang. All three women jumped and stared at one another.

"Don't answer," Teresa hissed at Amberlin as her hand went for it.

Amberlin pushed her chin out defiantly and picked it up.

"Hello?" she asked. She mouthed the word *James* as she listened. "No, of course she's not," she said, and listened for a protracted period of time. Delia hung her dress over a chair and sat.

"Now, why would we keep her from you? If we knew, and she *wanted* us to tell you, of course we would."

Teresa held her hand out and whispered, "Give it to me. Give it to me." Amberlin flapped a hand back to shoo her off.

"Yes, you're certainly invited to the open house. My understanding is that she's gone off by herself to think, but there's no animosity toward you that I know of."

"I know of some," Teresa said. Amberlin shushed her, nodded her head.

"Yes, I will. I'll tell her. Certainly. Good-bye, James."

She hung up.

"Oh, my," Delia said. "Is he calling the cops yet?"

"Not yet. He called before, all bent out of shape that we weren't getting back to him. I told him to come tonight. You heard me."

"Shit," Teresa said. "He won't."

"He might," Amberlin said. "Though I have to say he's shown all the spine of a jellyfish up to this point. But if he does, we have to let her go. And I really think she's ready."

"Because she ducked a jar of tomatoes?" Teresa said.

"Could somebody please tell me what's going on?" Delia asked.

"It's Christine. She ducked the tomatoes," Amberlin said, and when Delia rolled her eyes and groaned, explained more fully. Teresa, her back to them, washed vegetables and sorted them on the chopping block.

Delia looked relieved. "That's fabulous. So let's bring her up. What do you say, Teresa?"

Teresa turned to the counter and picked a heavy chopping knife from her knife block, ran her finger along the edge. She shook her head.

"No?" Delia said. "That's it? Just no?"

"Just no," Teresa said firmly, slicing a pepper in half.

"Well, who the fuck died and left you pope?"

"Delia," Amberlin remonstrated.

"No, I mean it. Teresa, you can't just say no. You can't act like nobody's involved in this except you."

"She's my responsibility," Teresa said.

"And she's our friend," Amberlin replied.

Teresa pulled the seeds and white core from the pepper before she raised her face and gave them each a piercing glance. "No," she repeated. "No. No. No. We will *not* untie her tonight. No." She turned her back on them and went back to chopping. Hard.

Delia pointed to the front of her head and tapped at it. Amberlin shook her head, then held up a finger for Delia's silence.

"Teresa," she said, "I really think it's okay now. Odds are, she didn't really want to do this in the first place. Many first-time suicide attempts are a cry for help. And it's a good sign that she came to you. Maybe she was even hoping you'd stop her."

"No," Teresa said.

"Pigheaded," Delia said. "You're being pigheaded, and I think we have a right to an explanation."

"No you don't. It's my family."

"Your family. Your family? And what are we, here? Outsiders? You think you gotta control the whole damn show?"

"Yes," Teresa said. "I do. This time, I do. I didn't try to force it with my parents when Nan was crazy and needed help and they were ignoring her. I didn't push to take Christine because my husband didn't want to. I didn't see a lawyer and get divorced when I should have because Donnie would be upset. Too many times I knew something and let it go. This time I'm not letting it go."

"Teresa—what're you talking about?"

"I'm talking about what I knew and didn't do anything about. Like Nan." Little pieces of green flew out from under her knife, and each of her words was echoed by a hit of the knife against the chopping block.

"Nan?" Delia asked. "What's she got to do with it?"

"Nan. My sister. The night before she shot herself, she called me from the rehab. To say good-bye."

Delia pressed a hand against the counter and supported herself against it. Amberlin grew still.

She might not believe in ghosts, but she knew when one had walked into the room, and at that moment Nan whispered her way into Teresa's kitchen and stood behind her sister.

"I asked her, 'Nan, whaddya mean, good-bye?' " Teresa said, not looking at the ghost. Just chopping and chopping at the pepper. " 'You're there to get well. Fourth time's a charm, right?' "

Amberlin took a few tentative steps toward her, then stopped. Nan took in a deep, sad breath and let it go. Teresa kept her eyes on her work, and when she spoke, her voice was tight and pained. "I knew she meant to do it. I knew it and I didn't do anything about it. God, I'm so stupid. So stupid about people. *Stupida,* stupid."

Teresa chopped and chopped and choked out words.

"I'm stupid, and I let my sister die, and my husband fuck around, and my kid stay angry at me. I didn't take Christine when I should've, but I won't let her die. I know you think it was wrong—I hit her in the head, I tied her up—but fuck that. For once in my life I did something instead of just shutting up and going away. And I won't I won't I *won't* let her die."

Nan's ghost shook her head. She turned and appealed to Delia and Amberlin, her expression a mixture of sorrow and impatience. You do something with her, she seemed to say. You see how she is.

Delia nodded, stepped to her, and put her hand on Teresa's. "I think," she said firmly, "you should put the knife down."

Through the blur of tears Teresa looked down and saw what her hand was doing—still working, still making food, still chopping at the vegetables. "God. I'm like that rabbit on TV," she said, sobbing. "I keep going and going even when I don't know why."

"You know why you keep going," Amberlin said softly, coming closer. "And so do we."

Their kindness pierced her more than any cruelty ever had, and inside her chest she felt as if an old tight cough were breaking up, but into tears that racked her body, poured out of her with words she never knew she kept under all that water, all that old, old water.

Amberlin led her to the kitchen table, sat her down, and poured Teresa a short glass of sweet vermouth. Teresa could feel Nan hovering at her back, pressing a hand against her shoulder, putting her face close to Teresa's ear, speaking into it so she could hear the words inside her head and inside her heart.

"We shared a room, and divided the closet in half. Scratched our initials on the wall," Nan said inside her. "We used to eat pizzelle with ice cream in the middle. Pizzelle sandwiches, in the middle of the afternoon in the summer because Grandma didn't want us to starve between lunch and supper."

Amberlin patted her arm, Delia patted her hand. She took a sip of vermouth. Her throat burned with words and water, as if fire was opening it up.

"We thought we could learn all the spells and fly and touch the stars. We used to get umbrellas and open them and jump off the top step trying to fly. We'd take sheets and make parachutes to jump off the picnic table with. We tried every way we knew to fly."

Teresa felt how wet her face was and that she needed a Kleenex. She felt Nan's hands pressed into her shoulders as if she were putting something into her, giving her something but all the while she felt as if she were crumbling, disintegrating, pieces of herself falling away, washing away in words and water.

And though Teresa didn't turn around to look at the ghost of her sister hovering behind her, she heard her voice speaking as clearly as if they were sitting at Grandma's table, talking about music and boys.

"We did fly," Nan said. "For a while."

Teresa shook her head. "I didn't fly. I didn't. Only you did, and you flew away."

"Yeah," Nan said. "I flew away."

"I couldn't stop you."

"No. You couldn't keep me, Teresa. I wasn't yours to keep."

Teresa put her head down on the table and let it stay that way. She didn't want to hear any more. It hurt too much. Amberlin and Delia looked at each other, and each took a step back. This was a moment for Teresa to be with her sister, and while they wanted to express sympathy, they didn't want to intrude.

Nan sighed patiently and continued, her words echoing against all the painful places inside Teresa's heart. "Remember what I told you? When I was in rehab? Remember?"

"I can't," Teresa moaned. "I can't."

"Yes," Nan said. "You can. I told you I want you to do something for me. I want you to cook yourself a big plate of pasta fra diavolo. Hot as you can make it. Hot so it burns the inside of your mouth and all the way down your throat."

And Teresa did remember. Fra diavolo. Before she killed herself, Nan had told her to cook fra diavolo.

"Then make a plate of brown rice, and cook it so it's almost not done," Nan continued. "Remember I told you to do that? Cook it so it stays rough and scratchy the way Mom made it sometimes. You wouldn't eat it, because you said it hurt. Make it like that, I told you. Remember?"

Teresa nodded.

"Okay. Eat the fra diavolo, and then the rice. And then, make tiramisu and eat that."

Teresa remembered, but she still didn't understand.

"Listen to me, dopey," Nan said. "You were always a dope. Just listen. It's magic. The hot sauce burns the skin off your mouth. The rice scratches your tongue and throat. Then there's nothing left but new skin, all thin and raw, so when you eat the tiramisu, you'll really taste it. Really feel how smooth it is. Nothing between you and the feeling."

"It hurts," Teresa said.

"Yeah," Nan agreed. "It does. Hey, dopey."

"What?"

"Remember what I told you? When you eat the tiramisu," Nan said, "think of me." Nan kissed her sister on the top of her head, lifted her hands from Teresa's shoulders, and whispered herself away.

Teresa remembered. Now she felt a dull ache in her belly, the remnant of sorrow and regret. She remembered the whole conversation, and that after she talked to Nan she tried to call the center and tell someone, but nobody answered at the main switchboard. That time difference—maybe the office wasn't open, maybe she got the number wrong. But she didn't know who else to call, and she told herself she was overreacting, being overly dramatic. And who was she to know so much anyway.

But she knew better, though she wouldn't trust her own knowledge, and her sister's death sat on her shoulders like a wingless angel from that moment to this. She had never made fra diavolo. Couldn't look at brown rice. Never made a tiramisu, though it was a common request from her customers.

Teresa felt a tap on her shoulder and raised her head. Amberlin was holding out a paper towel. She took it.

"Thanks," she said, and wiped her nose. "God, I hate crying. It's so undignified."

"It's a lot to hold in," Amberlin said.

"Yeah," Teresa said. "A lot."

"Well," Delia said, "anybody want to drink heavily? Because I was thinking about it."

Teresa blew her nose again. "You could get me another one of these," she said, holding up her empty glass.

"I don't know how you drink that," Delia said. "It's so sweet, it gives me a headache."

"Mother's milk," Teresa said.

"Comfort food," Amberlin agreed. "I'll take a scotch, myself."

They got their drinks and sat at the table, staring out the window, quiet, each one feeling the recent presence of ghosts.

Delia knew how you could be stilled by moments too big to comprehend. Amberlin knew how easy it was to make no decision instead of risking the wrong one. Each of them wished for some voice that would tell them what to do at the moment it needed doing.

"The thing is," Teresa said at last, "Christine could probably get out if she wanted to badly enough. I didn't tie her tight or anything. So I guess I figure that when she's ready to leave, she'll leave. When she knows she's safe."

"Maybe she needs permission," Amberlin suggested. "She thinks so much of you."

"Yeah," Teresa said, "wish I did. Nan had all the self-confidence in the family, and then that turned out not to be such a good thing. Made me wonder if it wasn't best to just keep your mouth shut and your profile low."

"You couldn't have stopped Nan," Delia said. "She did what she wanted, regardless."

"You think so?" Teresa asked. "That's how you saw her?"

"Well, I didn't know her like you did. She was pretty much gone by the time we got to be friends, but I remember thinking that she was like one of the fairy people my father used to tell stories about. Ready to slip off the edge of the world at a moment's notice. You were here." Delia picked a foot up and planted it down on the floor again. "Like that."

"That's one thing I'll say about you," Amberlin agreed.

"You're here. I think Christine's got some of that toughness in her too."

"She's gotta be resilient to grow up with Nan and still be okay. Sort of."

"What do you think brought it on?" Amberlin asked. "The holidays? James?"

"Mostly I think it's the anniversary," Teresa said. "Nan's seven years dead. It's time to let go. And she doesn't want to. Neither do I."

"Is that why you always talk about her like she's still alive?" Amberlin asked. "I think this is the first time I ever got it through my head that she's not."

"Huh," Delia said. "You're right, Amberlin. I do it too, without even thinking."

Whenever Nan's name came up, it was as if she were someone living very far away that Teresa no longer had contact with, so she never talked about what Nan was doing now. But at the same time she spoke about her as if she were still a vital force in the world, still affecting her and, in that sense, still very much alive.

"I guess," Teresa said, "she is."

Teresa swallowed the rest of her vermouth and let her face rest in her hands. She mumbled something the women couldn't hear.

"What?" Delia asked.

Teresa pulled her hand back. "I said Christine never cried. At her mother's funeral she didn't cry. I asked her about it, and she said she stopped crying for her mother years ago, but I didn't believe her. I thought maybe someday she'd need to cry and someone would have to be around to hold her hand. Someone who knew her mother."

"Hold her hand, or hit her on the head?" Delia said wryly.

"Well, that can help the tears get started too," Teresa said.

If Christine could feel really bad for a while, then maybe she'd be a little better. See her life a little more clearly. There'd be more room in her for being alive. That's what Teresa thought anyway. Now she didn't know much at all except that she was the one crying, and Christine, so far as she knew, was just the same as before.

"Look," she said, "I'll let her go after the party. Then I can follow her around, stay with her and not be distracted. Tonight, when everyone goes, I'll untie her and . . . and give her permission to leave. But if I let her go now, I'd never forgive myself if she actually did anything to hurt herself. So after the party, okay?"

"Okay," Delia said. "After the party. And we can all spend some time with her."

"I've got the name of a really good psychiatrist who specializes in grief," Amberlin said. "I met her once, and she's very warm. Very nice."

Teresa grinned. "You get a commission?" she asked.

"Of course not! Oh. That was a joke, wasn't it?" Amberlin smiled. "Okay. After the party. She'll be—well, I guess *fine* isn't the right word."

"*Alive* is the right word," Teresa said. She pressed her hands down on the table and pushed herself up. She looked at the clock. "Time," she said. "We've gotta move. God, I still don't know what I'm wearing. What're you wearing, Amberlin?"

"My bronze dress. The one you like. You should wear the green silk pant thing."

Delia leaned down and whispered to Teresa, "Good idea. Rowan likes green." Teresa rolled her eyes and Delia squeezed her arm and said, "Be right back."

She went into the living room and came back with a cobalt-blue vase that had two tulips and a spray of pink flowers in it. Under her arm was the Irish lace tablecloth.

She touched the pink flowers. "What's this called, Teresa?"

"Witches' broom," she said. "Why?"

"I picked it up on my way over. I'm gonna bring it down to Christine." She nodded toward the door.

Teresa chewed on her lip and watched her make the descent, which for Delia felt much easier this time, with the two women waiting upstairs and enough light around her that she could see.

She carried her glass of flowers as if it were the only one of its kind in the world. She stood in front of the plate Teresa had left the night before, which still had the ceci cookie on it. Christine was just a heap under a bundle of blankets. She was no bigger or stronger to Delia's eye than her father had been when the flesh left him as he was dying. No bigger or stronger than her children when they were first born. She had all the fragility of the dying and the newly born, and Delia wondered which one she would turn out to be when this holiday was over.

"Christine," she whispered, and waited. There was no answer, but the blankets moved, and her head emerged with her eyes open.

"I brought this," Delia said, showing her the flowers. "I thought you might like it."

Christine still said nothing, but she continued to stare at Delia, who waited to see if any more horrible visions of burning emptiness would appear in her eyes. But none did. Delia stood very still and listened in the gray light. She could hear her heart beating. Hear her lungs pulling in breath and pushing it out again. She could hear Christine breathing too, only that was more labored.

Delia was at a good point in her life. She loved her husband, her kids were great, her work was going well. She had a house, she could pay all her bills and afford extra for vacations and gifts. She had good friends. Very good friends. Her health was fine, and she had more energy than any one person deserved. She was happy.

And even though she knew it would change, because time changes everything, she didn't want it to. She wanted no tragedy or profound pain to interfere with the party she was having in her life right now. Maybe that was selfish. Maybe it was just wise. But in the face of a friend who had pain, it was certainly impossible. She couldn't wish it away, couldn't organize a better deal on this one.

Delia listened to the pain Christine wasn't talking about, and felt it enter her like a hand moving into her chest and wrapping itself around her heart, saying, "It's like this. Can you hear it? Can you feel it?"

She lowered her head onto her chest and listened, felt tears fall out of her eyes and into the vase she was carrying. She tried to gulp them back, but couldn't, and through the haze of water saw Christine staring at her, eyes wide and mouth gaping.

"I'm sorry," Delia whispered. She hadn't come down here to upset Christine more, make it worse by crying all over her. "I'm sorry," she repeated. "I just wish you were happy."

She put the tablecloth down, put the vase of flowers next to it, and turned away.

Christine watched her turn away, and when she was at the steps called out to her.

"Delia?" she asked. Delia stopped and turned back to her.

"Thank you," Christine said. "Thanks a lot."

She disappeared into her blankets, and Delia wiped her eyes and ascended the steps.

ABOUT EATING LIGHT

CHRISTINE HAD ALWAYS BEEN A LITTLE AFRAID OF the dark, and of night in general, since that was when her mother was most likely to get drunk and start singing too loudly or dancing too hard or get in a fight with her boyfriend. Night was filled with waiting for her. Waiting for the neighbors to call the police on them. Waiting for one of Nan's boyfriends to get too drunk and hit her. Waiting for Nan to pass out or throw up, whichever it would be that night. Waiting for the demons that would emerge from her mother, whom she loved and sometimes hated and sometimes saw in herself. She'd run from the darkness, toward anything that was light. This last time she had tried to get as light as she could and go away altogether. But she'd failed.

Or else she'd found the darkness under the light, which was always there, waiting to drag you down into it. She wondered, if she kept going down into it, whether there would also be light under the darkness. Maybe that's why Teresa tied her up. So she'd sit still long enough to get there in the quiet of the long night, the big dark, the winter solstice and its dreams.

She rested her head back on the pile of blankets, and the pipe next to her began to hum as a tap was turned on upstairs. There were all kinds of things happening in the cellar, she found. Hummings and little jolts of mechanics and creakings of wood. The scuttle of a mouse across the floor. The spider silently weaving its web above her. The furnace going on and off again. Water rushing through pipes. All the hidden necessities occurred here, and she had never known it because she was afraid of the dark. Afraid to see what lived down below. Afraid to come in out of the light.

She felt no inclination to try to undo her ropes and run away. Teresa hissed at her—something about putting a spell on them—but she didn't really believe in spells, and didn't think Teresa did either. Still, she didn't want to try. If she did, Teresa would most likely hit her in the head with a vacuum cleaner next. She figured she might as well wait until things calmed down. Then she'd be able to leave and do what she needed to do at her leisure. With dignity.

For now it was enough to sit and listen to the cellar do its work, listen to what walked inside her, deep down at the bottom of her, let it come out and play with the spiders and mice.

There was humiliation at the thought that Amberlin might tell the others she was just crying wolf because she'd ducked when jars came flying at her. They might read that as a sign that she didn't really want to kill herself but just wanted attention. Under that was the fear that maybe she did want to live after all. That seemed like such an enormous commitment to make right now, and she wondered if she'd ever actually made that commitment before. She was born. So she was alive. But had she ever said she wanted to live? Most definitely and with all her heart wanted to live?

It hadn't ever come up, really.

When Nan was alive, Christine was too busy making sure she stayed alive. When Nan died, she was too busy trying to figure out how to walk around as one person in the world, instead of being Nan's daughter. Too busy trying not to feel all the complicated feelings of her grief.

Right now, if anyone asked, she would say she didn't know what she wanted. She would say it took too much energy to want anything. She would say please leave me alone.

The furnace began its rattle and hum, and she sat up, looking for the small spark of ignition she could see through the little window part deep within it. Her space, she realized, was beginning to resemble a scene of ancient sacrifice. There was the great fire to burn the incense in. There was the blood of the sacrificial tomatoes all over the wall. Pieces of cheese and crusts of bread were left on the floor for the gods. One very important ceci cookie sat on a sacred white plate nearby. And next to that, there was a cobalt-blue glass with a red and a white tulip, a spray of pink broom, lifting their blossoms toward the gods.

The color pierced her. The red seemed to collect depth to itself. The white caught the light that filtered from the streetlight, through the cellar window, and shone too brightly through the ambient gray light. They reminded her of the sugar eggs she would see in store windows at Easter, which fascinated her. Nan had actually bought one for her once, and she stared at it for hours, constantly startled by the soft glitter of the shell, the little sugar birds and flowers inside.

The one her mother bought her had two ducks on a blue lake, with sugar tulips around it. As she sat and stared inside, she wondered what it would feel like to live in a world where everything was sweet and soft and contained. It seemed so quiet inside the egg, as if going inside would lend a hush to her life that she'd never find out here, where she sat in a dingy apartment with a mother who drank too much. Inside the egg it was peaceful, beautiful, and life made sense.

She looked around her now at the mosaic of vegetables on the wall, the nest of blankets, the tulips, and smiled wryly. It was quiet. Nothing much disturbed her. Maybe she'd found her egg, tulips and all.

But the tulips were bowls to catch dark and light, holding them, hugging them and radiating them out to her. They seemed hungry for her to see them, really see them. Hungry for her touch.

"All right," she said to them, consenting at last. She stretched herself as far as she could in the tangle of ropes, and her finger brushed against the soft petals of the red tulip. It swayed, and was still. She pulled herself back into her nest and rubbed her index finger against her thumb. The flowers were hungry for her touch. She was hungry too.

She was hungry?

The sensation was disturbing, familiar, and unasked for. She didn't want to be hungry. She had no intention of being hungry ever again. But she was anyway.

"I am hungry," she said out loud to see if it was true. Her stomach rumbled in response. There was an emptiness in her, and a sort of shakiness and a sort of yearning. Her teeth wanted to bite into something. Yes, she had to admit, these were all signs of hunger. She sighed. Her body didn't seem to recognize that she hadn't made up her mind to live.

She was hungry in spite of her intention to die. Did she intend to die?

She knew that upstairs the final preparations for the party were taking place. The women would dress, the waitstaff would arrive, the guests would come in and eat all the marvelous food. A part of her wanted to be there, maybe just out of habit, maybe because she thought the women must miss her presence. They'd become family to her, just as she was to them, and no matter how ticked off you were at family, you still missed them if they weren't there.

She wasn't sure if all of these rumblings and hummings inside her meant she'd changed her mind about staying alive. She had no reason to have changed her mind. Nothing else had changed. Nothing except her feeling, which right now was a combination of hunger, fatigue, and a stirring of interest in the world around her. Was that enough to stay alive for? The chance to eat, and sleep, and poke at the world to see if it was ticklish or not?

The red tulip and the white tulip sat in their cobalt-blue glass and absorbed energy in the form of light and darkness, radiating both back to her. Christine lay back down and stared at them, asking nothing of them, only listening to the rustlings and hummings that continued around and within her.

TERESA'S KITCHEN

WHEN AMBERLIN TOLD JAMES HE WAS CERTAINLY INvited to the party, he resisted the urge to shout at her that he didn't need an invitation, that he would be there whether they wanted him or not. After all, Christine was still his fiancée, as far as he knew.

The women, he decided, were trying to drive him away, trying to drive him mad, but he wouldn't give them the satisfaction of losing his temper. Amberlin was goading him, hinting that Christine didn't want to see him, but she talked as if she knew where Christine was. They all knew, he was sure, and they were trying to keep him from her.

Teresa wasn't panicked, and Amberlin was cool as ice. Probably between them and Delia—though he thought Delia liked him—they had Christine's head so turned around, she didn't know what to think or do. Maybe Teresa had finally talked her into leaving him. Or, as the cop said, dumping him.

But Christine wouldn't do it this way. She was too mature for that. They'd had discussions about the right and the wrong way to end a relationship, and had agreed that if it ever came to that, they'd be adult about it. No. She wasn't dumping him. Either Teresa was preying on her fears and talking her into staying away from him, or, more likely, she'd had some kind of emotional crisis—maybe even a psychotic break—and Teresa was hiding her from him. Thinking she could take care of it herself. He was surprised that the others would go along with that, especially Amberlin, but Teresa could be forceful. Stubborn. Pigheaded. And she was their boss, after all.

If the women knew where Christine was, as seemed likely, then they weren't worried about him finding her at the party, which meant she wasn't there. Unless they were bluffing.

He'd cruised by the house a few times earlier in the day to see if he could spot her. He didn't, but he thought he could see her car in the back driveway. It was hard to tell because of the angle of the drive and with Delia's car blocking his view, but it might be her car. And if so, sooner or later, she'd have to appear too.

As he came home, he wondered if he was losing too much of his own emotional cool, falling into a trap of too much heat and not enough thought. It was out of character for him to react this way, sneaking around and spying, calling repeatedly and being almost rude to women. He'd always considered himself a gentleman, and too sophisticated, too emotionally savvy for any of the strange behaviors associated with obsession. He didn't stalk. He didn't pry. He didn't spy. A relationship was based on mutual trust and respect, and had no room for that kind of behavior.

But this was different, he told himself. This wasn't about his ego. It was about Christine's safety and well-being. He didn't have to sink into melodrama to know what was right to do. He had to find Christine and get her away from the toxic influence that surrounded her.

He decided that instead of going to the party, he'd watch the party. If he saw Christine, he'd go in. If not, he'd figure out some way to get the police over there and search the damn house. It seemed like the most reasonable response.

FOR THE REMAINDER OF THE DAY, THE WOMEN WERE TOO busy to worry about anything except getting food onto plates, getting plates onto tables, getting tables set up, and chairs put out, and more food onto plates, more plates onto tables. Amberlin and Delia stepped down the cellar stairs every hour or so to ask Christine if she wanted anything, and reported back to Teresa that she was eyeing them with more curiosity than rage. But she didn't want anything. At least, nothing she would name.

The party was to start at seven, and by four, everything was ready and the waitstaff had arrived. The women went into Teresa's room and shook out their party clothes and their party faces and tried them all on.

"God, I'm getting fat," Delia said, smoothing the blue velvet over her hips.

"Fat?" Teresa said. "Are trees fat?" She put her face to the mirror and thought it looked tired, needed more mascara or something.

Amberlin came out of the bathroom draped in bronze satin, and Delia made an appreciative sound. "Thanks," she said. "I like it too."

"The confidence of youth." Delia sighed. She looked Teresa up and down. "You, on the other hand, are too thin. It would do you good to expand some."

"Yeah," Teresa said, running her hands down her waist, across her hips to her thighs. "Maybe it would."

"Do you think," Amberlin asked, "men ever do this? Stare into a mirror and criticize their looks?"

"Not often enough," Delia said wryly. "Let's go."

They descended the stairs from Teresa's room to the living room just in time for the doorbell to ring the first time. Teresa opened the door to Michael, who had his father and the children with him. Jessamyn greeted Teresa prettily, even curtsied in her red velvet dress, and was sufficiently admired.

"Will there be lots of people?" she asked Teresa.

"The house should be full," Teresa said. "Why?"

"I want them *all* to look at me," she said, twirling so that her skirt billowed out around her. "Everyone."

"Already it starts," Teresa said.

Anthony shook her hand and mumbled something, to which Teresa responded, "Y'know, if it gets boring, there's a TV upstairs in the room next to mine."

He moved his eyes this way and that, to see if his parents had heard. Then part of his mouth tried out a smile and he said clearly, "Thanks."

"Hey," Delia said loudly, "kids." She opened her arms and scooped them in, one at a time, kissed them each soundly, and then released them.

"Mom, you'll mess up my dress," Jessamyn complained.

"Would you believe I could have such a dainty girl, Teresa?"

"No accounting for genes," Teresa replied. "How are you, Michael."

He stooped down and kissed her cheek. He was a tall man. "Good, Teresa. You've met my father, haven't you?"

Teresa stuck her hand out. "At Jessamyn's birthday party a few years ago," she said. "Good to see you again." His hand was dry and cool in hers, his grin worked on only half of his face.

"Eh," he said. "Eh ka."

Michael found his father a comfortable chair and sat him down, and Delia, after chewing on her lip and looking worried, got him a good pillow and filled a plate for him, and the door opened for Sherry, who brought her guitar and set up a chair near the fireplace, where she'd spend a good deal of time strumming Christmas carols. As people drank wine and ate and relaxed, someone would start a sing-along, and her voice would ring out above theirs like a bell, but everyone would enjoy the sound of their own voice most.

Sherry looked at Amberlin as if she were the best treat to find under the Christmas tree, and the color rose in Amberlin's cheeks at her glance. They moved across the room to each other like water finding its level from a variety of sources, and Amberlin held out a hand to her. Sherry took it briefly, squeezed it, kissed her on the cheek.

It was an unobjectionable move, but the look that passed between them was so intimate, Teresa turned away, not wanting to invade their privacy. She pulled the curtain back on the window, letting in the blinking lights in the neighborhood, and seeing who might show up next.

A blue BMW was parked across the street. She stared at it hard, waiting for someone to get out, and then realized who it was sitting in the driver's seat. Her lips went tight. She pulled the curtain shut.

"Hail Mary," she said. "Blue BMW. James."

She opened the curtain a crack and peeked out. It was James, but he didn't seem to be getting ready to get out. He was fiddling with something on the passenger side, and then she saw him put something up to his eyes. Binoculars? She pulled the curtain shut again.

James was parked outside, spying on them. What a fool, she

thought. Her irritation at his stupidity was subsumed under the realization that he must be hungry sitting out there in the cold, and maybe if he had some food in him, he might not behave so badly. She'd make him a plate, and maybe they could talk like reasonable people.

No oysters, she thought. That would be bad form. But shrimp would be right. Jumbo shrimp and cocktail sauce. A piece of fried cod too, and a few mushrooms. And, of course, some of the small hot red sausages she got especially for the occasion. They were very small.

She piled the food on, got a cup of hot cider, and put on her coat and wrapped a scarf around her head. It would be cold tonight. Frosty and clear, and the moon at the full.

She left by the back door and walked down her driveway. As she went, she could see James staring into his opera glasses at her window. He was so intent on whatever he was watching that he didn't see her approach, and when she tapped on his car door, he jumped so hard, he hit his head on the roof.

"Anyone home?" she asked. "It's the Welcome Wagon." She held out the plate of food.

He rolled his window down, rubbing at his head. "More like the *un*welcome wagon," he said.

"You can come inside, James. You're welcome as long as Christine says you are, and she hasn't said you aren't. Yet."

James glared at her. "You're worse than any mother-in-law, aren't you?" he said.

"Only if you're very lucky, and get a little smarter than you are now," Teresa replied. "I brought some food. Here."

She pushed the plate through the window, and he was torn for a minute between wanting to refuse, and then catching the aroma that wafted to him from the plate. His stomach won over his morals, which Teresa approved. As he filled his mouth with shrimp, he pointed a finger at her.

"You know where she is," he said.

"What makes you think that?"

"Because if you didn't, you'd be out looking for her."

Teresa could keep silent about the truth, but she couldn't outright deny it, so she lifted a shoulder and let it fall. James clucked his tongue against the roof of his mouth and shook his head. He got a couple of sausages in his mouth and chewed hard.

"You, of all people," he said, "should know better than to try to keep Christine from the medical help she needs."

"Is that what you are to her? Medical help?" Teresa asked softly. "I thought you wanted to be her husband."

"I do," he said, bread and sausage spraying out of his mouth. "Of course I do, but you know what her family history is. Teresa, we had a fight. I'm afraid of what she'll do. And you would be too if you weren't so hell-bent on stuffing your feelings."

Teresa fixed her eyes on his mouth, which was chewing hard to deal with all the food he'd put into it.

"I'm not the one who's stuffing anything right now," she noted mildly.

"Very funny," he said. "But you won't laugh if she ends up like her mother, will you?"

Teresa shook her head. "Christine's not Nan. And she's not crazy. Sometimes I think you'd rather she was, which'd let you off the hook. Or make you feel like a bigger man or something."

James stopped chewing and tried to push the plate back at her, but she put her hands behind her back and wouldn't take it.

"Stick to what you know, Teresa," he said. "You know food. I know what's healthy and what's not."

"You think I don't know what's healthy? What's real?" Teresa said testily. "I lived with Nan. She was my sister. I knew her when she was well, and I knew her when she was sick. I can tell the difference."

"You wouldn't know healthy or real if it walked up to you and kissed you," James said, gesturing at her with a shrimp. "On the mouth."

Teresa put a hand on her hip and tapped her foot. "Come inside if you get cold, James. Stay out here if you want. Suit yourself."

She turned away from him, and he shouted after her, "I know she's in there, Teresa, but you can't keep her there forever. And if the cops show up with a warrant, you'll have no choice in the matter anymore."

Teresa continued walking until his voice faded as she reached the top of the driveway. She stood outside her back door for a moment, considering his words, considering whether they were a real danger or just words he made to fluff up his ego after a bad time of it. Probably the latter, she thought. If he really wanted to make trouble, or, more important, if he really wanted to see Christine, he would have come inside when she invited him.

She thought maybe she should go back and ask him why he didn't do that, why he didn't just come in and search the house now, but then, if he said yes, he would, she wasn't sure what he'd do. They were playing a pretty stupid game together, she thought. And she wished he would just go away.

Her cat brushed itself against her legs, and she bent down to pet him. "What're you doing here, sweetie?" she asked. "Didn't Delia put you down in the cellar?"

Apparently she forgot, Teresa thought. She picked up the cat and stood, coming up so quickly that she didn't see the figure of a man looming above her, and she almost bopped him in the chin with her head. Something flew from his hand and landed on the sidewalk.

"Oh," she said, taking a step back and releasing the cat, who scooted to wait for her by the door. "Oh." She peered through the semidarkness. "Rowan?" she asked.

"That's correct," he said, bending and putting his hands on whatever he'd dropped. She bent with him. "What is it? Did it break? I'm sorry, I didn't even see you there."

"It's okay," he said. "I didn't see you either. Not until I was right on top of you. Maybe you wanna put a light on back here?"

"Most people come to the front door," she noted.

"Habit," he said. "I'm a back-door man."

She laughed nervously and stood as he stood, holding the object he'd dropped out to her.

"Well, I might as well give it to you here," he said, and pushed it toward her. "Merry Christmas."

"But you already gave me a present," she protested.

"This is different," he said, and put something that felt like a small wreath in her hands. "Take it. It's a present for me too."

"Oh. What is it?"

"Mistletoe," he said, and he leaned down and kissed her.

She was inclined to pull back, but his lips were soft and seemed to say something she'd wanted to hear for a while, though they spoke very quietly, which meant she had to listen very closely. She stood still, letting him kiss her, listening to what his lips said. Then she moved closer, to hear them better, and he wrapped one of his large arms around her shoulders and helped her get closer yet.

James was wrong, she thought. She knew what was real and healthy when it kissed her on the mouth. And when it did, she knew enough to shut up and listen.

BREAD AND ROSES

THERE WERE, OF COURSE, ROSES. ROSES BURGEONING with red and glowing white. Roses layered in full bloom, wide open, spreading their fragrance, and roses in tight and graceful bud, the edges of their petals curling only slightly outward to give a hint of future blossom. The house was filled with the scent of them, sounding as a descant above the aromas of food and the crackling smoky smell of a fireplace at its job.

The house filled up with people, each of whom would go home with a full belly and at least one rose. For many of them Teresa would also make plates to take home, which was a tradition she remembered from every family party she'd ever been to. Weddings and showers and funerals and graduation parties alike, at the end some woman would be standing with an empty paper plate, saying, "Take some home for your kids?"

For your husband. For your mother. For yourself. Just take some, because the world is all about sharing food, isn't it? And since, today, I have so much to share, it would please me very much if you took some home.

Sherry played soft music at the fireplace, and guests who stood near her had a moment to stare at the fire dancing while they listened.

Later, when she took her break, Teresa would put on a tape of her favorite arias, sung by her favorite singers. Kiri Te Kanawa. Renata Scotto. Pavarotti and Domingo. Marilyn Horne and Marian Anderson.

As guests arrived and the house filled, she was busy greeting people, talking to customers, catching up with friends. Delia would make sure the right people got to meet each other, found someone to talk with who would be interesting to them. She had a talent for making people comfortable, and an instinctive sense of who would get along with whom. Her sensitivity in these matters ran deep, and though it seemed like a surface skill, it was really the skill of caring about what other people felt. She could mix them the way Teresa mixed flavors, always coming up with something good.

She led Mr. Byron, a VP at the bank, directly to Sister Anna, and they talked theology all night.

"Who'da thunk it," Teresa muttered, watching them lean close to each other and seeing Mr. Byron's pallid face flush with laughter as he waved his arms about. She most often saw him seated very still behind a desk, shuffling papers and speaking in precise tones in a language she still didn't understand. He'd held her hand through the process of incorporation, consulted with her about investments, worked with Delia on the books, and she never once suspected he would like to talk theology with a nun. But Delia knew.

"Hey there, Paul," Delia greeted the man who designed and built her kitchen years ago. "Come over here and meet Candy. She breeds huskies."

Now, what, Teresa wondered, would Paul have to say to Candy, who breeds huskies, besides come home with me and have some fun. But Delia had remembered that Paul had two huskies, which Teresa wasn't sure she ever knew.

Sometimes she worried about her capacity to connect with people. Maybe she spent too much time with her head stuck in a pot and forgot to look at what other people said and did. Forgot to see the people she cooked for. Or maybe in the last year or two, she'd gone into herself, like a seed waiting to sprout into something new. Maybe that's what Christine was doing now. Maybe they were both ready to come out and see the world again. Maybe.

A very large woman with spiky blond hair tapped her on the shoulder and complimented her on the ricotta and spinach torte.

"Thanks," Teresa said. "That was my grandmother's recipe." And all the while she tried to remember if she knew this woman. How she knew this woman. Had she invited her?

"Well," the woman said, laughing like an imitation of Santa *ho-ho-ho,* "I'd really like to get it for my magazine. Maybe you'd be so kind?"

"Sure," Teresa said. She believed recipes were of the oral tradition, meant to be shared at large. And this woman was very large.

She liked to laugh, though, and she tried it some more. "Ho-ho," she said. "This is a wonderful party." She threw her arms out wide. "Would you mind if I took some pictures for my magazine?"

"Not at all," Teresa said, hoping her magazine wasn't *Penthouse*. She tried to catch Delia's eye. This must be something she'd arranged. She wondered if Delia had told her about it, and she hadn't listened because she was too busy.

Delia's eye would not be caught, because she was busy with Jessamyn, who stood on a chair in front of a vase of roses, sniffing each one, one at a time, to see if they had different scents. Her husband stood behind her with his hand on her shoulder.

"Maybe," Teresa said to the woman, pointing at Delia and her daughter, "you should take a picture of that."

She looked over to the fireplace and saw Amberlin standing next to Sherry, her eyes bright, her mouth open in song, her long arm waving the music out in front of her.

"Or that," Teresa said, pointing to them. "That's Bread and Roses."

"Ooh," the woman said, "ho-ho-ho. What a good idea." And she darted for her camera.

Teresa took a minute and drew in breath before the next guest approached. As she spoke with this gentleman, an old and valued customer whose conference dinners she catered four times a year, Rowan came up to her with a plate of food.

She stared down at it, then gaped at Rowan. "For me?" she asked.

"You gotta eat too."

The portly gentleman agreed, and asked the question she heard so much. How did she stay so thin when she cooked so well?

"Cooking won't make you fat," she said. "Eating will."

"Not tonight," Rowan said. "I put an anticalorie blessing on everything. Go ahead." He picked up an olive and held it out to her. "My mother used to tell me olives are good for your skin. Makes it soft."

She'd never eaten at her open house. She always waited until it was over and had a plate of something by herself when she could relax. All these years, and she'd never eaten with her guests. Suddenly, that seemed miserly and wrong.

She smiled, and opened her mouth for him to feed her.

"Later on," he said, his quiet eyes scanning her for possibilities, "if you're good, I know where you can get some fresh figs."

Sherry took her break, and the tape played selections from *La Bohème*. Rodolfo sang of poetry and love. Mimi sang of sewing and love. Her hands were cold, and she died, but the magic that fell around them in the meantime was as beautiful as the roses in their vase, which Jessie sniffed and sniffed and sniffed.

Teresa, listening, could hear the voices of all her ancestors singing. They sang of the big things. Of the need for bread and roses. Of the need to live close to the bone, close to the heart, close to the center of things. She walked to the window to send them her special thanks, though she wasn't sure for what. For the privilege of good food, and friends, and a fire in the fireplace, and, for the first time in many years, a fire in her heart.

She stared out the window toward the west and the south, which was the quadrant of the night she supposed they would occupy, and instead saw James, sitting in his car, talking on his car phone.

"Mother of God," she muttered. "What's he up to now?"

"Who?" a voice behind her said, and she started. It was Amberlin.

"Don't do that to me," Teresa said. "Shh. Don't get upset. It's James. He's been watching the house all night."

Amberlin's face twisted into many different possibilities, and she felt her anger at him rising up as it had in the cellar. Teresa was right. He had hurt Christine, made her afraid for her own sanity. And he was still acting like a fool. She hissed through a tight jaw, "Christine's gun is still in your room. I could take him from here."

Teresa turned wide eyes to her. "Amberlin? Is that you?"

She shrugged. "I found my inner bitch," she said. "I'm enjoying her while she's around."

That could be fun, Teresa thought. Unleash Amberlin, give her a few jars of tomatoes, and let her go for him. Without the gun, of course. But no. She needed some other solution, because now he was holding up the phone and laughing wildly, pointing at it, mouthing words.

"What's he saying?" Teresa asked. "Can you tell?"

"I think—either the cops, or you're dopes. Maybe both. Maybe neither."

Teresa pressed her hand against her temples. He wouldn't. But if he did, what would the cops do? Search her house? Arrest her? Take Christine away? After all, he was a psychiatrist, and he could have her committed if she was a danger to herself or others. She knew the rules. She remembered them from Nan.

"Amberlin, what am I gonna do?" she asked.

"I think," Amberlin said quietly, "you have to let her go."

Teresa shook her head.

"If you don't, they might take her away."

A woman who ran a coffeehouse that Bread and Roses baked for squealed with delight as she came into the house, and made a beeline for Amberlin.

Teresa walked away, not wanting to engage in conversation. Rowan, she could see, was talking with Delia, and the conversation looked serious. Or maybe she was just getting paranoid, thinking they were talking about her, about Christine. Thinking James would call the cops. Still, her breath was too hard in her throat, and she had to get out for just a minute.

She excused herself to the guests who stopped her to chat as she made her way upstairs to her bedroom, where she retrieved Christine's purse. That was where the gun was. Maybe she should hide it. The police didn't like guns around the house, and she wasn't even sure if this was legal. Besides, if they didn't have the gun, how could they prove Christine was trying to kill herself?

But if she wasn't trying to kill herself, why was she tied up in the cellar? Any way you looked at it, it looked bad. She took the purse and went back downstairs and to the kitchen. She kept the doors closed for the party, so that she would have a retreat if she needed it. She could sit there for a minute and quietly try to think this through. At the open house, Christine would often do that. Sometimes she'd sit and smoke out the back door when she needed a break. Sometimes, just at this time of year, Teresa would join her and smoke a cigarette too. But she didn't want one now. She wanted to make a plate of food.

She got a ceci cookie from a platter of cookies. A piece of ginger trout. A slice of mango. Who could resist a slice of mango in the middle of winter? It was like eating a slice of the sun. And bread, of course. Some olives too.

She took the plate and the purse and descended the cellar stairs.

At the bottom of the stairs, she paused and let her eyes adjust to the absence of light. Christine saw her before she could see Christine.

"Hello, Teresa," she said from her nest. She'd grown accustomed to the dark, Teresa thought. She didn't know if that was good or not.

"I brought you a plate of food," Teresa said. "Your favorites. Ginger trout. Mango."

She could see her now, in dim gray outline, a plane of light spreading from the streetlight in front through the cellar window to grace her. She walked over and put the plate down in front of her. Christine nudged it away with her foot.

Teresa picked it up and looked at the food. All her best food, and Christine was refusing it. All her best, refused.

"You're not crazy, Christine, if that's what you think. Is that what James made you think, that you'll be crazy like your mother? Well, she wasn't crazy either."

Christine laughed derisively. "How do you know? You weren't there."

Teresa winced. That remark hit home. She hadn't been there for her sister or Christine. Not when they needed her most. Teresa felt herself deflate. She was shamed. Humiliated. But she couldn't bear the burden of her inadequacy anymore. It was part of the unchangeable past, not part of the malleable present.

"Look," Teresa said, "no matter what I got wrong, I wanted your mother to live. Only, she . . . flew away from us. From you. I couldn't keep her. Now I want you to live. I'd rather you were here and drunk or seeing Elvis in your bedroom at night than—than dead. Do you understand that?"

"I don't see any reason to stay alive if all it's gonna do is hurt," Christine replied.

Teresa turned her face away, sinking into herself. This negated every belief she had in life, in staying alive. In her own life. Until recently, she had really believed that trying hard, working hard, was all it took to have a good life. But in this past year that faith had let her down in almost every way it could. She kept talking, her voice sounding strange to her own ears, as if she'd never used it before.

"Maybe you're right," she said dully. "It does hurt like hell. And I guess I kept you here, thinking I could—not make it go away, but help you get through it to a better place. Where it feels good to be alive. But maybe I don't know where that place is anymore."

If she told herself the truth, Teresa had to admit that for the last year, she had often felt just as Christine did. At night when she went to sleep alone. In the morning when she woke up alone and said to her cat, "I'm still here," she'd also say, "So what? Who cares?"

Christine was paying attention to her now, her small, fair face turned up in the soft light, her forehead scrunching into a question.

"Maybe," Teresa said, "I'd do just what you tried to, only I'm too chickenshit."

Christine clucked her tongue and shook her head. "C'mon, Teresa. Give it up."

"What? Give what up?"

"You don't mean that. You're saying it to try and change my mind."

"Yeah?" Teresa said harshly, finding something of anger in herself. "You think so, huh? The hell with you. You don't know how many nights I was here alone, wanting to die."

Christine blinked back the darkness and tried to see Teresa's face more clearly. "Don't talk that way," she said hoarsely, a little confused, her eyes darting this way and that in the dark. "You wouldn't kill yourself for the wrong reasons."

"The wrong reasons?" she repeated. "Don't kill myself for the wrong reasons? And *you're* gonna tell me what the right reasons are? Because my son won't speak to me? My husband left me? My sister killed herself? Are those the *wrong* reasons? Well, how about because you won't eat."

She picked up the plate and grabbed the ginger trout and put it in her own mouth. "It's good food," she said, chewing hard. "Good food, and every hand on it is the hand of someone who loves you. *Loves* you, Christine, and isn't that a good reason to kill myself, when my love means nothing? Keeps nobody alive at all?"

She flung the plate away as if it were a Frisbee, and it smashed into the cellar wall behind her.

"Teresa, calm down," Christine said, and Teresa heard the fear in Christine's voice. She considered it carefully, and awareness of opportunity grew in her. She still had the purse in her other hand. She opened it, pulled out the gun.

She took a few steps closer to Christine and waved the gun in her face. She lifted the gun and held it to her head. "I can find my own reasons to die."

Christine reached for her, stopped by the ropes. "You don't mean it," she said nervously. "You aren't going to."

Teresa's mouth turned up in a wicked grin. "Yeah?" she growled back. "And what if you're wrong?"

Christine got her leg out of the blankets and kicked at Teresa, catching her in the ankle, making her stumble forward onto Christine, who reached for the gun. They grappled for it, Teresa holding it high in the air away from her.

"Goddammit," Teresa said, "get away. Get away."

Christine got hold of her wrist, her ropes keeping her from a full reach, but once she had the wrist, she held on hard.

Teresa tried to shake her off, but Christine had the grip of a pit bull, and all she could do was toss the gun away from them both. She did, and it clattered to the floor a few feet away.

Christine looked at Teresa hard, still gripping her wrist. "If I let go, are you gonna do anything stupid?" she said sternly.

Teresa blinked at her, then giggled. Christine blinked back, and then giggled too. Then they were both laughing. At themselves, at the stupid nest Christine was in, at the tomatoes on the wall, at the blue vase with tulips, at the music they heard upstairs, which was Tosca singing about art and love. At the cat, who wandered in at that moment and asked them with a polite *mrow* if he could eat the fish they didn't seem to properly appreciate.

"And you thought you were crazy." Teresa chuckled, wiping her eyes.

"I think it does run in the family," Christine said.

"We live hard. That's true. You just gotta get used to it."

Christine rested her head on Teresa's shoulder. "Do you think that's what happened to Nan?" she asked. "She couldn't get used to herself?"

"Maybe," Teresa said. "Or maybe her spirit was bigger than her. Or, maybe, Chrissy, she was a drunk."

"I tried to help her," Christine said mournfully.

"And it's time for you to stop trying, huh?" Teresa said. "It wasn't really your job. You were the kid. She was the mother. Remember?"

They were silent for a while, and then Teresa pulled back and looked at Christine. "I'm gonna untie you," she said, "but that doesn't mean you have to leave. It's just that—well, never mind. I'll explain later. But I'm gonna untie you because you're not crazy, and you really do want to be alive, and it will stop hurting so much. Okay?"

Christine nodded uncertainly. Teresa stood up and stepped hard on the gun, which she kicked away as she undid the intricate spider-web of knots she'd made, each knot a blessing to tie down whatever it was that wanted to hurt Christine. Each knot a spell to bind that away from her.

"Teresa," Christine said, "did you mean it? Were you really going to—use the gun?"

Teresa untied the last knot and lifted a thoughtful face toward Christine. "It's true I felt pretty lousy," she said, speaking carefully, "but . . . no. I wouldn't shoot myself."

"It was a trick?"

"No. I just wanted to show you how it felt, so you'd understand."

"I don't understand though," Christine said. "What keeps you alive when everything is falling apart? Why don't you . . ." Her words trailed into silence.

"Kill myself?" Teresa shrugged. "I got green beans in the freezer."

Christine waited for that to make sense, and when it didn't, she asked, "Green beans?"

"From the garden," Teresa said. "Can't kill myself while there's green beans in the freezer. And by the time they're gone, it'll be time to plant more. Maybe when they're ripe, Donnie'll be hungry for beans with mint and garlic. Maybe he'll come home for some. And maybe I'll have other company to feed too. So I better stick around, huh?"

Teresa stood up and took a step back. "I'm going upstairs. I should be at the party. You take your time."

She stepped over the gun on her way up and didn't pick it up. Christine sat in the gray light and watched her go before she stood and tested her own legs for their strength.

TERESA'S KITCHEN

TERESA EMERGED FROM THE CELLAR TO SEE DELIA'S and Amberlin's frightened faces on the other side of the door. They began whispering loudly and simultaneously at her.

"What?" she asked in a normal tone. "What now?"

"The police," Amberlin said. "Coming up the drive."

They heard a knock on the back door, and all three turned to it and stood very still, like deer looking into the headlights of an oncoming truck.

"I'll get it," Teresa said at last. She took a deep breath and opened the door, putting on her hostess smile. She saw an olive-skinned man with dark eyes and hair. His badge read OFFICER LOPEZ. "Merry Christmas, Officer. Can I help you?"

"Complaint, ma'am. Noisy party."

Teresa's tension left her as suddenly as it arrived. Was that all? But they weren't noisy. No more than they ever were. And besides, any neighbors she might disturb were sitting in her living room, eating her food. She always followed the Italian tradition of co-opting potential enemies before they called the police and complained.

"Is it the music?" Amberlin asked solicitously, coming up behind Teresa.

"Don't think so, ma'am," he said. "Report said someone was—um—carrying on in here. Said they were afraid there might be injuries."

"How funny," Delia said. "Maybe they meant one of the children. One of my children, probably," she added.

"Hey," Amberlin said, pointing at his badge. "We met you yesterday. At that accident. Remember? You directed us around it. And Delia"—she grabbed Delia's elbow and pulled her forward—"she was driving."

"Oh, yeah," Delia said, looking him up and down. "You're the one who doesn't believe in luck."

"Yes, ma'am," Lopez said, knitting his brows. "It was a bad accident. The snow. I'm glad you made it through okay."

Amberlin laughed lightly. "Thank you so much. I'll tell you what, Officer. Maybe you should come into the living room and look around, make sure everything is okay."

She took his arm and led him inside. Brought him through the kitchen, where his head picked up and he sniffed around. They kept going, into the living room, where the crackling fire and the soft pink Christmas lights made everyone look good.

His eyes grew wider as he saw the people, the flowers, the platters of food.

"Try some of Teresa's fillet of sole in green sauce," she suggested. "It might make you change your mind about luck."

Officer Lopez shook his head at Amberlin. He felt as if he'd just stepped into one of those fairy stories his *tía* used to tell him, where the spirit people took an unsuspecting man to a room filled with enormous banquet tables spread with fantastic foods. Only later would the man find out he'd been enchanted, and what he thought was one night was actually a hundred years.

Still, he thought, looking around, it might not be a bad way to spend eternity. He took his hat off. Delia took it from him before he could put it down and carried it to the guest room to hang it up with the other coats.

When she returned to the kitchen, Teresa was waiting, looking anxious.

Delia smiled. "She didn't say anything about introducing him to her girlfriend, I noticed."

"Maybe she found her inner liar too," Teresa replied.

She went to close the kitchen door, and would have succeeded, except that James's foot was stuck in it.

She looked at it, looked up his leg, looked at his face, which was angry.

"Teresa, I will not put up with this anymore. If you don't—"

"You're looking for Christine," she interrupted him. She opened the door wide. "Come in, and help yourself."

ON THE LIMITS OF LOVE

WHILE SHE STOOD IN THE CELLAR, STARING AT THE gun on the floor and waiting for her legs to decide what to do next, Christine thought about her mother. She was dead, and a great part of Christine's sorrow was that she'd spent so many years learning how to love her, and now had nowhere to go with that love. It was like a bank fund she couldn't spend. Or like a banquet she couldn't share.

But that didn't make the love itself go away, because it seemed love was an energy all its own. A force, like a hurricane, that wouldn't be stopped by death or drunkenness or madness, or even the presence of wings.

Teresa liked to listen to *La Bohème,* which Nan had also listened to a lot. Both of them said it was like visiting family, but Delia and Amberlin were irritated by it. Teresa would weep into a dish towel when Rodolfo noticed that Mimi's hand was cold and declared himself a poet. Why listen to something that makes you cry so hard, Delia would ask.

Teresa said because it was beautiful. Christine said that's just what Nan had said too. Delia just couldn't hear it. Teresa said you had to know the story. The beauty was in the Bohemians who tried to live free and love each other, who loved their art and each other and lived so big, it burst their hearts wide open, and they died. Or at least Mimi did.

What, Amberlin wanted to know, was so beautiful about that? To her it seemed messy and not very smart.

That, Teresa said, was the beauty. That it was messy and not very smart. A willingness to be messy and not very smart because that's what it took to live the life they wanted. There was great love in that, and not even death could take it away. The beauty of it was that they put love in the world, more limitless than death.

Love has no limits, Teresa said, and that's what makes *Bohème* beautiful.

Christine thought that was important, perhaps even true, in a fundamental way she couldn't quite grasp. Teresa wasn't saying love was the only emotion, or that love would fix your carburetor if it was broken, because she was a pragmatic woman and knew better than that. No. There was still the need for car mechanics and anger and grief and humility and pride and the whole smorgasbord of events and emotions it took to be human. One big sloppy mess that somehow makes the most ecstatic meal you ever had.

But Teresa was saying that love was without limits. That love encompassed the whole sloppy mess, and could bear it. You wouldn't bother to get your carburetor fixed if you didn't love your car, or love driving, or at least love getting to the places the car took you to. And you couldn't feel love if you didn't let yourself know grief. Couldn't feel anger if you didn't let yourself know love.

Love, that energy sitting at the center of the universe from the beginning, somehow took in all those other energies and transformed them into something like bliss. Something like life.

It was, Teresa would say, the heart of the sauce.

Christine wasn't sure, though, that she knew what love was. What it was made of. What the delicate flavors and aromas and textures of it were. What the sweet, sharp, hot, savory, salty, and delectable shadings were. Maybe, she thought, this was the first time she'd felt anything in a long time. She knew James was a good man, but she didn't feel it. She recognized all the important signs and symbols of a respectable, reliable, potentially interesting long-term partner, but her heart didn't feel happy or big when he walked into a room.

Maybe she'd picked James because he didn't ask her to feel too much. In fact, her stronger emotions frightened him, just as they frightened her. It seemed so much safer not to feel when you didn't know what would rush out if you opened certain spots in the heart. Or maybe she'd been trying to prove herself different from her mother, sane and whole and in control of her life, at James's expense. Surely if a psychiatrist chooses you, that says something about the quality of your mental health. And certainly she'd gone out of her way to show him repeatedly how calm and strong and full of light she was. The problem was, she couldn't sustain it, and in trying she ended up smashing castles.

Maybe all this was true. She couldn't be sure right now. All she did know was that she felt horrible when her mother died, and missed her even to this day. She knew she didn't want Teresa to hurt herself. And she knew the tulips looked beautiful, even in the dim gray light of the cellar. Perhaps especially in the dim gray light of the cellar.

And maybe all that was somehow love, which has no limits and takes in all the other emotions to soothe them or stir them up or complement them or remind you that it's necessary to feel them and be human and eat food and laugh and go on until you die of consumption, still singing of love.

Love has no limits. It's an energy bigger than the sun, which is why, sometimes, it scares us so very much.

Delia knew this, too, when she saw Michael walk into the party with his father. She saw the way he touched his father's elbow to guide him toward a chair, and how gentle that touch was. She saw how unafraid he was to lift his daughter high and toss her, because he knew he wouldn't let her fall. Teresa knew it when she saw Sherry walk into the party and flow like a river toward Amberlin, who stood chewing the end of her thumb, worry lines growing around her mouth. She knew it in the way Sherry didn't touch Amberlin until Amberlin extended a hand. Sherry knew it in the way Officer Lopez took his hat off and declared himself off duty, the way he stayed and told off-color Spanish translations of jokes to the magazine editor.

Amberlin knew it in the way Rowan's eyes followed Teresa around the room, and the way he would be at her side with whatever she needed—a drink, a napkin, a slice of marinated peach, as soon as some turn of her shoulder or shifting of her weight indicated her need to him.

And Christine knew it in the way the tomatoes decorated the wall, the way the tulips sat in their blue vase and drank what little light there was, the way Teresa chose to stay alive because of the green beans in her freezer, the way the women tended to her, each in their own way.

Teresa was fond of telling a story about the difference between heaven and hell.

If you toured hell, she said, you'd see a bunch of people sitting at a table piled high with every kind of wonderful food imaginable. The smells, the sights, would fill you with joy and hunger, and both sides of the table would be set, with people at each seat, but all the people would have one hand tied behind their backs and spoons with handles two feet long. With one hand tied, and handles that long, they just couldn't get the food to their mouths. So what you'd see was people seated at a feast, struggling to feed themselves and failing for all eternity.

If you went to heaven, Teresa said, you'd see the same thing. People at the table, one hand tied back. The best food. And those spoons with the great long handles. The only difference would be that the people wouldn't be struggling to feed themselves.

They'd be feeding each other.

Christine stood and thought about that for some time. Or, at least, it seemed like some time to her, though thought can pass as quickly as light. It feels like a long time, though, when the thought is good and it sinks from your head into your heart.

After she was done thinking, she picked up the gun and stared at it.

A clatter on the stairs made her lift her head. She squinted in the dim light and saw James.

"Christine," he said, walking toward her, breathless and nervous, "you're here. Thank God. I've been so worried. My God, what happened?" he added, looking around at the mess of tomatoes and pickles that decorated the walls.

"Amberlin had a little accident," Christine said, smiling, but not too much because she remembered she wasn't sure how she felt about him anymore, and was certain she didn't want to make that castle over again.

"Are you okay?" he asked. "Are you hurt? You haven't—hurt yourself, have you? Teresa didn't do anything to you, did she?"

Christine stifled her laughter. She didn't know how to begin to explain Teresa's therapeutic approach. She had a feeling it wasn't in any of James's books.

"I'm fine," she said.

"You're sure? Are you? Christine," he said, the tone of his voice changing. "Is that—a gun?"

She looked down at her hand. She was holding a gun. "Yes," she said. "It is. It was my mother's."

He put a hand out, palm up, and took a step back away from her. "Now, don't get—don't do anything rash. You need help. I can get you help. I can help you, Christine." He made his voice reasonable and calm and took another step away from her.

"I don't need help, James," she said. "Really. I'm okay."

"Of course," he agreed. "Sure."

He was humoring her. She could see that. She wondered how long he'd been doing that, and why he bothered. "You really think I'm crazy, don't you?"

"Now, Christine," he said placatingly, "you know I don't like that terminology. It's pejorative and inaccurate."

She took a step toward him. He took a step back. She saw that he was afraid.

"I wonder what you ever wanted with a crazy woman," she said softly. "Or maybe by the time you figured it out, you were in too deep and didn't know how to get out without embarrassment."

He shook his head. "I love you, Christine. I just want to help you."

She stared at him, listened hard, tried to get the word *love* to feel like something, but it wouldn't. It just wouldn't. Not the way he said it. Not the way he meant it. "And what if I don't need help?" she asked. "Do you love me then?"

"You do need help, Christine," he said with deliberate calm. "We've talked about this. About your mother. You know that suicidal impulses are just anger turned inward."

She bit back on a wicked grin that was trying to rise to the surface of her face, but it wouldn't stay away. She raised the gun and smiled a real smile at him.

"Not anymore," she said.

UPSTAIRS, TERESA STOOD AT THE CELLAR DOOR WITH Amberlin and Delia at her side. They were huddled together in the kitchen, discussing what they should do next, when they heard the gunshot.

Teresa's face went very white. She put a hand on Amberlin's arm and Amberlin held her up. But then events moved very rapidly. The door to the kitchen was flung open and Rowan's face appeared, his eyes even bigger than usual. He went immediately to Teresa and would have asked her questions, but many other people filled the door behind him, Sherry's and Michael's faces pushed their way through the crowd. Woven in with the voices asking questions and expressing shock, they heard the sound of someone running up the stairs at a good rate.

The cellar door opened, and James emerged, his face whiter than Teresa's.

"She's crazy," he gasped. "She tried—I don't need to be subjected to this kind of—"

Delia stepped forward with his coat in her hand, and he took it.

"She's crazy," he said more authoritatively, "and you're all crazy, and I'm going home. Merry Christmas."

And he stumbled out the door.

Teresa would have thrown herself down the stairs after that, except another pair of feet were rapidly ascending, and an arm emerged, holding a gun, at which point the other guests gathered at the kitchen door gasped simultaneously and stepped back.

Officer Lopez pushed through them, his hand on his holster.

Then Christine herself was in the kitchen, standing and squinting into the light. "Sorry, folks," she said, smiling and holding the gun up high by its handle to show she meant no harm. "I was downstairs getting some pickles for my aunt, and I found this. Didn't know it was loaded." She laughed heartily. Everyone else followed suit.

Teresa looked at Rowan, and he joined in the laughter, made a good job of getting everyone back to the living room. To the fireplace and the music and the food.

Officer Lopez scanned Christine, noting the smudges of dirt on her face, and the cobwebs in her hair. Christine blushed under his gaze and raised a hand to pat her hair.

"I always get so messy in that darn cellar," she said, smiling brightly. "I better go wash up."

Lopez held a hand out to stop her. "I'll take the gun first," he said.

"Yes," she said, handing it to him. "Of course."

He examined it, saw that there was another bullet in it, removed the bullet. "Is it registered?" he asked Teresa. "You have a permit?"

"Actually," Christine chimed in, "I think it was my mother's. She had a permit. Is it Nan's, Teresa?"

Teresa nodded mutely, then cleared her throat and spoke. "I was cleaning out closets and found it. Didn't know what to do with it, so I left it there."

Officer Lopez looked from Teresa to Christine. They didn't look like they were related, except in their smiles. Teresa's reminded him of his *tía*'s.

"I'll need to see paperwork for this," he said, "file a report."

"I'd be glad to," Christine said. "But . . . now? My aunt needs me for the party."

He looked from one woman to another. As a cop, he had to rely on instinct once in a while, and he thought they all seemed—maybe not harmless, but fundamentally sound. Besides, he didn't like that guy who'd made the complaint on them. He sounded whiny and arrogant at the same time, which was a bad combination. "I have to go call this in. I'll let the desk sergeant know I'm staying on the premises for further questioning. We can go to the station when I'm done." His mouth twitched from neutral into a slight smile that disappeared as quickly as it came. "It could take a while," he noted blandly.

Christine smiled, and he gave her a little nod before he got his coat and went out the back door.

As soon as he was gone, Christine turned a grin to Teresa, then Amberlin, then Delia.

"Got anything to eat?" she asked. "I'm starving."

DOLCE

OF COURSE CHRISTINE DIDN'T MARRY JAMES, WHICH was only one of the miracles that occurred that Christmas. James rather quickly married a very nice young woman he met at a singles function, a young woman who had never wanted wings.

Christine started grief therapy with the psychiatrist Amberlin recommended. She was a very well padded older woman who wore her graying hair in a bun and played opera for her to help her cry. Christine continued to work for Bread and Roses, and she started taking classes in things like metalwork and welding and stonecraft. It would be another year before she dated anyone, but then, she wasn't in a rush. Neither was Frank Lopez, who started coming over for Sunday dinners at Teresa's now and again. He was particularly fond of the way she made enchiladas, after a recipe he'd given her from his own *tía*.

Christine did stand up for Teresa when she married Rowan the following summer. Sherry played the music, and Donnie walked his mother from her house across the yard to where the wedding was held, down the grassy aisle demarcated by tubs of rosebushes that he would later help his mother plant. Amberlin and Delia stood on either side of Christine, ruining their makeup with crying as they watched

Rowan kiss Teresa under the trellis, and then they all kissed her, too, while the guests cheered and tossed birdseed at them instead of rice.

They took turns watching the house while Teresa and Rowan honeymooned in Italy, where Christine knew they'd put flowers on Great-grandmother Emilia's grave. Roses, of an old-fashioned kind that Rowan would pick. They'd have a lingering scent, and would include all Teresa's thousands of thanks for the recipes.

Delia's father-in-law moved in with them, and died less than a year later, but well before the annual open house, thank God, Delia said. The children were distraught. It was their first experience of death or loss. Delia let them cry and ask questions and be moody and confused for as long as they needed to, and Teresa brought great bowls of ziti to the funeral, and ceci cookies, which were their favorite.

Amberlin moved in with Sherry, although they decided it would be best to delay the question of children until both of them felt ready. Especially with Sherry getting signed on to one of the bigger folk labels, which meant she'd have to tour quite a bit for a while. It was wonderful, and it was difficult, and it was all Amberlin could do to keep up with her own emotions and describe them to her friends.

And the teller of these stories? Well, you would probably never say it was Nan, simply because she was dead when all of this happened. How could a ghost—or an angel if you prefer that—whisper in your ear what to say about this person and her heart, or that person and his actions. Who would ever think that this story, and all stories, are simply the whisperings of ancestral wings close to our ears. The stories we're told at night while we sleep, when we forget not to listen.

But if you've already ceased to believe in the precise possibility of wings, then let us tell you this, instead:

One day Christine sat down in Teresa's warm kitchen with Delia and Amberlin, Michael and Rowan and Frank, and asked their permission to write all this down. Over lots of pasta and good fresh greens and helpings of tiramisu that Teresa whipped up as they were talking, they told Christine everything they'd felt and done and been in her absence, and she told them everything she'd felt and been and done too.

And all the stories they told each other were food for their souls. And all the food they ate was good.

The Recipe for

FEEDING *Christine*

THE IDEA FOR *FEEDING CHRISTINE* WAS BORN, APPROPRIATELY, in a restaurant over crab cakes and fish chowder after our storytelling group, The Snickering Witches, had just completed a workshop at the Salem Witch Museum. Three of us, Lale Davidson, Cindy Parrish, and I, had been writing and performing together since graduate school almost five years previous. SuEllen Hamkins had been writing and performing with Cindy for over ten years. We had long cherished an idea to do a theater piece composed of food stories. At that lunch Barbara said, "Let's write a play about women and food."

"We need an event to shape it around, like the preparation of a feast," Cindy suggested.

"What if one of the women was trying to starve herself to death and the others were trying to save her?" Lale asked.

"And," SuEllen added, "each of the women is hungry for something different."

And so the brainstorming began.

Jobs, babies, and lives caused the idea of the play to be shelved, but I, who had written a few books already, decided to write this material as a novel, using the stories of the other women within it.

We gathered for an intensive writing session during which we traded stories of food in our lives—*tell of a time your father fed you, make a list of comfort foods, sexy foods*—and so on. Characters became more real in all their grace and stupidity. Conversations and writing contributions of the women went in the pot, and I stirred and stirred, melding their flavors into the stock. The manuscript went to agent Laurie Liss, who added her own essential revisionary touches. And when Beverly Lewis at Bantam accepted it, we celebrated with a feast, complete with tiramisu.

In this book you can taste the lives of all the women who put their hands on it and their words into it. Lale's stories of diets, Cindy's conversation about Despair, and SuEllen's observations about baking and beauty are just samples of the writing that sweetened the pot. Like many good meals, it took a gathering of women to make it happen, so that a world of readers can enjoy the results.

As Teresa would say, *mangia buona.*